Forbidden PLAY

FORBIDDEN PLAY

O'RYAN FAMILY SERIES
BOOK 2

KRISTIN LEE

Photographer: Lindee Robinson

Model: Drew @tat2_rider on IG

Cover Design: Dirty Girl Designs

This book is for my brother.
You were fun, fearless, and always the first to make us laugh—
often while hiding how much you were hurting. You faced
diabetes and two kidney transplants with quiet strength,
never wanting your pain to weigh on anyone else.
But you did love. You loved your sisters, your mom, nieces,
nephews, and your friends. Every single person I meet who
knew you says, "He was the best. Never had a bad word to say
about anyone."
We cherish every laugh, every photo, every memory.
You lost your battle here...
but in Forbidden Play, you get your happily ever after.
And I hope you know—
you were never a burden.
You were a gift.
Always.

ONE
NOELLE

"Noelle is oblivious. Still."

Bree's whisper slides through the bathroom like oil on water—slick, deliberate.

I freeze midstream in the stall, heart stuttering as my brain scrambles for context. *Oblivious to what?* My pulse roars in my ears, loud enough that I'm sure they can hear it. Because deep down, I already know exactly who they're talking about.

Brooks.

My boyfriend.

For over a year.

How could I be so naïve?

The ache in my chest is so intense that I know they can hear me breathing. Renee chimes in, almost sympathetic. "I don't know why Brooks stays with her if he has sex with other people. Why not just break it off and play the field?"

My teammates' laughter comes next, the arch in Bree's voice and Renee's rolling giggle stabbing me in the back as they dissect my life in a bathroom.

I should come out swinging from this stall. Say something cutting and clever, snap the way I do at home when my youngest brother, Witt, forgets to pick up the dog poop in the backyard and I'm the one who steps in it.

At home, with my family, I have an edge and humor and can whip up just the right words to make them laugh at exactly the right moment. Here, with girls like Bree and Renee, I'm always searching for the version of myself that fits in.

Holding my breath, I just listen.

"Noelle is too pure...too good." Bree says it like it's an insult. "Brooks is bored and just wants to have some fun, if you know what I mean." I can't see her, but I bet her eyebrows are wiggling. "Tabby actually knows what she's doing."

My stomach does an airplane barrel roll. Bored.

A pause. A girlish giggle that sounds sorry, almost.

"Her brothers are football legends. It's all about connections," Renee offers a snarky take on why Brooks has *me* for a girlfriend.

I peek through the slit in the stall, and something inside me hardens. There's nothing left in their tone but spite and that desperate need to be interesting by torching someone else's life.

And they're throwing the match on me and my life.

The bathroom is silent, but my ears are roaring, the blood pounding so hard behind my eyes I barely hear the door creak when I open it. Their heads pop in my direction. Their eyes land on me—wide, guilty, only a little sorry.

I square my shoulders, wishing I were anywhere but here. "How long?" I say, my voice small, too high. Not the voice I use at home. Not really *me*.

Bree just rolls her eyes. Renee looks like she may feel sorry for me as they both open their mouths to defend the gossip spewing from their mouths.

"Don't," I say quickly, holding up a hand as if that's enough to keep their words away. "I don't need your sympathy when you're spreading rumors or...truths. I just need—"

I break off, tears stinging. God, in front of them. Of course. I wipe my cheeks with the side of my hand.

Bree looks away, pretending she's not jealous of Tabby and me. Bree would do anything to get her hands on Brooks. Her words come out razor-sharp. "Months, Noelle. Tabby has been riding his cock for months."

Renée moves, takes a step, uncertain. "Noelle, I'm—"

"Don't," I snap, tears threatening to pour. Their false concern makes me want to throw a softball as hard as I can into their guts because that's what I feel like. Like I've been gut-punched.

Crying at home is one thing, with Greyson teasing me and tossing me a Nerf ball to shut me up, or Dad making dumb faces until I snort-laugh. But with these girls, it's pure ammunition.

A weakness.

I shoulder past them, not bothering to look back. I need air. Need to get away. I need to run. Run to where, though? I'm not going to Brooks. Not now. Not ever again.

By the time I make it outside, the sun is blinding, and the chatter on the quad drills straight into my skull. My throat is tight and sore from trying not to sob until I got past the main doors.

Why can't I make real girlfriends who would stand up for me? Take me aside and tell me about my boyfriend's extra-sex-curricular activities? It's not a new feeling. I've always been able to be me around guys—their intentions are obvious, their jokes simple. There's no hidden battle with guys, no shifting alliances—guys are just easier.

I laugh up a snotty sob, thinking about what my granny would say to me right now. "You're madder than a wet hen."

And she'd be right.

I'm sick of crying over Brooks skipping family events or, worse, ignoring me when he is around. But cheating? That's a whole new kind of hurt.

When I punch in Brooks's number, it goes straight to voicemail.

My mom would know just what to say. I hold the tears back long enough to force unplanned words from my mouth. "You're a cheater and a liar. We're over. Have fun with Tabby." That's all. But the tears fall once again. I wipe them away, and through blurred vision, I finally step off school grounds. I text Parker out of habit. He's my younger brother by eleven months. Mom always called us her twins.

> Me: You at home? I need to hang out
> a sec.

No reply. I should have known better since he's preparing for workouts, hoping a college other than Dad's will offer him a scholarship.

Every muscle in my legs burns as I jog to my rental house that I share with two male cheerleaders. As my feet pound the pavement, my backpack slams against my back over and over. College students don't run. We stroll, enjoying the sights and sounds of campus.

Two weeks from graduation, I should be wishing college would last forever. I've loved my classes. I can't wait to be a sports journalist, and I've loved cheering for my team and for Brooks, but most of it was make-believe, a fairy tale with a messy ending.

Did I come out with any real, true girl friends? No.

Did I find the man I wanted to spend the rest of my life with? I thought I did, but that's wrecked now, too.

In my room, I collapse on my bed, clutching the stuffed rabbit my mom gave me when I was three. "What am I going to do now?" I ask Bibby.

She stares back at me with her little blue eyes as if she knows the answer.

Greyson will know.

My brothers are all completely different. John David, or J.D., is by the book. Greyson is easygoing. Parker is gentle. Witt is—well, Witt. He rarely speaks and keeps to himself.

I grab my keys and head to Greyson's house. Even though he's ten years older than me, he's always been the one I turn to the most.

His truck isn't out front, but that doesn't mean anything —four-car garage. The Corvette in the driveway barely registers.

I walk in without knocking. In our family, doors are always unlocked. Always open.

The kitchen is half-lit. An abandoned bowl. A stack of playbooks on the counter.

And sitting at the kitchen table is someone I didn't expect.

Matt Stricker.

Quarterback coach for the Austin Armadillos, sitting at the kitchen table studying his iPad.

He looks up and smirks. "Lost?"

I roll my eyes—a familiar, practiced motion. "Just escaping the drama."

The normalcy of my voice surprises me. I sling my bag off my shoulder and grab a bottle of water like I live here. Honestly, I kind of do, considering I pop in for five-minute hangouts with Greyson's family all the time.

Matt leans back in his chair, watching me with that half-smile the guys always say *means he's about to talk trash.* There's something steady about him. Not a friend. Not a threat. Just... Matt. Greyson's best friend. He smells like chalk, sports detergent, and old leather.

Home base.

"No Greyson?" I ask, my voice as casual as I can muster.

"Paulina won another tennis match, so they won't be home tonight. I'm dogsitting." He glances over his shoulder at the golden retriever sleeping on the couch. "You look like hell, Noelle."

I laugh—a sharp sound, more real than anything since I left the bathroom. "Thanks. Just what a girl wants to hear."

Opening the bottle, I suck the water down, not realizing how much crying dehydrates me. I toss the empty bottle into the recycling bin for a score. I mumble, "I should have taken the softball scholarship, but I wanted to fly into the air and hope that men catch me."

"Cheerleaders can be scary," he says, watching me for a beat too long. "Something happen?"

There it is. The real question. I sink into the chair across from him, kick up my feet, and let my guard down for the first time today.

"Can I just... can we just hang?"

He gives a mini salute. "I'm not much for pep talks, but

I'm good at Madden. Or I could make you the world's worst sandwich."

The tension in my shoulders eases. This is why guys make sense—straightforward comfort, no drama, just shared space. A little banter and you've reset everything.

"We're not playing a football game. Do you do anything else?" Seriously. I've never seen him with a date or doing anything other than football. "How about Mario Kart?"

He snorts. "Only if I get to be Mario. Luigi freaks me out."

For some reason, I find myself laughing at the thought, like all my problems are vanishing because of my brother's best friend—Matt Stricker, older than me by more than a decade.

We head to the man cave for a little video game competition, and for a while, there's nothing but the sound of controllers clacking, me cursing at the screen when he shells me, and him laughing like he hasn't got a care in the world. Eventually, I forget the searing ache in my chest. It's just graphics, noise, and friendly competition.

Eventually, the questions will come, and I won't be able to hold back the tears. But here, in Greyson's basement with the man who seems to understand that sometimes silence is more honest than small talk, I feel like I can breathe again.

When he beats me on the Urchin Underpass level, he slaps his hand on my leg and squeezes my knee. "Doesn't matter the game, sweetheart. I always win."

My whole body tingles as the pads of his fingers press into my skin. And that cocky grin is to die for. Matt has saved me several times over the past year, always being there when Brooks was flirting or dancing with other girls. And I always loved how I felt in his arms.

Our eyes linger. Too long.

TWO
MATT

Holy hell.

I shouldn't want this. But as my palm rests on her knee, my body buzzes with this reckless urge to drag my hand up her thigh, right to the place I have no business even thinking about.

Not when her oldest brother is my boss and the other is the quarterback I'm supposed to coach. Not when she's... what, fifteen years younger? Enough years to get me excommunicated from every locker room I've ever set foot in.

And yet, here we are. She's grinning, flushed after losing to me at Mario Kart. I can't help the cocky smile that tugs at my mouth. "Doesn't matter the game, sweetheart. I always win."

My hand lingers on her leg longer than it should. I squeeze her knee, and she doesn't pull away. In fact, she looks up at me with those deer-in-the-headlights eyes, all wide and uncertain and so goddamn soft it makes my chest hurt.

I clear my throat and pull back, forcing my attention to the controller in my hand, pretending not to notice the way my body reacts to her nearness. "Rematch?" I ask, my voice lower than I mean it to be.

She lets out this little laugh—breathy, real. "You're just asking for another win."

I shrug. "Maybe I want to see if you can surprise me."

She looks at me a beat longer, and something flickers behind those eyes—a shadow that's got nothing to do with video games. She looks tired, older than she should for a girl getting ready to graduate from college. For a minute, I want to reach for her hand, smooth my palm over her knuckles just to see if the tension will ease up at all.

Instead, I ask, "You want to talk, Noelle?"

She chews on her lips like she's working hard not to fall apart. She's quiet for a long moment, way too quiet for Noelle O'Ryan, the girl who shouts over her brothers and fits right in with a locker room full of guys. The girl who dances like no one's watching, free and happy. Yeah, I've noticed every little thing about her since I met her.

Finally, she says, her voice soft and small, "Do you ever feel like you're the butt of a joke?"

Shit. Here it comes. I put the controller down, my full attention on her now. "You want the honest answer?"

As she nods, she fights her emotions with everything she's got. Tears well under her lids as her eyes flutter open.

I sigh. "More than I care to admit. But Noelle, I'm sure no one's laughing at you. How could they?" I almost say *you're perfect*, but I catch myself.

She blinks. One tear escapes, creating a black mascara path down her cheek. "Oh... everyone's laughing behind my back. My teammates all know, and I didn't. Why is the girl-friend always the last to know? I always thought I was above all the girl drama because I could hang with the guys, you know? But I was just stupid."

It's instinct, the way I move closer, positioning an arm behind her on the couch. "You're not stupid. And what did they know that *you* didn't?"

She shakes her head, bringing her feet onto the couch and hugging her knees to her chest. "I just... I didn't know. I mean, sometimes I thought he... maybe, but I didn't know for sure." Noelle's voice falters, and she puts her head on her knees, sobbing.

I rub her back like my grandmother used to do to make me feel better, waiting for her to continue. I think I know what has happened. Her boyfriend is the stereotypical jock who thinks the world revolves around him. I'll never forget how he danced with nearly every woman at Greyson's wedding, except for Noelle. She grabbed me and pulled me to the dance floor. I looked over my shoulder, and it didn't seem to be a blip on his radar.

Minutes go by with her wiping her eyes, and her nose is running. I don't want to get up to get a tissue, so I raise my shirt, tilt her head, and wipe her nose. She sniffs and cry-laughs before more tears fall.

Finally, she croaks out, "Brooks... he was cheating on me. Since... God, since forever, apparently. Even after." Her voice hitches, as she combs her fingers anxiously through her hair. "Even after last week. I thought I was making the right choice. I waited. And then I finally thought, okay, maybe this means something real. It was my first time. And then today..." Her voice breaks apart.

Her first time?

Noelle's shoulders tremble as she covers her face with her sleeve. I edge closer, not caring anymore about the list of a million reasons it's wrong to get this close to my best friend's sister. I just know she needs someone. Someone who won't judge her. But I promise you, I am judging her narcissistic boyfriend.

I wrap my arms around her, and she buries her face in the pocket of my shoulder, crying so hard her body vibrates. She feels so delicate and vulnerable that she might shatter if I hold her too tight, and I want to kill every asshole who's ever made her cry.

"I thought it meant forever, Matt," she says, her voice muffled and heartbreakingly young. "How stupid is that?"

I shake my head, rubbing her back. "It's not stupid. It's natural to assume that when it's your first time. Everybody wants to believe in forever at least once. You trusted him."

She lets out a shaky breath and lifts her head, her eyes huge, wet, shimmering—like something out of a kid's movie. For a moment, neither of us moves. She's looking at me like I'm a ray of sunshine after a thunderstorm, like I could clear all her heartache if I'd just try. And I know this is the exact moment I'm supposed to let go.

Don't, Matt. She's too young. She's Greyson's sister, not to mention the head coach's sister.

But then she presses her lips to mine—soft, uncertain, desperate. My resolve shatters. I should pull away; any smart man would. But my hand finds her jaw, my thumb grazing her cheek, drying her tears. For a moment, I just breathe her in—citrus shampoo, salty skin, hurt, and something like hope.

She kisses me, slow at first. She tastes like heartbreak and something dangerously close to new beginnings.

I kiss her back.

At this moment, nothing else matters. Not the age, not the O'Ryan name, not the rules I've drawn around myself for years to keep from having a real relationship.

All that matters is her.

THREE
NOELLE

When our lips meet, everything inside me goes still and electric at the same time.

My mind spins faster than the blades of a helicopter, but for the first time, I'm winging it with a man. Kissing a man without analyzing every detail. I refuse to let myself think—about anything except the scratch of his stubble and the faint taste of pineapple on his lips. For a second, it almost feels like all the hurt burns away, replaced by this wild, dizzying rush I've only heard about in movies but never truly believed could be real.

Oh God. This is Matt. Greyson's best friend. And I'm the one kissing *him*.

The moment my flesh presses into his, he doesn't respond with movement but with a sigh that almost sounds like relief.

But then. Then. He kisses me back, gentle at first—like he's giving me a chance to change my mind—but when I don't, his hand slides into my hair and pulls me closer. My whole body is buzzing. All the awful things Brooks ever said, all the whispers in the locker room, the stupid questions about whether I'm enough or that I'm a prude for wanting to save myself for marriage. Well, those voices go quiet.

Under the steady weight of Matt's hands, my problems and hurt vanish, and the world shrinks down until it's only us. Lips overlapping in sweet harmony. Again and again.

When he finally pulls away, I'm lightheaded and woozy from the rush. He looks at me like he's just caught himself doing something he promised never to do. I want him to kiss me again, but he hesitates, searching my face for something, trying to read me.

"Did that make you feel better?" His voice is low and scratchy, but there's a hint of shakiness underneath.

My nerves prickle against my skin. How do I answer this question? Did it make me feel better? More than better. "It made me feel something," I gasp, forcing another wobbly laugh. "Does that get me a starting spot on your roster?" I joke, humiliated that I kissed him.

My hand moves before I can think, brushing over the heat of him, the unmistakable hardness straining against his jeans. Electricity snaps up my arm. My mind goes blank for half a second. Matt inhales sharply, his eyes going wide. He grabs my wrist, gentle but firm, and I pull back, my cheeks burning.

"Sorry," he says, soft but urgent. "I just wanted to comfort you, and I crossed the line."

"Oh God, I'm so stupid. What was I thinking?" I spring from the couch, putting as much distance between us as possible. Standing in front of a picture of Greyson's family reminds me that all I've ever wanted was to have someone love me back the way my brothers love their wives.

Suddenly, I feel Matt's presence behind me, and all

those feelings I've had for him over the past year flood my synapses. It was a crush that I never planned to act on. A schoolgirl pining after her brother's best friend. But now that I know what his lips can do, I'm incapable of stuffing my feelings back into a bottle and corking it as if I've never had a taste.

"Noelle, you're not stupid. If you hadn't kissed me, I probably would have kissed you. It felt right in the moment... but it's not. Kissing you was wrong in every way. You're in pain and... you were trying to ease it. I hope it did. Because you're beautiful, intelligent, athletic, and..." he pauses, seemingly searching for the perfect words. "You're the perfect woman for someone."

Without facing him, I see his reflection in the glass frame. "But not for you," I huff. "Not for Brooks, obviously. Who am I perfect for? I'm pathetic, hanging on to Brooks, and for what? Why didn't he break up with me? He says he loves me. He took my virginity." My chin falls to my chest as I close my eyes, wishing I hadn't overheard Bree and Renee in the bathroom. Wishing I hadn't embarrassed myself by kissing Matt.

His palms fold over my shoulders and his thumbs press into the base of my neck, rubbing up and down. "He's young. That's not an excuse for his behavior, but in my opinion, you never challenge him or talk to him about what he's doing to you or how he makes you feel. Like at your brother's wedding... when he was ignoring you, you didn't talk to him. You pulled me onto the dance floor."

"You seem to be my fall guy," I say, sniffling. "You know, like my stunt partner does. Catching me when I fall."

"Go to him. Talk to him and decide: either a clean break

or figure out if your relationship is worth repairing. I'll always be here for you... as a friend."

"I broke up with him over voicemail. But you're right, I need to give him a piece of my mind."

He kisses the crown of my head as his hands slowly skim down my arms, silently erasing the kiss we shared just minutes ago. He turns and begins walking up the staircase.

"Matt. Wait. Can you at least tell me if you liked the kiss? Brooks has a rule against kissing."

His head snaps toward me. "No kissing? Not even his girlfriend?"

"He gives me pecks, but not ones with emotion or... desire." I'm ashamed to even use that word. I've never felt desired.

Matt rubs the stubble on his jaw, his brows curling to meet in the middle. "Noelle, you're a perfect ten. And that kiss may have been an eleven."

He stares at me for a few seconds, flooding my body with warmth. "Thank you," I whisper.

FOUR

NOELLE

Privacy.

Brooks shows up at my house over the weekend and asks my roommates for privacy. Of course, they do what he asks; they're starry-eyed over the first-round draft pick. We had exchanged a few texts, and he badgered me into giving him one hour when he got back into town from New Orleans.

The guys leave, shooting me a hopeful look over their shoulders as they walk out.

Leaning my butt against the couch with my arms crossed, not daring to look into his eyes, I say, "So, what do you have to say for yourself?"

His body nears mine, and the ache in my chest grows stronger. He slides his palms up my arms and back down, lulling me into his embrace. He pulls me to his chest, and I can't help but cry.

"Shh... I'm sorry. It won't happen again. I'm so sorry." His apology seems genuine. "Noelle, I was wrong and had too much to drink. I got caught up in the moment."

"How many moments? Bree made it sound like you've slept with Tabby repeatedly," I say.

He strokes my hair, pulls my head back, and peers into my eyes. "I made mistakes. I love you. Forgive me."

'But why would you... after we...?"

"I was drunk, but that's not an excuse. I won't ever do it again. Trust me."

My mom used to say it takes more energy to hold a grudge than to forgive, so I nod, thinking that's what she would expect of me.

Brooks leans in and pecks me on the lips. "Good. You're all mine, Noelle."

I don't know why I can't express what I'm feeling with Brooks. Why can't I argue with him, kiss, and have makeup sex? I have heard it's passionate, and maybe that's what we're missing.

"So... Hamlin is having a party tonight. Do you want to go?" Derek Hamlin is a linebacker on our team "This is probably the last time we'll all be together."

"Aren't you coming back for graduation?" I ask.

"Yeah, but after I walk the stage, I'll have to fly back out to New Orleans. Back-to-back meetings with my agent, a corporation for licensing rights, and then a realtor to look for my own place."

Disappointed, I look down at my shoes. "So, you won't be at my party?"

"No. I wish I could. I mean, do you want me to cancel with the shoe company?" he asks, lifting his brows.

"I wish the Armadillos would have drafted you."

"Me too, but since they went to the championship game, they didn't have the opportunity. My draft stock was way too high." His voice is full of overconfidence and swagger.

Brooks's phone rings, and he walks outside to talk on the front porch. He talks low, and I tiptoe into the kitchen to eavesdrop. I know that's wrong, but even though I forgive him, it doesn't mean I trust him. But everyone deserves a second chance, right?

"Hey, who was on the phone?"

He hems and haws. "Sorry, I'm sworn to secrecy." Brooks laughs, but something isn't right in his voice.

I sway up to him, slide my arms around his waist, and grab the hem of his shirt with my hands. Maybe if I initiate sex, it will make him feel desired. Maybe that's what's been wrong—neither of us has felt wanted so badly that we can't wait another second for clothes to be strewn across the room. But when I get to the point that he needs to raise his arms for me, he stops me.

"Don't you want to have makeup sex?" I ask, my heart popping a few stitches that were holding it together.

"I do, but I only have a few hours to get the rest of my stuff packed, and I'm meeting Professor Reinhart to take my final exam."

"Oh, okay. Should I meet you at the party?"

Brooks reaches for my hands, squeezing them. "Could you? Or I can pick you up, but it will make us both late."

My shoulders fall just a bit, hoping we could ride together so I could show the catty girls that Brooks loves me. "I'll just meet you there. I know you're busy."

He hugs me and kisses me on the cheek. "Great. I knew we could work this out."

Walking into the party, the first person I see is Renee. "Hey, what are you doing here?"

"Brooks and I are back together."

Her eyebrows practically reach her hairline. "Really?" Her eyes are as big as I've ever seen them.

"I know you think Brooks is too good for me. But we worked it out, and I'm giving him a second chance."

She folds her lips over her teeth. It's clear she doesn't approve. "Second chance, right."

"Renee, I've enjoyed cheering with you. When you're not around Bree, you're nice, but you're a different person when you're with her."

Renee grabs my hand. "I don't want him cheating on you. My dad had a five-year affair with his coworker, and my mom kept believing him every time he said it was over. It tore our family apart. Now I have to split myself in half because of their stupid mistakes. You're the one who's too good for Brooks." Her voice trails off as Bree bounces in.

"Thanks, but just quit gossiping about Brooks and me."

"Hey, who's ready for Jell-O shots?" Bree screams with her hands raised, working hard to be the life of the party.

"None for me."

Bree rolls her eyes and grabs Renee's elbow, snatching her toward the kitchen. I walk around until I find Brooks and some of the team playing cornhole outside, so I find a seat next to one of the players.

"Ready for graduation?" I ask.

"I haven't found a job yet, but my parents own a manufacturing company in Steele, Texas, so I guess I'll work there until I do," he says, like he's disappointed in himself.

We all have these grand visions of what we'll be when we grow up, and athletes expect to go pro. It's what they've dreamed of their entire lives, so when reality hits that only a few go on to play professionally, they get depressed. Their world is turned upside down.

"I haven't found a job either. I'm interviewing for a sports reporter position for a new start-up the week after graduation. I don't know which sport, but if it's football, then I think I'll have a chance since my dad and brothers don't shut up about it."

"Don't sell yourself short. Lots of women have families that love sports, but they don't. You love competition. Sometimes I'd look over at the cheerleaders and none of the other women beamed like you."

I smile, and my body feels warm. Is he flirting with me? No one has dared to in over a year. Everyone bows down to Brooks Pendleton.

"Yeah, I do love football—all sports. Even hockey. My brother Parker played college hockey, but now he's doing football workouts for Baylor, Texas, and Texas A&M. And I would bet he chooses A&M because my brother J.D. hates them with a passion."

"Even now?" he asks.

"Well, since he has players from A&M on his team, he teases them. But under it all, he's a Longhorn."

"But your brother Greyson didn't follow him there. I guess we all need to make our own way, don't we? Are you glad you came to this university and met Brooks?"

My tongue gets stuck in my throat, and I have a difficult time answering, so I just nod.

"You deserve better, and I'm pretty sure you already know it." His chair scrapes against the concrete as he gets up. "He's not who he says he is."

His fingers graze my shoulder, and there is pity in his eyes.

When he leaves, another couple takes a seat next to me. She sits on his lap, and they're kissing and giggling, flirting and drinking. The perfect couple, in my opinion. Being together should be easy, but with Brooks, it's a freaking job. I spend most of my time waiting for him. When will he notice me? I've been here twenty minutes, and he hasn't even winked my way, waved me over, or jogged over to kiss me and say hello.

Keely asks me, "Are you moving to New Orleans with Brooks?"

"No." That's when it hits me that Brooks and I never even discussed it after he was drafted. Did he assume that I wouldn't leave my family? I probably wouldn't unless we were engaged, but why didn't he at least ask? Right now, I need to be close to home. Parker and Witt need me. J.D. and Birdie recently had a baby girl, Henley. Sutton and Greyson have one on the way.

She seems surprised, but then her boyfriend yells over to Brooks, "Your girl is staying here and not moving with your ugly mug. What are you going to do without her?"

Brooks straightens his spine, and a red tint travels up his neck to his face. "Football."

I hear a few snickers, but I don't turn around to see who it is. Instead, I stand and yell, "Bree, where are those shots?"

The guys cheer me on as I do one shot. Then two more. Brooks is watching, fuming. I rarely drink if I'm not somewhere safe. During my freshman year, a guy put a date rape drug in one of my teammate's drinks. She was never the same. A month later, she quit the team, dropped out of school, and moved home. A few of us called to check in, but she would never answer, then she'd text us saying she was working or whatever. After that, I assumed she didn't want any memories of this school, this team, or the guy. Word spread about who the guy was, and soon he was gone as well.

Inside, the music pulses so hard it thrums in my chest. A disco ball flashes in the living room where all the furniture is pushed against the walls. Bodies are pressed together—dancing, jumping, losing themselves in the sweaty chaos. I laugh, half-wild, the flavor of hard seltzer buzzing on my tongue as I join in, dancing with anyone who grabs my hand, male or female. For a moment, I'm light—untouchable.

Then Jake—tight end, always grinning—spins me like we're on some neon-lit tilt-a-whirl. Spinning. Spinning. Free, until I'm suddenly not. The room tilts and my stomach lurches up my throat, fierce and unstoppable. I pinch my mouth closed to push it back down.

"I'm... I'm..."

Jake's steadying hand pulls me. "Let's get you to the bathroom."

He steers me across sticky floors and swings open the bathroom door. Inside, a girl kneels in front of a guy, head bobbing, lost in him. But it's not just anyone—I know those sneakers. White leather, neon trim, stupidly expensive. Brooks. My Brooks.

His eyes snap to mine, wide and guilty, but the girl just keeps going, swallowing him like he's special. My vision blurs. Rage and nausea war inside me. Jake tugs at my arm. "Let's get out of here."

I don't move. Not yet. I stumble forward, my focus locked on Brooks, and he fumbles, trying to peel her off. Something dark wells up in me, hotter than fury. I open my mouth to scream—only to feel everything I've kept down all night expelled right onto her perfect hair and his now-limp dick.

"Fuck, Noelle," Brooks shouts.

"My hair is ruined," the girl gripes under her breath, but when her head turns, I realize it's Tabby.

"Good. Best of luck. If he cheats on me, he'll cheat on you too." I spin toward the door and lose my balance. Jake steadies me and takes me outside.

"Can I call someone for you, or can I take you home?"

I'm such a fool. Why did I forgive him? My body aches from the liquor. Unlocking my phone, I give it to him. "I don't know. Maybe my brother."

"You want me to call your brother? Like the quarterback for the Austin Armadillos?" he asks, his voice scratchy.

"I have four brothers," I mutter as the lights dim and my eyes close.

I have no idea how I got home or who took care of me, but I have a raging headache, and my stomach is growling. When I finally turn over to look at the clock, there are pain meds, water, and a note.

You need to eat.
Bagels in the kitchen with your
favorite cinnamon cream cheese.

There's no name on the note, so I'm assuming it's one of my roommates. Maybe they were at the party. I don't remember seeing them, but in all honesty, I don't remember much. Except my boyfriend's penis in a mouth that wasn't mine.

One kiss and I can't push Noelle from my mind.

The memory of her lips haunts me. What else haunts me is seeing her in this condition at the party. Noelle's friend used her phone to call Greyson, and Greyson called me, desperate for someone to pick her up immediately. Greyson and J.D. had taken their family to visit their grandmother. He tried Parker first, but he was M.I.A., and he didn't want to involve their dad.

I put the address into the GPS, drive over, and pick her up. Change her out of her reeking clothes. I try and fail at *not* letting my eyes linger on her body. She's fit and athletic, and when the back of my hands brush against her silky-smooth skin, it's impossible to ignore. It's been a week, and I'm betting that she doesn't remember that I'm the one who picked her up. Unless her brother filled her in. I've been avoiding the subject with Greyson by stating, "It's none of my business."

Today is her graduation. Her family is throwing a party

at Sloane's, the fanciest spot in their little suburb outside of Austin.

I tuck her present into my pants pocket, throw on my gray suit jacket and my black felt cowboy hat, hoping to shield my eyes from Noelle and her family. I don't want them catching on to my feelings, so a little shadow over my eyes should do the trick.

The restaurant has plants adorning the entrance, cascading from the ceiling like a waterfall. "Good afternoon. The graduate appreciates you being here. Your name?"

"Um, Matt Stricker." Damn, this is more formal than I expected.

"Sir, you'll be sitting at table four."

"Thank you."

I step into an oasis of twinkling lights strung in every direction and throughout each tree. The chandeliers aren't the typical ones you would find in old mansions; instead, they're made of light-colored wood with curvy, bubble-like faceted crystals hanging from several branches.

J.D. and Greyson wave me over to the bar, which glows with golden lights and amber liquid arranged on the shelves. Some bottles are sitting on books, some angled like photos.

"Glad you could make it," J.D. says as he shakes my hand. He's the head coach of the Austin Armadillos, making him my boss and a friend.

Pressing my lips together, I smile. "Wouldn't miss your sister's graduation. How's she doing?"

Greyson's brows furrow. "What do you mean?"

"About Brooks. She came by when I was house-sitting. She seemed down. Said Brooks was..."

I don't have a chance to finish my sentence when Sutton,

Greyson's wife, flings her arms around me. Sutton is also my boss since she's the general manager of the team, but she's become more like a sister to me. We hit it off from her first day on the job, and she's responsible for Greyson and me becoming best friends.

"Matt! You're looking handsome."

"Don't I always?"

I wrap her in an embrace when I notice Noelle over her shoulder in the distance. The wind is knocked from my chest —she's wearing a white, strapless short dress. Her hair is half up, flowing down her back, and the hem of her dress hits mid-thigh. My eyes travel down her legs, and I mentally scold myself for even thinking about her in this way.

Why is my dick twitching?

"Hey, thanks for picking up Noelle last weekend," Sutton whispers in my ear.

"Anytime. I'm here for the O'Ryans."

We break the hug, and Greyson says, "You never really told me what Noelle said that night. All she told me was that she got drunk."

"She passed out. Her roommates weren't home, so I put her in bed and put some water by her bed. Did she tell you why she was drunk?" I ask, looking between them.

"Nope. She holds things close to the vest when she doesn't want people to know." Greyson sighs. "Noelle wants people to believe she's this badass, but our mom's death affected us all in different ways. She wants to be like Mom instead of being herself."

"Are Brooks and her still broken up?" I inquire casually.

J.D. and Birdie join us, with their baby girl Henley on J.D.'s chest, swaying from side to side. "Broken up? Really? When?"

"That's what I was getting ready to say. When I was dogsitting, Noelle came by. It was obvious she had been crying. We played some video games, and finally, she told me that Brooks was cheating on her and she broke up with him. Maybe that's what spurred the drinking binge."

Greyson listens without interrupting. It's his gift. He understands why Noelle would come to him with her problems, but he realizes she never told him anything about it.

He twists his lips and finally opens his mouth, only to close it again. He gives us a head nod to look behind me.

"Guess they're back together," Sutton says, her tone full of disappointment. "But she must make her own mistakes, Greyson O'Ryan. If you demand that she does one thing, she'll do another."

Greyson marches in their direction, and I follow to keep him from ruining his sister's graduation party. He loves Noelle with all his heart, which is why I'm ashamed of kissing her. When they are within earshot, I hear Noelle say to Brooks, "You're here." I can't tell if she wants him to be or not. Her face is expressionless.

Brooks grabs her hands. "I wouldn't miss your graduation. You mean the world to me."

Greyson takes another step, but before he can erupt, Noelle shakes her hands loose and crosses her arms over her chest. "Leave."

"No, baby. We hit a snag, but we can work it out. Look, I bought you this." He reaches into the purple gift bag he's carrying and pulls out a diamond necklace. He's obviously gotten his signing bonus with New Orleans.

Her eyes go wide, and I assume that's all it's going to take for her to take him back. We stand waiting for her response. She closes her eyes and says, "I've moved on. Please leave."

He jerks her arm, and I lunge for him, grabbing his elbow. "Get your hands off her, or I'll break them."

Brooks shakes me off and says, "What's wrong with you, old man? You want what I have?"

Yes.

"What did you say, motherfucker?" I grab him by the shirt. He has a few inches on me and is probably on some illegal supplement.

"Stop. Both of you. And for your information, Brooks, I traded up. Matt and I are dating," Noelle adds.

I stand there, my hands flexing at my sides, heat rushing through my chest so fast I almost don't register what she says until it's hanging in the air like a live wire: *"Matt and I are dating."*

Time stops. Brooks blinks, shock flickering into something ugly. Noelle's brothers—Greyson and J.D.—are stone-faced, like boulders ready to roll. Her other brothers are behind Brooks. Parker smiles like he's enjoying the show, and Witt is expressionless. Her dad's jaw clenches so hard I hear his teeth grind.

For a heartbeat, nobody breathes. I catch Noelle's gaze. Her eyes are level, daring me to contradict her, but something almost pleading shimmers there—a silent apology.

Brooks laughs, humorless, the sound splintering the hush. "Are you serious right now? You're with...him?" He jabs a thumb at me, his knuckles white. "What, you break up with me and go straight for your brother's quarterback coach? You've got serious daddy issues."

Greyson starts forward. "Watch your mouth, Brooks." His voice is like gravel, and J.D.'s knuckles are turning white, his nostrils flaring. To be honest, I think it's more at me than at Brooks.

Her dad, Mr. O'Ryan, just stares at me, betrayal and disbelief twisted across his face. "Matt?" His voice is a low warning. "Is that true? With my daughter?"

I swallow hard. Part of me wants to set the record straight, but Noelle is standing there with her chin high, her arms wrapped around herself like armor. Her eyes beg me to go along with the charade, so I nod. "Yeah. It's true." The words land heavy, as real as the pounding of my heart.

Brooks's skin turns redder than a hot pepper. "Un-fuck-ing-believable," he snaps, his fist closing around the necklace. "You really are a liar, Noelle. And you..." He glares at me, his voice breaking. "You're pathetic." He tosses the bag at her feet and storms out, shoving past Greyson so hard the doors rattle behind him.

She picks up the necklace and throws it across the room.

For a breathless moment, the room is silent except for the echo of Brooks's exit and their grandmother popping champagne in the background. She steals the show at every family event I've been to, but not this one. No one can top what just happened here.

Noelle holds her hand over her heart, and I take my place beside her. Her brothers exchange looks—Greyson is furious, J.D. is betrayed, and both are looking at me like I've just punted a puppy off the porch.

Mr. O'Ryan steps between us—tall, broad, and protective. "Matt, this—this is wrong." The words cut deeper than I expected.

Noelle hugs herself tighter, trembling but silent. I slide my arm around her back and whisper, "It will be okay."

Greyson rounds on us, his voice low and cold. "You've got to be kidding, Matt. I trusted you. You're my best fucking friend." I've never seen Greyson's face as hot and red as it is right now.

I try to speak, but I need to let them get their anger out.

"I don't want to hear it." J.D. glares at me. "You know better, Matt. She's just a kid compared to you."

The disappointment in their eyes stings like nothing else.

Noelle looks down, her shoulders slumping. For a second, I wish I could disappear. We end up cornered in a quiet dining alcove when the uproar dies down. Noelle's shaking and won't look at me.

"Can we all go into the private dining room? I promise I'll tell you everything. Please," Noelle begs.

Her immediate family and I go into the other room, her brothers fuming. "What the hell is going on?" Greyson asks, his voice taut, laced with fury. "Matt, I swear I'm going to kick your ass."

Greyson bumps his chest against mine when Noelle shouts, "Stop. Stop! Just listen to me. It's not Matt's fault."

Parker mumbles, "Sure seems like he's taking advantage of you."

"No. He's saving me from the humiliation of Brooks Pendleton. Please, just everyone sit." Noelle commands everyone's attention.

Sitting around a table decorated for a princess, with pink crystals flickering against the lights and dark pink flowers as the centerpiece, everyone takes a breath and waits for Noelle to speak.

"I overheard my teammates say that Brooks was cheating on me. When I talked to him, he apologized and promised it would never happen again. But at our last college party... I found him in the bathroom getting... I'm sorry," she whispers. "I just... I needed Brooks to believe I'm over him. I just wanted him out of my life for real."

Risking a glance at her older brothers, I see the emotion on their faces. The one that can't believe Brooks hurt their little sister. It's J.D. who blurts out, "I'll ruin him and his career. Where does he live?"

Greyson scoots his chair back, and it scrapes across the floor, sounding nearly as angry as J.D. Noelle gets up, wraps her arms around his waist, and lays her head on his back. "Just let me deal with him. My way."

Her voice thickens as she looks at me, tears blurring her eyes. "Will you—can you please just go along with it for a while? Just until it blows over? Give Brooks a taste of what it feels like to not be wanted anymore."

I take a shaky breath. For a split second, hope flickers in my gut—hope that maybe this could be real, not for revenge, not out of desperation, but because she wants me. But the look in her eyes douses it.

"Yeah, if your family is okay with pretending," I manage, my voice rough. "Whatever you need, Noelle."

Even if it leaves me without my best guy friend.

Greyson's not a fan of the idea, based on his jaw grinding.

She nods, relief and regret warring in her expression. "Thank you, Matt. Just... until Brooks gets the message."

I force a smile. "Of course." But inside, disappointment gnaws like an open wound, and I wonder if I'm really the one who just got played.

"Dad? J.D.? Greyson?" she urges them to say something. "I just want Brooks to understand how it feels to be tossed out like last night's leftovers."

Witt, the youngest, mostly silent brother, says, "Fake it 'til you make it, right?"

A smile slides across Noelle's face. She stands and hugs him. "Exactly."

"I'm sorry he treated you so badly. I hated hearing you cry when you would come home from school."

"Thanks, Witt. I didn't know you paid attention." He shrugs like it's no big deal, but it is. It is to me.

Greyson says, "Before I agree to anything, I want to know how we got here and why you chose Matt."

"Because he's hotter than a ghost pepper tamale, and Brooks knows Matt's been there for her when he was ignoring her at the wedding last year. Now leave the girl alone. This is her life." Their granny has a sparkle in her eyes like she's proud of Noelle for thinking fast on her feet. "If she needs to prove something to Brooks, then let her."

Mr. O'Ryan says, "Who in the hell has ever heard of fake dating? Especially with a man more than a decade older. It doesn't look good."

Granny raises her arms and rolls her eyes. "Oh, hell, Robert. People have done it since the dawn of time. You want to make someone jealous? Find a guy willing to take you out and show the other one what he's missing."

Birdie pats her baby on the back. "Granny's right. If Matt's willing to put his dating life on hold for a bit for Noelle, then what's the harm?"

My dating life is nonexistent. Greyson and Sutton know my reasons, but not J.D. and Birdie. I asked them to keep it between us, and they have.

Mr. O'Ryan lets out a heavy sigh. "Touch my daughter inappropriately just one time, and I'll skin your ass."

"I understand. I had no idea Noelle was going to pitch

that we were dating to Brooks. Because we're not. But I felt at that moment it was the right thing to do to protect her."

Mr. O'Ryan gives me a short glance before looking at Noelle. "I appreciate that, but sweetheart, why didn't you come to me and tell me what was going on?"

"I was embarrassed. My teammates were talking behind my back, and what girl wants to tell their dad that their boyfriend has his penis in other people?"

"Well, then tell me." Greyson looks devastated that Noelle didn't tell him.

"I came to tell you, but you were gone, and Matt was there instead."

Sutton leans over, always the executive, and says, "Noelle has lots of people here to celebrate. We need to go out as a family, united behind her and Matt's dating revelation. We can deal with the fallout later, but Brooks needs to think this is real. Deal?"

Everyone nods. Granny can't wipe the smile off her face. She loves Sutton like her own daughter.

"All right. Let's go."

Standing up, I take Noelle's hand in mine. "You ready?"

"Thanks, Matt. I owe you."

Yes. Yes, you do.

And I'm thinking of all the ways I can call in that *I owe you.*

"Everyone's staring at us," I say through clenched teeth, ventriloquist style.

My family isn't altogether on board with our fake dating, but they won't embarrass me by outing me.

"Those are the looks you get when you say you're dating a man fifteen years older than you." Matt places his fingers on my back, touching me with only his finger pads, and guides me to a group of my friends from high school.

He hovers at a comfortable distance to keep up the appearance that we're dating and turns red when he overhears one girl saying, "Wow, I need an older man. He's a five-alarm fire that I wouldn't want to put out."

I put my hand over my mouth and whisper in her ear, "I know, right? We just recently started dating, though."

Paulina, Sutton and Greyson's now-adopted daughter, runs up to me and pulls me over to the side. "Dad is stewing over there. When did you fall in love with Matt?"

"Paulina, we just started dating. We're feeling things out.

But remember when he danced with me at the wedding?" Paulina shakes her head aggressively. "Well, I knew then that he was my savior and he would be there for me when I needed him. You'll understand when you're older."

"I do understand. And guess what?" She switches the subject. "Trevor asked me to go to the movies. His parents are coming into town and taking us. Can you believe Dad said I could go?" She's practically bouncing with excitement.

"Yes, I'm sure Sutton is the one who made that decision."

"Mom wants me to have some experiences she didn't have."

Yeah, and your dad doesn't want you to have the experiences he had.

Across the room, my dad is deep in conversation with Parker and Matt. Matt laughs, and it seems a little too forced. Is he nervous or just playing along?

I scan the crowd and spot my older brothers throwing daggers Matt's way. Mom used to call it the old stink-eye. But the tension between them helps—if they acted totally fine with me dating Matt, everyone would know I was lying, grasping for anything to stop the hurt Brooks inflicted. This performance is perfect.

Sutton taps the microphone, thanks everyone for coming, and says, "Noelle's dad would like to say a few words."

He clears his throat and looks at me. "Noelle is the light of our family. Free-spirited, but not wild. Even though her revelation today may make me change my mind." Subtle laughs hum through the room. "She's nurturing but not suffocating. She's direct and confident with us, her family. Maybe that means I did something right. Her mother was supposed to be here for this."

When he says it, I find Witt in my peripheral vision, and he's as stoic as they come. Witt never talks about his feelings, but I know it must be hard on him not having grown up with Mom at all.

"Anyway, I know she would be proud of the woman you've become, Noelle. And I want to read something she wrote in her journal when you were four years old."

My sweet Noelle, the heartbeat of our family. You make each one of us smile with just a laugh or one of your many questions. And when I catch Greyson and John David playing princess with you, drinking out of tiny teacups and protecting their little princess with fake swords, I realize that you will have plenty of people that will always be there for you. And I love how Parker is only a year younger, but you act like he's a baby. You pull people into your orbit, and they can't get out. My wish for you is that you find a career you love and a person in life who will give you as much joy as you give everyone else.

My dad has one errant tear slowly making a trail down his cheek, and I can't help but attack him like the little girl I once was. "Thank you. You're the best dad."

"Congratulations on your big day." He squeezes me tight.

"Okay, no more sappiness," I say. "Thank you, Sutton and Birdie, for making this party so chic. I don't deserve you two. Thanks for being my estrogen in a family of testosterone. And for being the women who put up with my brothers. Everyone, eat up. And in true O'Ryan family tradition, the back room is also set up with games and contests. Like 'Guess My Age' or 'Where in the World Am I?'"

I stop and chuckle. "Just guess a football game and more than likely you're on the right track. Am I at a high school game, one of my college games, one of Dad's, Greyson's, or J.D.'s, or a professional game? So you must say the city. There's also a brand-new virtual reality simulator that Witt coded so that you can immerse yourself in ten different activities. Have fun."

A line of friends waits in a circle to hug and congratulate me, but when I look around, I can't find Matt. When I'm finished and starving, Matt comes up to me with a plate full of food.

"Here, you need to eat at your own party. Isn't that the point of being a princess... to be waited on and taken care of?" His voice is as smooth as silk but quiet, and I just let his words linger in the air. It feels good for someone other than my family to care about me. Brooks never made sure I ate. Like, at the party, he could have been with me and made sure I didn't get too drunk, but instead he was betraying me.

"Thanks. Where did you go?"

His chest hiccups with an internal laugh. "Had to take some medicine and needed water. You're dating an old man, you know?"

He shoves one hand into his pocket and hands me an organza bag. "This is for your graduation."

"You didn't have to...money would have been fine," I tease. But then I pull it open and gasp. "It's perfect."

"It's not a diamond necklace."

I bump my shoulder against his arm, playful and flirtatious. "Well, you weren't my boyfriend until an hour ago, so I'll forgive you." It's a crystal ornament with my name and graduation date on it. "It's beautiful. Why did you buy an ornament?"

"You mentioned that you collect Christmas ornaments at a cookout one time, so I thought..."

Cutting him short, I fling my arms around him and hold him as tight as I can. "Thank you. It's so thoughtful." Not once has Brooks bought me a Christmas ornament, despite me talking about it all the time.

"Crap!" Parker yells by the chocolate fountain, and as people gasp, I see chocolate all over his khaki pants. "It looks like I've shit myself."

The more I attempt to hold in my laughter, I can't. Parker's eyes narrow, but my cheer mate Elise brings him a wet cloth, and she can't decide if she should clean him up. He takes the cloth and dabs. Greyson says, "I have shorts in the truck. Want me to grab them?"

Parker nods his head, and soon everyone has forgotten about his mishap and a makeshift conga line forms around the chocolate fountain. I nudge Matt and tease, "You should join them. I bet you can do a killer conga."

Matt's cheeks tint pink. "The last time I danced was with you at your brother's wedding, and I twisted my ankle. I don't need an injury. I have a feeling being your fake boyfriend will cause enough damage," he whispers.

"No guts, no glory," I say, dragging him with me to the conga line. My brothers join in, and it seems their cooling-off period is over. Everyone is celebrating. Parker has his hands on Elise's waist, and we scream and snake around the event.

Finally, it's over. The guys load up Matt's truck with the gifts. Birdie and Sutton insist that I go home and that they'll clean up since it's my day.

SEVEN

NOELLE

An odd but strangely satisfying day.

Outside, the breeze is soft, and Matt opens the passenger door for me. The ride is mostly quiet. My window is down, and the whirring of the engine and the rustling of the leaves make me comfortable in the silence. But after a few minutes pass, I say, "Thanks for putting up with all this."

Matt glances over with a close-lipped smile. "No problem. I didn't mean to get in between you and Brooks. But when he... I just lost it."

"Don't worry. Sometimes I just say what comes to mind instead of thinking about the consequences. It's almost like I'm scared I won't be able to say it later because that person may not be there."

"Like your mom?"

I nod, thinking about what she would have worn to my graduation. What would have been different about today? "To be honest, you played the part perfectly. You made today fun for me, and I haven't truly felt that in a long time."

He turns into my driveway, opens my door, and starts

filling his arms up with presents. Turning the key, I open the door and say, "Just take them to my room, last door on the left."

"I know where your room is."

"Oh, that's right, you picked me up from the party last weekend." My lips curve and I can't help the giddiness inside me.

I nod as I set a stack of presents in a corner. After he gets the last load, he asks, "How long do we need to fake being a couple?"

Shrugging, I answer, "At least a month. Maybe longer."

"Let's make some ground rules."

"I agree. There must be rules." I salute him like he's in charge.

"No catching feelings. I don't do girlfriends. And only until Brooks believes it and turns his focus somewhere else. Men want what they can't have."

I force a grin, ignoring the way my heart does a stutter step. "Deal. What should we do to seal the deal?" I joke.

He holds out his hand. "Shake on it."

"Boring. You are old." I press to my toes, kissing him on the cheek. "Your turn."

"You want to seal the deal with a kiss on the cheek? Maybe you're the one that's boring."

"Well, if you want more, all you have to do is ask?" I say, teasing, loving how his face gets red.

He leans down, and his breath floats over my skin, which instantly prickles. It's as if he's teasing me before he finally opens his lips and gives me the best kiss on the cheek ever.

EIGHT
MATT - KENTUCKY

Damn, it's loud.

If there's anything louder than a stadium packed with screaming fans, it's a pack of ten-year-old boys playing football, each trash-talking more than the next. I never thought I'd be more afraid of a birthday piñata than I was when a defensive end barreled at my blindside, but here I am—dodging water balloons and neon cupcakes in suburban Kentucky.

After playing professionally for a couple of years, I became the quarterback coach for the Stallions, where Logan Warren was the quarterback. Then we were together at the Louisville Heavyweights until I needed to make a change and ended up with the Armadillos. I've been lucky in my career to coach top talent and create bonds of friendship, which is why I'm here.

Logan catches me watching the chaos and claps a big hand on my shoulder. "Admit it, Matt, you're reminiscing about the glory days when we won the National Title and the Super Bowl."

I grin and shake my head, watching his daughter Evy race across the grass, her hair flying wild. "No, I'm thinking these kids are a tougher crowd than the SEC ever was. Besides, I'm going to win the Super Bowl this year. How's retirement?"

Reed jogs over. "Hey. Greer and the kids want to play against the old guys. Can we take them?"

Reed was Logan's and his wife Harper's roommate in college and played professional hockey for ten years. Now, he's retired too. "We can. I don't know about you," I chuckle. "How are all the kids? How many do you have?"

He starts naming them, "Caleb, Cannon, Carly—"

"A whole basketball team. Even has a sixth man," Logan teases. He looks at Reed. "Has Caleb decided to take the hockey or football scholarship?"

"Hockey."

Greer yells, "Dad, come on."

The guy's eyes light up like children at Christmas time. I wonder if it's having kids that makes them happy or if they would be this happy anyway. Logan punches Hagan, his brother-in-law. "Let's go."

"Why don't they want to play baseball?" Hagan asks.

Growing up in a small town, I played baseball, basketball, and football, so I say, "Easy question. You can't hit anyone in baseball. Not as fun."

"Yeah, I'm beginning to think I'm the only smart one in this group," Hagan says, shaking his head as we run over the big field.

I'll say this: these kids are as competitive as they come. Logan passes me the ball, and suddenly I have one kid, Cannon, leaping onto my back. The kid must have a forty-inch vertical jump. Two more are tugging at my legs, leaving me to face-plant into the bluegrass.

Greer is the quarterback for the kids' team, and it's evident that Logan has worked on his mechanics. He's smooth at ten years old. We're tied at eighteen, not having extra points in backyard play, when Logan's wife, Harper, yells, "Time to eat."

All the boys complain loudly, "No, the game's not over."

Logan whistles, getting their attention. As soon as he does, they take off toward the food table.

Admiring the rolling green hills and tree-topped land, I ask, "Do you like living out of town?"

"Yeah. It's still close to the hospital for Harper and the private school the kids attend. And the interstate is only five miles away, so it's a great jumping-off point."

"Do you feel like you're missing something by retiring?"

"No. Been there. Done it all. Now it's time to be with my kids and Harper."

Adalee, Hagan's wife, strides over, hugging me. "Didn't know you had come in."

"This guy keeps inviting me." I've been to nearly every one of Logan and Harper's kids' birthday parties. After coaching him two years in college and nine years in the pros, Adalee gets distracted by a cupcake-grabbing kid and rushes over to intervene.

"If you ever retire, I'll pay you to train Greer when he gets a year or two older." Logan swipes his hand over his face. "You'll probably have kids by then."

"Me? Nope. Not in the cards for this guy."

He laughs, but his eyes narrow—he always did spot trouble before most. "Are you regretting moving to Austin? Is something wrong?"

Might as well get it all out. I nudge him toward the grill, away from the shrieking chaos. "So...you know Greyson O'Ryan?"

Logan's eyebrows shoot up. "Of course. Problems with your new golden boy?"

I exhale and run a hand over the back of my neck. "Yeah. No. Maybe," I stammer. "It turns out his little sister, Noelle —she's all grown up. And I may have gotten myself tangled up in a fake dating situation with her."

Logan chokes on his beer. "You're kidding. Greyson's little sister? What are you, a glutton for punishment?"

The answer is yes.

"She needed help shaking off an ex. I ended up playing the part. The whole thing blew up at her graduation party. Her family... let's just say, none of them are thrilled that the guy she's fake-dating was the starting quarterback at his high school when she was in diapers."

He whistles, low. "What is that, a ten- or fifteen-year age gap?"

"Fourteen, but yeah." I turn my beer in my hands. "Greyson is ticked off even thinking about me dating his sister, even if it's pretend. Coach is barely speaking to me, and their dad looks at me like I just stole the Hope Diamond."

He cocks an eyebrow, but there's a smirk tugging at his mouth. "Have you..."

"We kissed one time when she found out her boyfriend, Brooks Pendleton, was cheating on her."

"The same guy New Orleans drafted?" he asks, his brows furrowing.

I nod. "One and the same. Total dick."

He scrapes his fingers over his chin. "So? Will this 'fake'

thing stay fake, or are you about to end up on the wrong side of a shotgun wedding?"

"Don't even joke. Like I said, no kids for me." I shake my head, but a traitorous flicker of hope twists somewhere low in my chest. "We promised—no lines crossed, no feelings. It's just for show."

Logan gives me a look—one he used to give rookie wide receivers when they were a little too sure of themselves. "Yeah," he says, "good luck with that. If it's nothing, why do you look like you're in too deep?"

We let his question roll around in our heads because I don't know the answer. Something just feels different.

I glance back at the birthday party. Girls are screaming—unlike the boys, it's high-pitched, but my mind's a thousand miles away, thinking about blue eyes, graduation dresses, and how impossible it is to keep something fake when I can't stop thinking about her.

Logan holds my gaze for a second longer, then it breaks as I feel a soft tap on my shoulder.

"Matt!" Harper's voice is all warmth and sunshine—even after all these years, Logan's wife still greets me like family. She leans in, pecks my cheek, and Greer barrels into me with Roscoe, their doodle, pulling at the leash and sniffing my ankles.

"I can't believe Roscoe still has as much energy as a ten-year-old," I tease, ruffling Greer's hair.

Harper gives me a doctor's once-over, that sharp blend of affection and medical assessment only she pulls off. "You look good, Matt," she says, her eyes narrowing in a friendly inspection. "Taking care of yourself?"

I grin. "Trying to. My numbers have been good lately. Daily shots. You know the routine."

But then I rub my eyes, blinking at the late afternoon sun, and Harper's attention sharpens. "You sure? Anything bothering you lately?" She's a pediatric surgeon but deals with the ramifications of diabetes all the time.

I shrug, squinting again. "Honestly? My vision's been a little fuzzy the past few mornings." I try to brush it off. "Probably just allergies or, I don't know, old age catching up."

Her doctor mode clicks in—brows knit, smile gone, careful. "Matt, with your diabetes, any changes in your eyesight can be serious. Have you gotten your eyes checked recently?"

"Not since—" I hesitate, then wave it off, "well, not in a few months. I'll make an appointment. Promise."

She gives me a look that could make any linebacker sit up straight. "Don't put it off. If it gets any worse, call me, okay?"

"Scout's honor," I say, though something twists in my stomach. I glance down at Roscoe's soft fur and Greer beaming up at me, then over at Logan, who's pretending not to listen—but his frown says he is.

"Thanks, Harper," I add softly, "for looking out for the old guys."

"You're not old, Matt," she says, smiling now as she pulls Roscoe away from another guest's hamburger. "Just... not invincible."

She and Greer head off, Logan trailing after, but her concern lingers, settling in next to everything else I'm carrying.

NINE
NOELLE

My first official interview.

Staring at my reflection in the sun visor mirror, my hands shake as I dab a fingertip under each eye, smoothing out the faint trace of mascara that always mutinies when I need things to go right. Sideline reporter," I mumble to myself. College is over and a big-girl job awaits. Professional Noelle. Even after practicing a polished and approachable smile, the jitters threaten to take over. I tell myself that if they don't hire me for this position, I have another interview next week with that startup sports streaming service.

"Get out of the car," I utter. My brand of pep talk is talking to myself. The network's office is in a bright steel building that looks the color of the team with the star on their helmet when the sky is clear blue. It's like an invisible thread drawing me closer.

When I step into the conference room, the panel waits: two senior producers, a guy from talent management who looks barely older than me, and—because the universe finds it hilarious—a framed photo on the wall of my brother

Greyson, grinning mid-photo-op. The wall is full of photos, but there are three larger than the rest, and he's one of them.

The first half of the interview is questions about my time as a reporter for the campus station, the sports I covered, my cheerleading career, and how I balanced college with being an athlete. I hit all the talking points.

The producer raises my resume, which mainly consists of grades and sports, with no mention of me being kin to any of the talented O'Ryan men. Then his eyes flick between my name and the photo on the wall.

"And you're Greyson O'Ryan's little sister, right?" one of the producers asks, her tone not quite neutral.

The guy from talent management leans in. "Everyone in this town knows your family. You must have some stories from the inside, huh? What's it like having two brothers in pro sports and a college coach for a father?"

It's the question I always get, and the one I hate the most. "My brothers are loud, competitive, and stubborn," I say with a well-worn smile. "I've never known a life without them being on top. I was young when they were in high school, but I wouldn't trade a moment of being dragged to their games when maybe I should have been at sleepovers with girlfriends. And my dad is just my dad."

His eyes gleam. "Would you be comfortable interviewing your own family? The public loves that stuff—personal perspective, and you could get us angles no one else can."

"I thought this job was for a sideline reporter. Of course, I would interview them if I'm covering an Armadillos game or my dad if I'm assigned to a LaGrange game." My voice comes out a little softer than I want. "I just want to tell stories that haven't already been told at my dinner table. I want to know what's happening now."

"You do realize that in a job, you don't get to cherry-pick what you cover." The female producer glares at me. Why do women always look at me as if they hate me? *Do I have a resting bitch face?*

"Yes, ma'am. I just want to make it on my own. My brothers made it on their talent, and I would like a chance to prove mine."

There's an awkward beat—a hum of respect or irritation, I can't tell. The questions move on, but I feel like I've shut a window I was supposed to leap through.

Afterward, one of the producers walks me out. "Thank you for your honesty, Noelle. We'll be in touch soon."

Soon.

As I step outside, sunlight bounces off the chrome bumpers in the station parking lot. My shoulders sag. I dial my dad. Voicemail. Sutton—voicemail. Parker—voicemail. Even Birdie, who answers texts in the middle of workouts, lets it ring. Not Greyson or John David either. Weird. Everyone's usually eager for information.

I tap out a message to Matt, my thumb hovering as I search for something breezy.

> Me: Obviously you haven't had a girlfriend in a long time. I haven't seen you since my party. Want to meet up for milkshakes after my ego recovers?

I stare at the screen. Three dots appear, vanish, reappear.

> Matt: Milkshakes? Sorry, can't.

Me: Matt, please. No one's returning my calls or texts.

Matt: Did your family take off without telling you? I'm out of town until tomorrow.

Me: Oh, okay.

Even my fingers typing on my phone sound sad. Am I sad because he's out of town? Or because my family isn't responding?

The dancing dots remind me of a handheld game I used to play in the stands of football games where it's filled with water and you push the button and try to get the cherries in a basket. Just up and down.

When I'm about to type *where are you*, he finally sends another message.

Matt: I don't like milkshakes. I have a better idea.

Me: If you say a protein shake, I'm blocking your number.

Matt: I'll meet you at Sprouts tomorrow night. Their wheatgrass shots are sweet.

Me: Wow. If I wanted to drink salad, I'd just gnaw my way through Sutton's garden. And I'm not sweet; I'm more of a spicy pickle.

Matt: (laughing emoji)

Me: What? I am.

Matt: Didn't say you weren't. Tomorrow at six.

TEN
MATT

Sprouts Cafe smells like someone mopped the floors with kale and antiseptic.

It's my fault I've been lax about my diet and my body is revolting so it's time to get serious again. I'm glancing at the wall of probiotic sodas when Noelle breezes in—hair a little wild, skin a little pale, eyes shadowed with something soft and uncertain. Maybe it's the overhead lighting, or maybe she doesn't know how to act regarding our fake relationship. I know I don't.

She spots me, aiming that smile in my direction, and for a second, I almost let myself relax. I forgot how much trouble her smile could spell. That slight upturn of those pink lips and the shy drop of her eyelids.

"Hey, Coach Grumpy," she says in a sing-song voice, nudging me and moving into my personal bubble. "Have you been avoiding me since my graduation party?"

My laugh sounds kind of like an old pickup truck that revs but won't shift. "I was the perfect fake date at your party. Why would I avoid you?"

So many reasons.
Greyson's sister.
My problems.
She may as well be a million years younger than me.

She studies my face too closely, like she's searching for clues. "Seriously. What have you been doing? Something seems off." She pauses, tilts her head. "Mysterious trips out of town... and you text like someone's holding your phone for ransom."

I grab a container of granola and study the label, more for the distraction than the sugar content. "Just... stuff. Friends. A couple of birthdays. Appointments." The last word hangs, awkward, like a QB pump-faking in the pocket one too many times.

She catches it immediately, her eyes narrowing, all big-sister stubborn in a little-sister package. "Appointments?" she echoes. "Like doctors?"

My shrug is more exaggerated than I intend. "It's nothing. Just regular maintenance for old folks like me." I muster up my best *let it go* scowl, but she just beams brighter.

"You're not *that* old," she smirks. "Now for this wheatgrass... whatever the heck that is. I bet I could take you in a shot competition."

"It's not alcohol, you know." I snort, then say, "Thought you never had one. You don't have..."

She grins. "Two, please!" she calls, waving down the barista, who looks unhappy to be here. A few beats later, we're handed tiny glass cups of murky green. I raise mine. "To new adventures and my very first—"

But she presses it to her lips, slams the liquid, pulls a face, and barely breathes. "Oh god, oh god, oh god!" Her chair falls over, and she races toward the bathroom. I hold the door as she drops to her knees on the cold tile, the sour stench of bile already rising. Everything inside her surges out in a hot, wet rush—green at first, then yellow flecked with bits of her lunch.

I crouch, the floor biting into my shins, and gather her damp hair in my fist, strands sticking to my fingers like wet rope. She lifts her head, lips trembling with a slurred "sorry," and then another spasm hits. Warm vomit splatters my chest, soaking through my T-shirt.

Great. I cannot catch a break today.

Half-worried, I watch as she tries to stand, eyes watering, mouth twisted in something between horror and apology. "I think I just joined a new kind of cult," she moans, then frowns at the rancid mess on my shirt.

"Sorry," she murmurs. "Let me—oh god, it's everywhere —" She grabs a fistful of recycled brown paper towels, and before I can stop her, she lifts the hem of my shirt to mop off the worst of it.

That's when she freezes, eyes landing on the white circle of my glucose monitor, stuck low on my abdomen with half the tape peeling up.

"What's that?" she blurts, then blushes, like she's caught me smuggling contraband.

"Nothing," I snap, tugging my shirt down. "Just tech. We're not actually dating, so you don't get access to my secrets."

She raises an eyebrow, not buying it, but she lets it slide. "Wow, mood. Did you wake up on the wrong side of the protein powder this morning, Coach?"

I can't help it. The corners of my mouth twitch. She has this relentless optimism, that goofy, push-my-buttons-and-see-what-happens spirit that drives me insane in every possible way. Part of me loves it. Part of me wants to run screaming.

"Am I not allowed to have a bad day?" I shoot back, a little softer this time.

"I've just never seen you be this short with anyone." Noelle leans in with a sly smile. "You promised to be my fake boyfriend, which by extension means my emotional support. It's in the contract. Fine print, obviously."

I finally let myself grin, just a bit. "Is that before or after the 'no feelings' clause?"

She cackles, and it's like an arrow to the heart. The good kind.

But my chest tightens. She doesn't know how right she is. I know I'm grumpy. I know I'm being a jerk. But keeping my distance is easier than letting her see just how quickly she's gotten under my skin.

"Are you ready to go back out?"

She splashes her face with water, then dabs it dry. When she makes a little "o" with her mouth, my mind goes straight to wondering if she would make a similar face when she's having an orgasm. I shake my head to rid myself of the thought.

Does it help?

Not in the slightest.

I follow behind her and order two waters from the bartender before we reach our table.

Pros of fake dating Noelle O'Ryan? She's a firecracker. Real, raw, too bright to look at straight on. She makes me remember things I thought I'd boxed up just fine.

Cons? Everything that matters. She laughs like my demons aren't scary. I work for her family. I'm her brother's best friend. Her oldest brother is the head coach. And I'm hiding things from her—invisible things, the kind that can blow up a whole life without warning. And I'm worried it's the beginning.

She sighs, then grins. "You know, dodging questions makes you even more suspicious. Should I be checking your pockets for illegal kale?"

"Only if you want to find sugar-free mints and lint," I deadpan, attempting to understand the emotions I'm having about my best friend's sister.

She snorts. "Well, thanks for meeting up... even if the wheatgrass attack nearly killed me."

I tap her arm, softer than I mean to. "You survived. Tougher than most rookies I know."

She glows for a second, and damn if it doesn't make my day a little less heavy. I search for a distraction. "So, do you have any other interviews lined up? Or did you terrify the network suits with your honest answers again?"

Her eyes light up and she launches in, describing the questions, the panic, the bit about her brothers and the photo wall, all while my own pulse thrums unevenly, the way it always does when I'm around her. I let her talk, stealing glances when I think she's not looking. Even if we're just faking it, Noelle breathes life into me after some not-so-good news. I've never been so taken with a woman. And I don't have a clue what to do about that.

It's a universal law in the O'Ryan house that dinner is loud, messy, and slightly hazardous to your physical or mental health.

When the whole crew here it's slightly chaotic, but I wouldn't have it any other way. My brothers act like every household item is a football—throwing glasses, utensils, or whatever is in reach.

Tonight's spread is chaos on steroids: J.D. and Birdie carrying in chicken wings with all our favorite flavors. My personal fave is the bone-in garlic parmesan ones. Flats only for me. Sutton slices watermelon. Dad has the deep fryer going with homemade fries. Parker grabs the roasted vegetables from the oven, transferring them to a bowl. Paulina sets out plates, and even Witt emerges from his cave long enough to roll his eyes at Parker's playlist.

Family banter is the soundtrack. "You call that music?" Greyson shouts over the thump of Parker's phone, grabbing tongs like a weapon. "If you start dancing, I'm leaving."

"Says the man who once did the worm at his wedding,"

J.D. fires back, and Paulina snorts her lemonade through her nose.

"I was just practicing my moves." Greyson grabs Sutton by the waist, kissing her neck. "Gotta come up with new moves to shake the defenders."

Birdie waves a hand for calm, gesturing for everyone to sit. "Let's hold off on the sports talk. We have a couple of weeks before you're back at it, so let's talk about something else."

Sutton jumps in. "Noelle, give us the scoop. Any news on job interviews? I know you've had a few." Instantly, every head swivels, some hopeful, some dreading more football talk.

"It's between me and two other girls for the sideline reporter gig. I'm cautiously optimistic, which means I already stress-bought three blouses I can't afford."

Dad shakes his head. "Noelle, please don't act like you're destitute. You have everything. And if you need anything, just tell me."

I know he's right, but I try to live as my mom would have wanted and take responsibility for myself. "Sorry, Dad." He just grins as everyone fills their plates.

Sutton rolls her eyes. "Just don't let Aunt Birdie style you," she teases. Sometimes Aunt Birdie forgets she's not on stage and wears fishnets to the local pizza parlor. She and Sutton are opposites. Sutton is classic and simple. Birdie is edgy. Both are fun and easygoing.

Leaning across the table, Paulina, who is still at the age where asking any question is fair game, pipes up. "Are you still dating Matt? He's so cute, and he's got drawings all over his arms like Daddy draws."

"Not the same kind, kiddo. If you're done, take your dish

to the sink and put the brownies on a plate," Greyson rumbles, giving me what he probably thinks is a subtle glare, then looking at the tattoo on his wrist. He feels that one single tattoo is a moral failure.

He turns to me. "Plus, you have no reason to be around Brooks anymore, right, Noelle?"

My cheeks go warm, and my mind snags on that afternoon in Sprouts. Matt with his faded country music tee, his biceps flexing when he lifted his shirt to clean my puke, his inked skin scrawled down his arm, rib cage, shoulder, and that gadget fixed just above his waistband. I didn't mean to gawk, but the sight made my pulse stutter—a little bit of intrigue, a little bit of worry.

What was it? A medical thing? He shut me down fast when I asked, and now I keep returning to it, my curiosity itching.

Dad clears his throat, eyeing me in that *what aren't you telling me* way. Probably trying to reconcile whether the tattoos or the dating is the bigger worry.

"Umm, we're seeing how it goes. Brooks has been texting me, so we're posting some pics." Before I can deflect or expand, my phone buzzes on the table. Unknown number.

Every instinct screams *scam*, but I answer anyway.

"Hello, is this Noelle O'Ryan?"

I clamp down on a gasp. "Yes, this is she."

"This is Tricia from the Network. We're thrilled to offer you the sideline reporter position for our league coverage this season."

"Are you serious?"

"Yes, you'll need to come in for orientation tomorrow," she says and then sends a schedule to my phone. "Do you accept?"

"Yes."

For a heartbeat, I can't breathe. Dad is staring now, everyone silent except Parker, who's shoving half a roll in his mouth. "I got the job," I manage, then I cover the bottom of the phone. I whisper-shout, "I got it! I got the job!"

The table erupts. Sutton shoves her glass up for a toast, Birdie squeals, and even Witt cracks a smile. Dad looks prouder than he did when Greyson got drafted.

Back on the call, I try to keep my cool. "Thank you! When do I start?"

"We'd like you to cover rookie introduction events for all the teams in our region—starting next week. Your schedule will include a visit to New Orleans for the Blacksmiths' training camp, Austin for the Armadillos, Oklahoma City, and Dallas. Maybe Atlanta."

Inside, anxiety tap-dances with excitement. Rookie days. New Orleans. *Brooks.*

I hang up and the questions rain down. Dad wants details. "What's your first assignment?"

My mouth runs on autopilot. "I'll be covering rookie days for every team around here. I'll have to travel—New Orleans, Austin, Oklahoma City. Do interviews, social content, sideline reports... the works."

Greyson whistles. "They're giving you the hard stuff right away, huh?"

Sutton pats my shoulder. "You're ready."

"Does that mean you'll see Brooks on assignment?" Birdie asks, concern lacing her voice.

"I—I guess maybe." Nerves crawl up my spine. "When is your rookie camp?" I ask J.D. Before he can answer, I continue, "If Matt's not busy at rookie camp, can he tag along? That should make Brooks believe it."

Greyson slaps the table. "Anything to make this fake-dating go away."

That gets J.D.'s attention. "Actually, Matt's taking a little more time off. Officially, he won't be back until training camp starts. If Matt agrees to tag along, it's fine with me. But, Noelle, that's a lot to ask, especially right now."

I'm not sure what he means because J.D. sometimes talks in theory instead of speaking directly.

Birdie just takes this in stride, but it's like the rest of the world tilts beneath the table. "Wait... What? Why would you give your quarterback coach time off during rookie days?" I sputter.

J.D. shrugs, and Sutton, who is also the general manager of the team, puts on her professional voice. "Matt needs a few extra weeks. He's been coaching since he was twenty-four. Matt has earned some freedom." He takes a deep breath. "Technically, he's still working. He blows up my phone hourly with schemes and ideas."

Greyson and J.D. share a quick glance—*they know*—but the rest of us are still staring, open-mouthed.

Witt's voice cuts through the confusion, quiet but sure. "It's about time some things changed around here. Dad says we're supposed to be open and honest."

All our eyes go wide. "So, are you going to tell everyone about your pen pal?" I ask. "Today I got the mail, and there was a letter to Witt in a girl's handwriting."

"That was an invitation to an in-person tournament later in the year," he says, shaking his head at how stupid I could be.

Dinner resumes with baby talk and how Greyson's tennis courts are now being used by a foundation that helps kids who are struggling growing up in a single-parent household. But my head's spinning. When the leftovers are boxed and everyone drifts away, I slip outside into the Texas twilight, phone in hand.

I dial Matt. When his voice clicks on, I don't even say hi. "I'm the new official sideline reporter for ESPN. I'll be doing rookie days, all over the region."

There's a beat where I swear I hear his smile even through the phone. And for a second, all the nervous energy dissolves in the warm Texas night.

TWELVE
MATT

My phone buzzes on the coffee table, cutting through the heavy quiet. When I swipe to answer, her voice, bright and electric, chases away the depressing thoughts filling my night.

"I'm the new official sideline reporter for ESPN!" she blurts out, exuding sheer happiness. No hello, just breathless pride. "I'll be doing Rookie Days, all over the region."

For a hot minute, I'm grinning like an idiot, even though nobody's around to see. "No kidding?" I say, finding myself sitting up straighter, invested in anything she says. "Proud of you. You're a big leaguer now."

"Don't say it like I'm a baby. Well," she admits, "It's a start. I get to cover the camps, the new guys. And, you know... New Orleans."

The name lands with a thud in my chest. New Orleans. Where Brooks is. No doubt she'll be around him, interviewing him. I've known many guys just like Brooks—they want a girl only so no one else can have her, not because they're in love.

I drag a hand over my face, searching for the right words —any words that don't sound like a jealous, washed-up old man. "That's... a hell of a gig. I'm sure you'll impress the coaches right away. Congrats."

She laughs, a little softer now. "Have I impressed you?"

Do I speak my truth?

You've had me hooked since the first time I heard you laugh. Hell yes, I'm impressed.

Nope, can't say that, so instead, I say, "Everyone who knows you understands that you can do anything you put your mind to."

"Thanks, I hope I can handle it. Even with seeing Brooks, I can do it."

My voice hardens before I can help it. I wish I could blame the tone on sugar levels, but it has nothing to do with diabetes and everything to do with the ache in my bones when I picture her anywhere near that guy. "Have you spoken to him since your party?"

"He's left a few voicemails and texts."

The realization hits as hard as a punch to the temple. I'm not just being protective; I'm fucking jealous that she hasn't blocked his calls. "And have you returned them?"

I can almost hear her shaking her head, like her hair is brushing against the phone.

"I haven't. Don't worry, I made sure he believes we're a couple. He's upset that I'm dating someone so old who has nothing to offer me in the future. His words, not mine."

Fuck. Maybe he's right. What do I have to offer Noelle?

"You shouldn't have to deal with him alone."

There's a beat of quiet—something shifting between us. "That's what I wanted to ask." She's playing it cool, but I know her too well; excitement is tangled up with nerves.

"J.D. said it was fine if you came along. To New Orleans. And, you know, the other stops if you want. For appearances."

"Appearances," I echo, half-annoyed that maybe she is only thinking of this as platonic. Half of me wants to scream, *"I want more,"* but that's not fair to either of us, or to J.D. and Greyson.

"Unless the famous Matt Stricker is too big-time to slum it with a bunch of rookies who have consumed too many energy drinks and sideline nobodies?" She fills the silence with her usual playful attitude. It's truly what draws people to her. She's endlessly optimistic on the outside, but it makes me wonder if that's her protective shell.

I snort. "I'm the most down-to-earth guy around. Honestly, the coaches won't want me there. I'm a coach for the opposition."

She laughs again, her voice full of summer heat and spark. It runs right through me, and God help me, I want nothing more than to say yes. But something hardens in my chest—a chill that's lingered since Harper's warning, since my vision blurred in the morning sun. I won't let her see; I keep it hidden, same as always.

"Why have you been so distant lately? Is this what you do when you date someone? Pull away?" she asks, her concerned tone weighing on me.

"We're not dating. This is a fictional relationship," I say.

"I know." I hear the frustration in her voice, and it's not my intention to upset her. "Are you just being this way with me or with everybody?"

"Noelle," I let out a heavy breath. "I can't do this."

I let the silence stretch—maybe too long. The old Matt

would have joked it off. But something's twisting inside me. "Noelle, I don't want to give you the wrong idea."

"Hey, don't take credit for my genius, albeit spontaneous, idea. Just say yes, Matt," she goads. "You'll keep me from throttling Brooks, which will keep me out of jail and on the sidelines."

She bristles, as if she senses something more in my tone.

"I don't know." My voice comes out rougher than I want. "Maybe you're better off with one of your girlfriends. Make it a girls' trip." I have enough on my plate right now, and Noelle just confuses my emotions.

Even through the phone lines, I know she's bristling at my tone. My suggestion. There's an edge now. "Oh, right, because you think I don't have loyal girlfriends." Her laugh sharpens, razor-bright. "That's original. 'Noelle only hangs with guys because of sports.'"

I wince. That one was below the belt, and I know it. Truth is, I get why guys flock to her. She's the only person in every locker room who talks football like it's her first language—and cares who wins, who loses, and who gets left behind. But I can't tell her that. Not now, not with my own walls up.

"That's not what I meant."

She sighs on the other end, her voice softening. "Maybe. But yeah, sometimes it sucks being the odd girl out. You try growing up the only sister in a family like mine, then act surprised when you get football cards instead of nail polish at your birthday parties."

I can picture her, pacing the length of her backyard, barefoot, annoyance bright in her cheeks. There's a lump in my throat that won't go down.

"You know I didn't mean it like that." I rub a thumb over my temple, wishing I was better at this. At her.

"Forget it," she mutters. "Look, I just thought...you might want to come. For me."

God, how am I supposed to say no to that? Especially with that hope, fragile as it sounds through the phone. I want to say yes *for* her. Hell, I want to say yes for myself, even though every instinct in me says to run. Protect her—from Brooks, from disappointment, from whatever's coming for me that I'm not ready to admit.

But I've never been good at walking away from her, not since that kiss that broke the shackles off my heart. And every small touch, laugh, or smile ever since.

"All right," I manage, my voice just above a whisper. "I'll come. For appearances, right?"

She laughs, but softer this time—like I just lifted something heavy off her shoulders. "That's all we're doing, Coach. Just a little make-believe. A girl's entitled to that once in her life."

Anger rolls through my veins that Brooks cheated on her, more than once, from what I gathered from her family.

My heart's pounding in my chest, the thump uneven. "Don't call me Coach. I'm not yours, and I haven't been a boyfriend in a long time, so forgive me for not being good at it."

Her reply is quick, bold in a way that only makes her more dangerous. "I'll consider that a challenge."

There's a hush between us, some current crossing the wire that neither of us wants to name.

"Let me know the schedule, and I'll see if I can make it happen for sure. But if I can, I'll support you in New Orleans."

"Yes, sir." Her imitation is terrible, but it makes me want things with her. Totally inappropriate things. "See you soon, grumpy." Long after she hangs up, Noelle's laughter hangs on like fog on a fall day.

For appearances, I tell myself. But in the quiet, it sounds a hell of a lot like a lie.

The Oklahoma sun has no mercy.

By nine in the morning, my ESPN polo sticks to me in places I haven't felt since cheerleading. The turf has fuzzy steam rippling from it like a mirage. I steady my mic, breathe from my belly the way Birdie taught me (it's always good to have a professional singer in the family), and lock my eyes on the camera's red tally light.

"Good morning from Oklahoma City," I say, bright but not bouncy, the way I practiced. "I'm Noelle O'Ryan with ESPN at rookie minicamp, where coaches are getting their first in-depth look at this draft class. Can they bump this five-win team from last year into a contender for a division championship?"

The producer's voice crackles in my ear. "Clean. Keep rolling. Two more takes for safety."

I nod, close my mouth, and wet my whistle. I think about how my mom used to say that. I'm not sure if I remember her saying it or if I'm recalling things J.D. and Greyson say. Taking an inward breath, I repeat the sound bite. The words come out smoother the second time, then the third, and my shoulders drop a half-inch, relieved.

This isn't the first time I've been on a sideline with a mic, but it's the first time for a football game. I've always been cheering. My experience has been with baseball and soccer for the most part. Coach Laramie jogs over and explains today's schedule. "You have complete access, just don't distract them during instruction."

"Yes, sir. Is there anything unique or secret that you'll be covering that you don't want us to show?" I ask.

"Great question, O'Ryan. Not today. Maybe tomorrow. I'll let you know."

O'Ryan. No one has ever called me O'Ryan like I'm one of the guys. Like I'm just as important as J.D. or Greyson. I like it.

This is my job. My shot, and I'm ready. Trying to cool off, I pull at my shirt three or four times, fanning myself. It's no wonder he called me O'Ryan, considering I'm almost as sweaty as the players.

I pivot off-camera, walking down the sideline to catch the rookie receivers working on drills, and I see Josiah Dream, who played for my college team. When the coach blows the whistle for a water break, he runs over to me, giving me a big hug. "Wow, I didn't expect to see you here. I heard about you and Brooks. I'm sorry he's such an ass."

"Thanks, now I have two people's sweat on me," I joke as he squeezes me. "I'm so excited to start my career, so show me some skills today, and I'll make you front-page news on the midnight broadcast."

"You got it, Noelle. You'll be the face of the network in no time. I better get back."

"Thanks, Josiah. Good luck."

A playlist hisses out of a portable speaker, all bass and bravado.

"Ma'am, are you waiting on eighty-seven?" a staffer asks, dragging a tall, dimpled wideout toward me.

"'Ma'am' makes me feel forty," I tease, lifting the mic. "But yes—Devonte?"

He grins like he's never had a bad day. "Yes, ma'am."

"Devonte it is," I say, swallowing a laugh. We angle so the team logo is visible behind us. My producer gives me a thumbs-up. "Okay, Devonte—first day with the big boys. What's the speed like out here?"

"It's fast," he says, eyes bright. "But I'm faster."

I grin. "Bold."

"Gotta be."

Smiling, because I feel the exact same way. If we don't believe in ourselves, who will?

We trade a few more questions—footwork, routes, who's mentoring him in the room. He slips once and calls me "ma'am" again, then apologizes like I'm the person who can make or break his career. Believe me, I'm not nearly that important. I let him off the hook with a nod.

His confidence is contagious. When we wrap, he asks if he can shout out his mom. He does. The camera guy chuckles. I pretend I'm not melting from his love for his mom and the heat.

Segment, B-roll, segment. My day becomes a loop of light and shadow, flashes of helmets and white towels, and the slow drip of my own sweat down my spine. I sip warm water between takes and send a quick text when my hands aren't full.

> Me: First interview done. No fainting, no mic drops, no profanity.

I watch the typing bubble blink and vanish, blink and vanish, and then:

> Matt: Proud of you, Butterfly.

> Me: Butterfly?

> Matt: You're spreading your wings.

> Matt: Don't forget to hydrate. And eat something with protein. Not just gummy bears.

I snort. He knows me too well, but not as well as I would like. I snicker while staring at my phone.

> Me: You say that like gummy bears aren't a food group.

That's when I realize he knows a lot more about me than I do about him.

> Matt: You should treat your body like a temple. Healthy foods.

> Me: Maybe you should teach me how, Coach.

> Matt: Don't call me Coach.

The bubble appears again and lingers. I picture him in the quarterbacks' room in Austin, hunched over a laptop, laser-eyed and bossy. But I remember he's not there, and something flips in my stomach. I'm beginning to feel this thing with Matt is beyond revenge on Brooks.

I like him. More than as my brother's best friend or my white knight saving me from a crappy boyfriend, but as someone who makes my heart smile and gives me goosebumps just from thinking about him.

I tuck the phone into my back pocket and head for the linebackers.

Around noon, the heat hardens into a wall. I feel it when I step into the sun—the way it presses on my skin and turns my head cottony. My last interview is with a rookie who can't stop giggling on camera. I laugh with him, and then, when I step out of the frame, my vision blurs at the edges; people become outlines without faces.

I bend my knees and breathe. I'm fine. I am.

"Hey, you good?" someone asks. Footsteps scuff. It's Josiah again, helmet tucked under his arm, sweat gleaming on his forehead. "You look a little—"

"Don't say pale," I warn, forcing a smile. "I prefer 'gorgeous' or 'mysteriously luminous.'"

He chuckles and extends a half-empty bottle of lemon-lime Gatorade—the good kind, the kind that tastes like Little League and childhood. "You should sit. It's a hundred degrees."

I eye the bottle, then Josiah. "You're offering your backwash? That's how documentaries start."

He looks horrified. "Oh, my bad. I can run and..."

"I'm kidding," I say, taking it and tipping it up. The salty-sweet drink hits my tongue, and I suddenly realize I'm parched. I swallow twice and hand it back. "We'll pretend the CDC approved that."

He laughs, relieved. "Noelle, take care of yourself. We

wouldn't want you to have a heatstroke on your first day in action."

"Got it. Now go run faster if you want to be on the highlights tonight," I say, waving him off.

When he jogs away, I sit on the edge of the sideline bleacher for exactly ninety seconds, the aluminum branding the backs of my thighs, my stomach doing a slow barrel roll. Nerves, heat, dehydration—I pick a culprit and point at it. Then I stand, fix my ponytail, and march back to the field.

The afternoon crawls, but then I get sprayed by an errant water bottle and wear it like cologne. Every time I slide the mic flag into my palm, the network name catches my eye: **ESPN**. My stomach swoops. In a good way.

By the time the producer finally says, "We got it," my legs feel like they belong to a much older woman and my brain is fried. I help coil cables anyway, because my dad didn't raise me to stand around while other people work, then the crew and I step onto the shuttle with a sigh that comes from my toes.

My phone vibrates as we pull away.

Matt: You alive?

Me: Technically. A rookie shared his Gatorade with me.

Matt: You drank after a player?

Me: He has dimples. I assessed the risk.

Matt: Noelle.

Me: I know him. I'm not a savage.

> Matt: Hydrate. Eat. And stop collecting rookie DNA.

I bite down on a smile that's too big for my face and tuck the phone against my chest. The window of the producer's car vibrates against my temple. The world streaks past in tan, green, and heat.

By the time I reach the hotel, the nausea has settled into a slow wave. I ride the elevator with two kickers and a box of delivered salads and try to breathe through my mouth. My room key sticks, then relents.

I drop my bag and peel my polo off like it's a sticker, then stand in front of the vent blowing out some much-needed cool air in my sports bra until my goosebumps hurt. I pull on my softest thing—an old, thin, gray Armadillos tank Matt once handed me when I spilled iced coffee on myself while watching Parker practice with the team last year. He gave me the look of a man trying to decide between sighing and strangling me, then threw me his tank that was strewn over his shoulder. He tossed it with a gruff, "Cover the crime scene." I never gave it back. Sorry, not sorry.

I flop on the bed and scroll through the photos the cameraman took of me for promotions—the one where my hair blows just right, the one where I look too serious, the one where I'm laughing with my whole face. I pick two and text them.

> Me: Your fake girlfriend is officially ESPN material.

> Matt: You look like you were born on that sideline.

Me: I only tripped once. Maybe twice.

Matt: I'll need to review the film.

Me: Nerd.

Matt: Accurate.

The nausea swells, then fades. I chug hotel water, grimace, and reach for the mini pretzels because I hear Matt's voice in my head: Protein, Sunshine. And salt. I nibble, stare at the ceiling for a beat, then thumb out another message.

Me: A rookie called me ma'am like eight times.

Matt: He's polite. I like him.

Me: Of course you do.

Matt: Did he look at you?

Me: I mean… I was holding a microphone.

Matt: Noelle.

Me: Don't worry, Coach. I told him my fake boyfriend is very scary and hates germs.

My phone buzzes without the courtesy of the three waiting dots. Incoming FaceTime.

I hesitate just long enough to swipe my hair into a lazy

knot and adjust the tank so it doesn't swallow me whole, then accept the call.

Matt's face fills my screen—too close at first, beard shadow darker than usual, eyes soft. He looks tired.

"Hey, Butterfly," he says, and the gravel in his voice reaches me all the way here. "You didn't pass out on live TV. I'm impressed."

"Low bar," I say, smiling. "How's Austin?"

He leans back; I catch a sliver of the QB room—whiteboard graffiti, a blinking projector, a coffee mug that's probably been refilled a dozen times.

"Hot, loud, and one of the rookies thinks 'progression' is a type of protein shake."

I groan. "Tell me you didn't yell."

"I used my 'firm teaching voice that your brothers love.'"

"Wait. J.D. said you were taking a few weeks off."

"A few days here and there, but not the whole week every week."

"Why?"

"I have things to take care of."

"What things?" I ask, then soften when his smile tilts. When he doesn't answer, I admit, "I... miss home."

He hears the wobble and straightens. "You okay?"

"I'm fine," I say automatically, because that's what you say. "But the water in the hotel tastes like chemicals."

"Did you eat?" His tone slides into protective mode again.

I hold up the pretzels. "Gourmet dining."

He sighs in a way that says he wants to DoorDash me a steak and personally watch me chew it. "Next time, call me when you feel off."

"And hear 'hydrate and eat a protein bar' in stereo? Hard pass."

He opens his mouth to protest and then pauses, his gaze snagging on somewhere below my collarbone. His eyebrows rise, then his mouth curves like he's trying not to laugh.

"What?" I demand, squinting at the screen. "Don't you dare say my face looks weird."

"Oh, your face looks great," he says, far too relaxed. "It's just—how do I put this delicately—you might want to do something about those."

"Those—"

I follow his line of sight down and realize my tank is doing me zero favors in the air-conditioning. Zero. "Oh my God."

I slap a pillow to my chest so fast I almost drop the phone. Heat rushes to my cheeks, impossible and instant. "You're the worst," I mutter, not meaning it at all. He's quite the opposite.

"I'm simply observing," he says lightly. "Journalistic integrity."

"You're not a journalist."

"I'm method acting then." He tries and fails not to laugh. "I mean, if a rookie noticed—"

"No rookies noticed," I say, mortified and weirdly... not. His voice softens the mortification into something fizzy and ridiculous.

"Good," he says. "Because I'd have to drive up there and run a clinic on eye discipline."

"You can't bench the entire rookie class."

"Watch me."

"You're very intimidating through an iPhone," I deadpan.

He leans closer until his eyes fill the frame, green and intent. "I don't like guys looking at you like you're... available."

I forget how to breathe for a second. The pillow is a furnace. "We're fake, remember?"

"Yeah." The word is quiet. Not untrue. Not the whole truth. "I remember."

Silence buzzes. The air conditioner kicks on and flutters the corner of the curtain. I can hear my own pulse in my ear like it's close to the surface.

I clear my throat first because I always do. "For what it's worth, I was too busy not fainting to flirt."

"You could've called me before you almost fainted," he says, grouchy again to hide whatever else that was. "I would've told you—"

"To hydrate and eat protein," I chorus. "Yes, Dad."

His mouth twitches. "Your actual dad would make me run entire stadiums for letting you get dehydrated."

"My dad would make you run stadiums for breathing near me," I say, and we both grin because it's true.

His eyes tip to the pillow again, playful now. "So, are you going to fix your, uh, wardrobe malfunction or are we pretending that's not happening?"

I narrow my eyes and adjust the pillow with exaggerated primness. "I'm maintaining my modesty."

"Good call. Hotel AC is brutal."

"You noticed."

He lifts a shoulder. "I notice... things."

I swallow. I should steer us back to safe ground now, talk about cover-two looks or airport food, anything that doesn't feel like standing on a high dive. Instead, I let the softness sit with us. It doesn't feel like drowning. It feels like floating.

"Hey," he says after a beat, gentler. "You did great today."

"Even when I almost face-planted?"

"Especially then. You're tougher than most guys I coach." He pauses, looks away like he's measuring something, then looks back. "You belong there, Noelle. On camera. On that field. You've always belonged."

My throat tightens fast. Tears threaten in the embarrassingly immediate way they always do when someone says exactly the thing I've been white-knuckling for. I tilt the phone so he can't see my whole face in case it betrays me.

"Thanks," I say, voice a little raw. "That means more than... you know."

"I know," he says softly.

We talk about nothing for five more minutes—the motel art that looks like it was painted by an AI that's only seen football fields, the rookie who slid in his cleats like a cartoon character, the way the rookies smell like a high school summer.

When the yawn finally sneaks up on me, it takes my entire face hostage. I don't even get to be cute about it.

"Okay," he says, smiling. "Bed. Now."

"Bossy."

"Always," he says, and his smile shifts into something almost shy. "Text me if you feel off in the night. I'm serious."

"I will," I say, and I mean it.

"And eat a real breakfast."

"Do donuts count?"

A smile slips out as he's shaking his head. "I will hang up."

I laugh, and the laugh tips into another yawn. "Night, Coach."

"Night, Butterfly."

I end the call and the room goes too quiet too fast. The pillow is still clutched to my chest like a shield. I toss it aside, stare at the ceiling, then slide off the bed and pad into the bathroom to splash cool water on my face. The mirror shows a girl with sun-kissed cheeks, tired eyes, and a gray tank that needs to be retired from video calls.

My stomach rolls once, then settles.

"You're fine," I tell the girl. "You're just tired."

Back in bed, I pull the covers to my chin and reach for my phone one more time. A text lands before I can type.

Matt: Proud of you. For today. For everything.

I breathe out and feel something in my ribs unclench.

Me: Miss you. But in a professional, ESPN-approved way.

Matt: There's no form for that.

Me: I'll make one.

Three dots. Then:

Matt: Sleep. Hydrate. And maybe… find a thicker tank ;)

I grin into the dark like a fool and toss the phone to the nightstand. The AC hums me toward sleep. Somewhere between the last conscious thought and the first dream, I realize I am not thinking about the heat anymore, or the mic in my hand, or even the way my name sat under the ESPN logo and made my heart stutter. I'm thinking about a grumpy quarterback coach who notices things, and how dangerous it is that I like that he does.

The drive to New Orleans is supposed to be easy.

But Noelle O'Ryan has a way of turning a four-to-five-hour *easy* drive into provoking me at every turn. She's got her bare feet propped on my dashboard, toenails painted the color of cotton candy, humming along to some pop station. The guy singing sounds like a little girl who sings about three octaves higher than any human should be able to.

I shouldn't look at her legs, but I do. They're stretched out, tan and smooth, and every time she shifts, my focus goes straight to wondering about what's under her skirt, how soft her skin is between her legs, and arguing with myself about keeping physical distance between us.

"Feet off the dash, Butterfly," I say, giving her a side-eye. "You're leaving prints all over my windshield."

She smirks. "I'll leave them everywhere if you don't start driving like someone born after 1950."

I snort. "The truck's older than you. Show some respect."

"It also rattles when you hit sixty," she fires back, grinning. "You sure it's gonna make it to Louisiana? We should've driven your Corvette."

"Don't insult the truck. She's sensitive."

"*She?*" she says, drawing the word out like it's a dirty secret. "You named this old thing? What's her name? I bet it's Betty."

"Holly. My dad bought her used for my Christmas present when I was in high school," I say, reminiscing. "She can do one hundred miles per hour. Dare me."

She cackles. "You're kidding, right? We'll end up splattered on the road."

"And here I thought you were adventurous."

"Are you daring me? Sure. I know *Holly* can't go that fast."

"Holly has a V8 engine, not some turbocharged four-cylinder that's made now." We're on a straight stretch of the interstate, so I press pedal to the metal, literally, and the truck stutters for a half-second, then picks up speed—seventy, eighty, ninety.

Noelle rolls down the window, screaming, hair whipping in the wind. I've never seen anything so pure and happy. It's breathtaking. I can't take my eyes off her when I hear a prolonged honk from the vehicle in the other lane as I drift dangerously close to it. I swerve quickly, and Noelle slides across the bench seat against me. Not going to lie, I love the way her body molds into mine.

"Okay, okay. Slow down."

"Apologize to Holly for doubting her." I keep my foot on the gas.

"You want me to say sorry to a truck?"

"Yep."

Noelle huffs. "Sorry, *Holly.*"

I grin. She grins as she rolls up the window, but I catch the little tilt of her head when she watches the scenery pass by, the nervousness hiding behind all that sass. She pulls her backpack with her ESPN badge clipped to it, into her lap like it's a security blanket.

I soften a little. "You're gonna kill it, you know."

She looks at me like she doesn't believe it yet. "You think so?"

"I know so," I say simply. "You were the star of late night on the network last week with Oklahoma City."

"In whose mind?"

Mine. I recorded it and watched it on a repeating loop.

"The viewers'. Didn't you see the ratings?"

"Umm... was that when I was sweating so much that my ta-tas were showing?"

Ta-tas. God, I love her.

"Noelle, the segment with you was the highest rating of the hour. And I didn't notice the ta-tas." That last part, a complete lie. I notice everything about Noelle O'Ryan. Expelling a big breath, I lay my hand on her knee. "Are you freaked out about seeing Brooks? You know we don't have to fake all of this if he's really what you want."

Her lips twitch, and for a second, the tension drops. Then she plops her backpack on the floor and starts fiddling with the radio, landing on some old '90s country song. "I guess I'm more loyal than I should be."

Fuck, that's a shiv to the ego. She's still hung up on him after all he did to her.

"Loyalty is in your family's DNA. It's a good quality."

"This is torture."

"Seeing Brooks?"

"I can handle Brooks. No, these songs on the radio. Why

didn't we drive your Corvette? Now that would have been fun."

She laughs, a real one this time—and for the next few miles, we let the highway fill the silence.

By the time we roll into New Orleans, the air's thick enough to chew. The facility's got that new turf smell—fresh paint, sweat, and ambition. I can already hear the rookies running drills before I even park.

Noelle hops out of the truck, slipping on her sunglasses and pressing her badge to her lanyard like it's armor. "You good?" I ask.

"I'm fine," she says, too quick. "You go do your coach-y thing. I'll go be professional."

"Professional," I echo, smirking. "Try not to trip over any microphones this time."

She swats my arm and walks off, hips swaying just enough to make me regret talking.

Inside, I find a few familiar faces—some of the same staff from when I coached in Louisville. They're running rookie drills, trying to make sense of raw potential.

"Stricker!" one of them calls. "Slumming it with us today?"

"Guess I missed the gumbo," I joke, shaking hands. "Just here to watch, not to interfere."

They trade looks. "We're just doing basics today," one says, lowering his voice. "But tomorrow we'll have to keep you off the field. Team rules. Rookie Media Day."

"Understood." I keep my voice neutral, even though it feels like a kick. I came here to help Noelle, to make sure she doesn't get swallowed up by the chaos. But rules are rules.

"So, are the rumors true? You're dating a recent college grad and the head coach's sister?"

"Yeah, she's one of a kind." I hate lying to my friends and colleagues, but I need to make sure they believe it, and I hope they ride the hell out of Brooks.

"Jesus, do you have a death wish?"

Maybe I do. "From Brooks? No. You know he's a real douchebag."

"I was thinking more about Greyson and J.D.," he says, raising both his eyebrows.

"They weren't happy at first. Still probably aren't, but they're supportive."

Across the field, I spot her—head tilted back, laughing at something. Brooks Pendleton stands beside her, helmet under his arm, his hand brushing a piece of her hair away from her face. He's grinning that same smirk I used to see on rookies right before they throw an interception.

Something sharp lodges in my chest.

She's smiling back. Not the big, unfiltered Noelle smile —the polite one. The one she uses when she's trying too hard. My hope is she's just trying to get through the day without punching him. She values her new job and wants to be the best at it.

Apples don't fall far from the tree, and there's no doubt she's just as competitive as the rest of the O'Ryans.

Still, when he touches her hair, I feel my jaw lock.

A staffer beside me whistles low. "Seems like Brooks is already working his charm again."

"Yeah," I say, tight. "That's his favorite play. Draw her back to convince her he means it this time. But I have faith she knows his game plan too well now to fall for his lies again."

Brooks says something else, and then he jogs back toward

the huddle, glancing at me over his shoulder. The bastard _winks_.

At me.

I swallow a curse, shoving my hands into my pockets. "Let's go to the field," the offensive coordinator says, but I don't hear a damn word after that. I'm scanning for Noelle and the cameraman. They set up on the sidelines.

When she's finished with a couple of interviews, I grab a water from the huge cooler and stride over to the ESPN side-line reporter. "Hey, you promised you would hydrate." I hand it to her and rub her back. Her lips curve, a quiet smile filled with thanks, the kind that speaks louder than words ever could.

After getting lost in her eyes, Brooks runs over, tunneling his fingers through his golden mane.

"I'm ready."

My body stiffens as Noelle shifts and says, "Okay." She turns to me. "I'll be done in a few hours. I'll just meet you at the hotel." Her expression unfolds like she's letting a secret slip out, making sure Brooks understands that she and I are still dating.

"Senior citizens sleep in separate beds, right?" Brooks asks with a deep belly laugh.

"Hah. Not us. We have too much fun sleeping together. Knock 'em dead. I have a video meeting with the Armadillos staff. Can't wait for tonight." I lean down and give her a lingering kiss. Gotta make him believe, right?

The look on Brooks's face is priceless. His jaw drops. His eyebrows hit his hairline. If she wanted to make him believe we're in a true relationship, he seems convinced right now.

There. I did my job.

But there is one problem: I want everything I just insinuated. Want her lips on mine.

Dinner that night is at some trendy spot near the hotel—dim lighting, candles, jazz bleeding through the walls. She's glowing from the day, still in work mode, talking about the interviews she nailed and how the head coach complimented her prep notes.

I want to be proud. I *am* proud.

But every time I picture Brooks's hand in her hair, I want to put my fist through something.

She notices. Of course, she does. "You've said maybe four words since we sat down," she says, leaning forward. "You planning to keep glaring at your gumbo, or do you want to tell me what's eating you?"

"Nothing."

She grins, but it fades quickly when I don't bite. "Matt, come on. You've been weird since the facility. Did something happen?"

I push my spoon away, staring at the table. "Not worth talking about."

"Bullshit." Her tone is pure O'Ryan—stubborn, relentless. "If you're mad, say it."

I lean back, jaw tight. "Just tired."

"Liar."

We finish dinner mostly in silence.

When we get to the hotel, she drops her bag on the bed and spins on me. "Okay, spill it. You've been brooding like it's your full-time job. What's wrong?"

I shove my hands in my pockets and turn to the wet bar, searching for bottled water. "I said I'm fine."

"You're the worst liar I've ever met," she says, crossing her arms. "Is it something I did?"

My temper snaps before I can stop it. "You really don't see it, do you?"

Her eyebrows knit. "See what?"

"Brooks," I bite out. "The way he looks at you. The way he touches you like he still owns you. And you just... you just let him."

Her mouth falls open, and she pops that perfect fucking hip. "He brushed my hair out of my face, Matt. I didn't respond."

"You fucking smiled at him like he's the drip of chocolate at a fondue fountain."

Her head tilts and her eyes narrow. "I did not. I faked it. I was doing my job."

"He was flirting. And he knows exactly what he's doing. You want a man that treats you like shit, is that it? Can you not see it?" My voice comes out rougher than I meant it to, chest tight. "He's playing you."

Her eyes flash. "This is my career. You think I don't know that? I just didn't want to make a scene."

"I wanted to make one for you," I admit, and it's the truth that stings most. "You don't deserve that. You deserve someone who'd burn the damn field down before letting a guy like him near you again."

We're standing too close now, breathing the same air. She's flushed, her chest rising fast, her eyes darting between mine.

"Matt," she whispers, softer now. "Why do you care so much?"

"Because—" I start, but the words choke off. Because I do. Because I can't stop. Because this fake thing hasn't felt fake in weeks. Even if it's mostly been texting and video calling, the conversations have felt real. Hell, I felt something the first time I saved her from being humiliated by Brooks.

She tilts her head, and that's all it takes.

One beat, then another, and our mouths collide.

The kiss is sudden—frantic, messy, real. Her hands clutch my shirt, mine cup her jaw, and for a second, everything stops spinning.

There's no noise, no Brooks, no rules. Just her.

When we finally break apart, we're both breathing hard. She looks up at me, lips swollen, eyes wide and glassy. "You done being mad at me?"

I huff out a laugh that sounds half-broken. "Not a chance."

"Good," she says, her voice trembling, "because I'm not done with you either."

Once. I had sex once with Brooks.

But the kiss Matt just gave me surpasses the sex with Brooks by a mile. Whatever just happened with Matt feels like a completely different sport. Like I've been playing back-yard catch my whole life and suddenly someone dropped me into the Super Bowl under the lights.

My lips tingle. My lungs forget how to pump air. I'm still standing in the hotel room, fingers curling into the front of his shirt, when I realize I've stopped breathing.

"Breathe, Butterfly," Matt rasps, his forehead resting against mine. His chest moves hard against my hands, so at least I'm not the only one sucking air like I just ran suicide drills in the gym.

"I am," I whisper. "I think."

His eyes search mine, soft yet regretful. My heart plummets because I know that look. I've seen it on Brooks after every apology, every *"it won't happen again,"* every time he decided I was too much or not enough.

But Matt doesn't look disgusted. He looks... wrecked. And like he's choosing his words cautiously.

"I shouldn't have done that," he says hoarsely.

My stomach drops. "Oh."

He squeezes his eyes shut like the words hurt him too. "That's not what I mean." His hands slide down to my shoulders, thumbs brushing my collarbones like he's memorizing the shape there. "I mean I shouldn't have lost my temper first. I didn't want the first time I really kissed you to be because I was jealous and acting like a Neanderthal."

First time. Really kissed you.

My brain zeroes in on those words like a reader annotates a book.

"So, you've been planning on *really* kissing me?" I ask, voice shaky but trying so hard to be my usual snarky self. "Are you ahead of or behind in your kiss schedule?"

His mouth curves, barely. "Smartass."

He starts to step back, but everything in me goes tight. I tighten my hold on his shirt so he can't go anywhere without me. "Don't," I say, more desperate than I want to sound. "Please don't pull away and pretend this didn't just happen."

His gaze snaps back to mine. Something fierce flashes there. "You think I could pretend that kiss didn't happen?" he asks, low. "You think I haven't been trying *not* to imagine it for months?"

Oh.

Months?

My heart stutters. I feel the floor tilt just a little. "Then why do you look like you're about to put yourself in timeout?"

"Because I'm me and you're you," he says, almost helplessly. "Because your dad threatened to skin my ass, your brothers have access to an entire professional weight room, I'm fourteen years older than you, and we're supposed to be faking this."

He gestures between us like there's something visible hanging in the air. There is. It's called everything.

"I know all of that," I say quietly. "It doesn't change the connection between us. It's been there for a long time, for me anyway." My lids fall as I gather the courage to come clean. "I've had a crush on you since the day we met at J.D.'s house. But who did I lean on every time Brooks ignored me, cheated on me, or flirted with women when I was right there? You. You're the one I felt safe with. I mean, I never thought..."

"I'm glad you feel safe with me, but this is wrong."

Gazing into his eyes, I pull on his shirt, wanting him to listen, and say, "This is right. Maybe not forever. But now it's right."

Silence hums between us, thick and electric. The air conditioner kicks on, sending a cool breeze over my over-heated skin. I suddenly realize how close we are—his hands still on me, my palms still pressed to the hard planes of his chest, like my body decided this is home without asking my brain.

"Tell me to stop," he says, his voice threaded with something raw. "And I will. Right now."

I should. But I'm a Texas girl and we don't admit our mistakes, at least not quickly. This is complicated and messy and probably a terrible idea. We're in a hotel room in another city because I dragged him into my drama. We're fake dating to teach my ex a lesson. My family barely agreed to this arrangement. But here we stand, Matt breathing me in like

I'm oxygen. I feel... seen. Wanted. Like maybe I'm not the girl everyone gossips about behind her back.

"I don't want you to stop," I admit, throat tight. "Not tonight."

His jaw flexes. I watch the battle play out in his eyes—loyalty to my brother versus desire, logic versus whatever this is. Finally, he exhales sharply, like he's making peace with losing.

"Just tonight. Just once," he murmurs.

"Are you only good one time?" The joke catches between a wispy breath and a laugh as I think about that Toby Keith song my dad used to mumble around the house.

He shakes his head and steps forward, backing me up until the back of my knees hit the edge of the bed. The room shrinks, and the only thing I feel is his hands sliding up my arms, fingers tracing over the curve of my shoulders, up my neck, cupping my face again.

"This, okay?" he asks.

I nod, unable to look anywhere but at his mouth, practically melting at being touched like I matter. "Yeah."

He kisses me again, slower this time. Not frantic, not messy. Just...deep. Measured. Like he's tasting each second. I lean into him because standing on my own isn't possible.

His lips move against mine with a certainty that he's right where he wants to be. A surety I've never felt before. Brooks always kissed like he was doing me a favor on the way to something else. Matt kisses like the kiss *is* the point. Like it's enough. Like I'm worth the time.

A soft sound escapes my throat—half sigh, half something more—and his hands drift back into my hair, cradling the nape of my neck as if I'm something precious. My whole body hums.

We stumble backward together, his knees hitting the mattress next. He sits and pulls me with him, and suddenly I'm straddling his lap, knees sinking into the bed on either side of his hips. I freeze.

"Is this okay?" I ask, cheeks burning. I've never...sat like this with anyone.

His hands immediately settle at my hips, big and warm and steady. He rubs his thumb in a slow circle on the side of my waist. "If you were any more okay," he says gently, "I'd be dead. You can move if you want. Or not. You're in control, Noelle."

I swallow, my heart beating a furious tattoo against my ribs. I am not used to being told I'm in control. I'm used to Brooks just taking. Not giving. I didn't know this existed.

I rock the tiniest bit, just to see what happens. Matt's breath hitches, his finger pads pressing on my hips—not saying *stop*, just letting me know he feels it.

My hands skate over his shoulders. The fabric of his shirt is soft under my palms, stretched tight over muscle. I want to feel his skin. My stomach swoops, but I don't back away from it.

"Can I...?" I tug lightly at the hem of his shirt.

His eyes flame hotter. "Yeah," he murmurs. "You can."

I grab the bottom of his shirt in both hands, and he lifts his arms, helping me drag it up over his head and throwing it onto the other bed. The sight of him bare-chested knocks the air out of me. I've seen him at practices in a T-shirt, sweaty and irritated and all-business. But now my focus is on his body, not the entirety of him. His body is like a piece of art, telling his story in pictures inked over one side of his upper body.

There are scars—small ones, a few jagged, one longer near his side. I drag my fingers along it without thinking.

"What's this from?" I whisper.

His jaw ticks, but his voice stays even. "Old surgery."

I file that away for later because I can hear there's more to it, but tonight isn't the night to dig. Tonight is not about his past. It's about whatever we're creating right now, one breath at a time. He grabs my hand gently and moves it to his chest.

"You look..." I search for the right word. Not hot, even though he is. Not handsome, though that too. "Solid, like one of those guardian statues they put at the gate of a grand estate. Only with better abs."

He chuckles, low and a little disbelieving. "That's a new one."

Has he been with lots of women? Of course, look at him.

My hands skim down his chest, there's a dusting of hair there, and then around to his back. His skin is warm, alive under my palms, muscles flexing when I grip him a little tighter.

He lets his head fall back for a second, eyes closing like he's trying not to explode. When he looks back at me, his gaze darkens.

"Your turn," he says softly.

My heart slams into my throat. "My turn for what?"

His fingers toy with the hem of my shirt now, barely grazing the sensitive skin at my waist. It sends a shiver arrowing up my spine. "I want to see you. But only if you want that too."

Brooks never asked if I *wanted* anything. It was always assumed that whatever was happening to my body was for the guy. That my job was to be pliant, quiet, and grateful.

I lick my lips and nod. "Like, naked?" He's seen me in

bathing suits and skimpy cheer outfits, but this...butt-naked with my brother's best friend. It's a whole other level of nerves popping inside me.

"As much as you want me to see." His eyes soften with something that makes my chest ache. Reverence. That's the only word I can come up with.

"Okay."

"Okay," he says, voice calm even though I can feel his pulse racing where my hands rest. "Arms up."

I lift my arms, and he peels my shirt off slowly, like I'm the most beautiful present under the Christmas tree. The one with the glittery gold bow with tails you pull to unwrap. Cool air hits my heated skin, and I shiver, hyperaware that I'm sitting on his lap in just my skirt and bra now.

He doesn't lunge. He doesn't grab. He just looks. His gaze travels over me, careful and thorough, like he's memorizing every inch.

"Damn, Noelle," he murmurs, almost to himself. "You're beautiful."

The words land so deep I feel them in my bones. I duck my head, heat flooding my face. "Brooks never..." I stop myself, folding my lips over my teeth.

Matt's fingers lift my chin gently, making me look directly in his eyes. "Don't compare," he says quietly. "I promise I'm nothing like him."

"I know."

He studies me for another long, quiet beat, then his hands skim up my skin, slow and respectful, pausing any time my breath catches.

"You okay?" he asks again.

I nod. It's a blur of heat and disbelief that I'm nearly naked with Matt. "Yeah. Feels... good."

"Good is good," he says, thumbs brushing along the line where fabric meets skin. "You tell me if anything doesn't. We stop. No questions asked."

I believe him. I believe him so much my core aches.

I want more. I want to know what all the fuss is about, the thing other girls whispered about in locker rooms like it was some secret club I'd never get access to. I want to understand my own body instead of pushing my feelings aside and just being there for the man, wondering why I don't react the way I'm "supposed" to. Even though I've only had sex once with Brooks, it was his desires that were fielded.

When his fingers dip under my skirt's waistband, his eyes silently ask for permission with an almost imperceptible nod.

"Please," I say, surprising myself with how sure I sound.

Matt lifts me to my knees, and I hear each metal tooth of the zipper unlatch. He moves one of my knees between his legs and eases the skirt down, letting it fall somewhere behind him on the bed. Now I'm in just my bra and underwear, practically sitting in his hands. Every instinct in me screams to dart under the covers, make a joke, deflect. But I stay. I sit there and let him peruse my body.

He swallows hard. "You have no idea what you do to me," he says, voice rough. "I want... everything. But I'm not rushing this. Not with you."

Everything inside me trips over that last part. Not with you. Like I'm not just some impulse. I'm something he's choosing to go slow for.

He leans forward, pressing open-lipped kisses along my collarbone, each one leaving sparks racing under my skin. My fingers dig into his hair almost without my permission.

He makes a quiet sound that does very confusing things to my insides.

"Tell me what you like," he murmurs against my skin. His hands glide up and down my back in long, soothing strokes. "What feels good. What doesn't."

Panic flickers. My brain goes completely blank, like he just asked me to solve a calculus problem in the middle of a hurricane.

"I... I don't know," I admit, my voice small. "No one's ever really asked."

He stills, pulling back enough to see my face. There's no judgment there. Just a kind of quiet fury I know isn't aimed at me.

"He never asked?" Matt says, and I don't need him to clarify who he means.

"No." I try to laugh it off, but it comes out thin. "He had... rules. About what he liked. What he didn't. And we only had sex once. I don't truly know what I like."

The admission makes me feel naked in a way the lack of clothes doesn't. But Matt doesn't flinch, just smooths his thumb over my lower lip.

"Okay," he says softly. "Then we'll figure it out together. At your pace."

My chest squeezes so tight I almost can't inhale. "What if there's nothing to figure out?" I whisper, voicing the stupid fear that's sat in my gut for years. "What if I'm broken? What if all this hype about how amazing it is and I'm just... a tomboy that doesn't work right?"

My eyes burn suddenly. Damn it. I did not schedule tears for tonight.

He notices—of course he does. "Hey," he murmurs. "We

don't have to do anything more than kiss. Hell, we don't even have to do that. You just say the word."

"And what if I don't want to stop?" I ask, my voice shaking even as my hands grip his shoulders like I'd gladly anchor myself to him and never move.

His gaze darkens. "Then we go slow," he says. "And you tell me what feels good as we go. I promise I'll cherish every inch of your skin. Show you the intimacy you deserve. We don't have to get it all perfect tonight. This isn't a test. There's no scoreboard."

No scoreboard. No grading. Just... learning.

I let the idea sink in, surprising myself with how much calmer it makes me.

"But you said this is a one-time thing."

"I lied to myself. Not now."

"Okay," I say, breathing him in. "How do we... start?"

He smiles then, small but real, and it does something ridiculous to my insides. "We already did," he says, kissing me again, softer this time.

He leans us backward, shifts us gently, rolling so I'm on my back and he's beside me instead of on top, one arm tucked under my shoulders, the other spread across my stomach like he's anchoring me there. It's protective, not trapping. He could move away in a heartbeat, but I could too.

Tattoos cover one side of his upper body, and for some reason, it revs my engine, faster than *Holly's*. I'm completely lost in all things Matt Stricker.

Matt takes his time kissing me, and it feels like he's writing a song on my lips. I don't know if it's so I don't forget or so he won't.

Believe me. I won't forget.

My fingers trace the patterns of his tattoos as I soak in every new feeling. His hand wanders along my hip, the side of my thigh, the dip at my waist. Every pass leaves a burning sensation behind.

Not frantic, not rushed.

One hundred percent lost in the moment.

My whole body feels like it's humming, but not in a panicked way. More like someone finally tuned me to the right station.

He pulls back just enough to whisper, "Do you want me here?"

"Yes."

He trails his mouth along my jaw, down the curve of my throat, pausing whenever my breath catches. "Here?"

"Yes," I groan.

His hand slides up my arm, fingers weaving with mine above my head, grounding me even as I feel like I might float away. "Here?"

"Yes," I say again, a little shocked at how sure I sound now, especially since I no longer have my hands to touch him or urge him to stop or continue.

But like the gentleman he is, Matt keeps checking in, keeps listening, adjusting when I flinch or go still, repeating what makes me sigh. It's... new. All of it. Not just the touch, but the care. The attention. Like he's invested in my experience, not just his own.

Time blurs. It could be minutes, could be hours. All I know is that I'm breathing hard and my skin feels alive in ways I didn't know it could, and nothing has really "happened" by locker room standards. No score. Just this slow, steady opening, however, I do feel his length hard against my thigh.

At some point, he rests his forehead against mine again, both of us panting lightly. His thumb strokes the side of my neck and slides down my breastbone. It's so gentle yet lights up every nerve in my skin.

"Still with me?" he murmurs.

"Yeah, hmm," I utter. My voice sounds wrecked. A field after a storm, muddied but finally rinsed clean.

He closes his eyes, exhaling shakily. "You're killing me, you know that?"

"Is that... bad?"

He laughs under his breath. "Not even a little. I just... don't want to push. I've wanted you for so long, Noelle. I have to keep reminding myself this isn't a dream."

Something in my chest loosens at that. He's not just in this because I'm convenient or because of some revenge plot. He *wants* me.

"What if I want you to push a little?" I ask softly. "Not in a scary way. Just... I don't even know what I like. I don't know what I'm supposed to enjoy or what's just me trying to be what a guy wants."

His hand stills on my skin, his breath falling on my face.

"No 'supposed to,'" he says, firm. "There's only what *you* want. What your body responds to. What makes you feel good. We can take our time and figure that out."

My heart starts beating so hard it's almost distracting. I lick my lips, nerves and wanting and something like hope tangling up in my veins. "But it's not just about me. I want to make you feel good too."

He opens his eyes, and I swear I've never seen anyone look at me the way he's looking at me now. Not like I'm a trophy girlfriend or an obligation. Not like I'm some fragile little sister. Like I'm... everything. The sun that warms his body. The moon that lights his nights.

I hold his gaze, the words bubbling up before I can overthink them to death. "Matt," I whisper.

"Yeah?"

My fingers tighten around his where our hands are still tangled above my head. My throat feels tight, but the words come anyway.

"Teach me."

SIXTEEN
MATT

Teach me.

Every hair on my body stands at attention. My mind runs a two-minute drill in fast-forward. A million scenarios. A thousand what-ifs.

Can I follow through with this?

She needs someone forever. That's not me. Not now.

If her brothers find out, I'm out my best friend and my job.

If her dad finds out, I'm a chalk outline.

If *she* wakes up tomorrow regretting this, I'm the guy who ruined the only good thing I've had in years. Not to mention my friendship with Greyson and my coaching position with the Armadillos.

I weigh all of it against one undeniable truth: being here with her feels right in a way that terrifies me. For the last couple of years, my rule has always been *no strings*. No one that makes me want more than a fuck.

I swallow. "Butterfly..."

She's watching me like I'm a cliff she's decided to jump from. No flinching. Brave in a way that makes my chest hurt.

"Let's find out what you like first," I say, because that's the only play that matters.

Her breath catches. "Okay."

I brace a forearm by her head, roll my palm down her side, slow and deliberate—over ribs, to waist, back up in a lazy pattern that lets me listen. She's on her back, hair messy against the pillow, pupils dark and wide. The room hums with the air conditioning and the sound of both our breathing.

"Talk to me," I murmur, keeping my voice low. "If you want more, you pull me where you want me. You're calling the plays."

Her mouth tips up. "You're really going to make this a sports metaphor?"

"It's my love language."

She laughs—soft, shaky—and I feel it where my hand rests at her waist. "I like that. I understand it."

I sweep my thumb just under the curve of her rib cage. I feel the fine shiver that runs through her core, and I store that information away: right there. Good. Again, slower. She exhales like I found a live wire.

"Here?" I ask.

"Yeah," she breathes. "There."

I keep a gentle rhythm, then shift, tracing the line of her collarbone with my knuckles, down the slope of her shoulder, up the tender inside of her arm to her palm. I lace our fingers and bring the back of her hand to my mouth, pressing a kiss there. Her lashes flutter.

"You're...gentle," she whispers, like it's a discovery.

"I can be," I say. "I can be anything you need me to be." Lord knows I want this more than once.

Color rises in her cheeks. She squeezes my hand and nods at the narrow band of fabric across her back.

"Can you—" She swallows. "I don't know where my arms are supposed to go."

"Wherever you want." I sit her up enough to slide my palm along her spine. "May I?"

Her yes is a whisper that feels like a vow.

I find the clasp on her silky bra and work it with careful fingers. There's a soft give, fabric easing. I don't rush. I'm not here to tear anything away; I'm here to erase every bad play Brooks called and draft a new one.

"Still good?" I ask.

She nods, eyes on mine, all trust.

I shift my touch to safer borders—collarbone, sternum, the clean lines of her shoulders—mapping without taking. She arches a fraction, like her body's answering something it didn't know to ask.

Her breath hitches. She bites her bottom lip in concentration, as if she's listening to herself.

"What are you feeling?" I ask.

"I don't know. Your touch is...it's all so foreign to me," she says, voice hushed. "Like...I can't believe this is happening."

"Me either," I admit, honest in a way I don't recognize from my old life. "But I'm not going anywhere right now."

Her eyes shine and her lips curve upward.

I kiss her—slow, patient, a steady cadence instead of a scramble. She leans up into it, and I feel her hand slide around the back of my neck, her thumb finding a rhythm at my pulse like she's calming herself by counting me.

I whisper against her mouth and she shivers. "I love the way your breath hitches when I kiss you."

She says, "I like it when you kiss me... but I keep waiting to mess it up."

"You can't mess this up." I drag my nose along her cheek, the curve of her jaw. "It's all about staying in the moment."

I explore in inches—her jawline, the dip beneath her ear, the slope where her neck meets her shoulder. Each time I pause and ask; each time she answers in a sound that makes my chest go tight.

"Here?" I murmur, brushing my mouth down the line of her throat.

"Yes," she says, the word a sigh that slides through me like a heatwave. She tilts, offering more, and my self-control hits a wall I have to breathe through. I keep it slow. Not because I'm a saint. Because she deserves *slow*. She deserves to feel chosen at every single step.

"Matt," she whispers, one hand fisting in the duvet, the other tugging at me until I settle half on my side, half braced above her, so she has weight and space. Safe, not pinned. Present, not crowding.

I thread our fingers and press them back to the pillow, just like she liked before. "You're still in control."

She nods. "I like... when you hold my hand like that."

"Copy that." I lace them tighter. "What else?"

"I like when you... talk," she says, embarrassed by how earnest that sounds. "When you tell me what you're doing. I don't feel lost then."

I could kiss her for that alone. "I can talk." My mouth curves. "I can coach."

She snorts a laugh that turns into a gasp when I glide my

palm down her side again, slower, letting the heel of my hand warm her through her shirt.

"Breathe," I say, matching her inhale with mine. "In through your nose, out through your mouth. Don't chase it. Let it come to you."

She mirrors me, pupils wide, her chest rising in time with mine. "Like this?"

"Perfect." I mean it. Christ, I mean it.

The self-recriminations try to crowd back in—her brothers, the job, the age gap, the way my body has been running on reserves I don't like admitting—but none of it holds in the same room as her trust. None of it is louder than the sound she makes when I trail a line of slow kisses down to her chest. I kiss the bouncy mounds of flesh, careful not to get close to the nipple. I want her desperate for my touch. She arches and shimmies on the bed, attempting to move where she wants my mouth.

"Tell me more," I ask, my voice rough with need.

"I like... when you slow down right at the spot that makes me want to rush," she says, discovering it as she speaks. "I never knew that part."

"Slowing down is how you feel everything," I say. "Rushing is how you miss it."

She looks at me like I said a thing she needed to hear in places that have nothing to do with tonight. I feel it land. I catalog it for later, something to come back to and talk about. Does she feel she's been rushed through life and hasn't been able to stop and smell the roses?

I move carefully, sitting with my back against the headboard and bringing her up with me, settling her across my thighs so she has height, leverage, and my shoulders to hold on to. She blushes at the new angle, then relaxes when she realizes I'm just... there. Breathing with her. Letting her look at me the way I've been looking at her.

"Better?" I ask.

She nods. "I don't feel so... observed. I feel... with you."

With you. The words knock around in my ribs like they're searching for a home. I grip her hip and squeeze once, a promise.

"Tell me if you want me to move." I tip my head against the wall and smile. "Or tell me to stay right here and just let you get used to the view."

Her eyes flick down my chest and back up, and that blush goes pretty and defiant. "Maybe I *am* looking."

"Good." I rest my free hand over her heartbeat and feel it kick. "Look all you want."

She does. Her palm skates over my shoulder, down my arm, and returns to the spot high on my chest she's already claimed. I don't correct her, don't steer. I let her explore, the same way I want for her. When she sighs, I answer with a low sound I don't bother to swallow.

"You like that?" she asks, a little wonder sneaking in.

"I like *you,* figuring it out in real time." I angle my face until our mouths are only a hairsbreadth away. "I like your voice when you tell me what you want."

She bites her lip, then lets it go. "I want... more of your mouth on my skin."

"Where?" I ask, soft.

She points, shy but sure, and I follow—from her neck to the pulse point down to her gorgeous, stunning breasts. Not big by any means, but they have the most beautiful light-pink nipples, hardened by desire. I work my way down and give each breast the attention it deserves.

Noelle arches into me, wanting it harder, so I nibble on

each perky peak until she's grinding against me. My dick is so hard it's aching, and with every front-to-back movement, her body weight takes over and her center covers me.

She melts against me in slow increments, a long surrender that feels like a trust fall. I'm so gone I forget to breathe until she says my name, and I find oxygen again.

"Still good?" I ask.

Grinding. Dry rubbing has never felt this pleasurable.

"Better than good," she says, her breath punching out on the last word. "This...this feels like I'm here. Not trying to be what someone else wants."

My jaw tightens on its own at *someone else*, but I let it go. This isn't about him. This is about her, and the way she's unfolding in front of me is like a play you designed that finally worked.

"Noelle." I choke out her name, my voice full of emotion, and I notice a slight shake to it. "You're the kind of woman that any man in his right mind would want." I smile into her sternum, kissing her dead center. "The best part about sex is designing your own plays. Making your own playbook."

She huffs a watery laugh. "You're such a dork."

"And you like me that way."

"I really do."

I kiss her again to shove these emotions far back.

Be in the moment. Don't ruin this.

The weight of everything I haven't said sits heavily in my chest, but I hold the line, keeping it where it belongs—inside me, not between us.

"Teach me how to please you."

"You are pleasing me. I've never been so fucking pleased."

She shifts, instinct chasing instinct, and I have to catch

my breath. I tighten my arm around her and press my nose to her temple, grinding down on the groan that wants out. She slides down my legs, ass in the air, looking like a cat stretching, and damn if she isn't tugging down my underwear. "I want to feel you."

"My cock?" I can hardly contain myself, but inside I'm repeating, *Stay slow. Stay present. The point is not to prove anything; the point is to be here with her and let her body talk.*

"You're shaking," she whispers.

"Yeah." My laugh scrapes. "You have that effect."

"Me?" she asks with a lilt in her voice. She truly doesn't know how fucking sexy she is.

"Absolutely."

Looking up at me under her mascara-laced lashes, she runs her fingers over my erection. The pads of her fingers are so delicate, yet I've heard she can throw a softball sixty miles an hour.

She's quiet for a beat, her fingers exploring my velvety head and the shaft, and places an open-lipped kiss on the tip. My cock jerks, and she lets out a little chuckle. "Did you make it do that?"

"No. I can, but no, it was a reflex. It just wants to be in your mouth. But that's not what I want right now. I want to feel how wet you are and have you come on my fingers."

I do want her lips wrapped around my shaft, but I want to see her come more.

"You're so direct."

"You wanted me to talk, and I'm just being honest." I slide down the headboard and roll her onto her back. My finger roams her legs while I suck her nipples into my mouth, and that's when she places her hand on top of mine and guides it between her thighs. She's dripping wet, and damn, I want to taste her, but this needs to come first. Noelle wants to know what her body responds to, and so far, she has responded to every sensation, no matter how big or small. She loves to be kissed everywhere, and I plan on showing her how I'm going to make love to her pussy with my mouth, but not yet.

I sink one finger inside her, and she grips my wrist. "Oh, yes."

Pumping and tickling her inner walls, she moves my wrist fast. Hard. I can't help but smile because if this fake dating lasts much longer and we get more opportunities, it will not be slow. I think my butterfly will spread her wings and try all kinds of things she has no idea exist.

Baby steps.

A few minutes later, I have two fingers inside her and my control is wearing so thin I may come without any aid from her. She's arching. Squirming. Moaning. It's turning me into a volcano ready to explode. She holds my wrist in place. Two fingers inside her and my thumb pressing against her clit. Her muscles start to contract, and damn, she's strong. Her pussy has me locked in place. Her juices cover my fingers and drip down her thighs as she pants, "Oh, oh, oh, I'm..."

"I know, Butterfly." I pull my hand out and wipe her arousal over her lips, then kiss her, tasting her sweetness as she floats in pure happiness. But I can't take it anymore. I wrap my fingers around my shaft, giving it a few pumps as the sensation starts at my toes and travels like a freight train.

When she comes back to reality, she sees how hard I'm dragging my hand and the strain on my face as I try to control myself. She says, "You're supposed to be teaching me."

"Spread your arousal on your hand and grip me hard.

Slide up and down, touching the rim and going slightly above and back down to the balls." I sense her hesitancy, but I know all it will take is one touch from her. "It's how I like it."

She slides that perfect palm up and down. Her delicate fingers caress my heavy, velvet head, and a growl rages from my throat, shooting cum in all directions. I haven't been with anyone in over a year. Hell, I knew I could have come without much assistance because she's the most beautiful, interesting woman I've ever known.

I let out a deep, intense growl, and when my body relaxes, I fall onto my back. My skin sticks to sheets covered in cum.

A slow smile curves her lips. "Note to self—do not provoke you. That growl was something else."

I throw one hand behind my head and tuck her into my side. I feel like I'm right where I'm supposed to be, but outside influences keep the doubt well within reach. Maybe doubt isn't the correct word; it's about betraying my best friend and their whole family.

Noelle's nails travel over my tattoos, and I know the next question will be, *Do these have a meaning?* Instead, she moves down and circles my glucose monitor. Seconds tick by before she asks, "So can you tell me your secrets now?"

Surprised, I frown. "I don't have secrets. What you see is what you get."

"When I asked what that was," she says, tapping the skin next to the monitor, "you said we weren't dating for real, so I don't know your secrets. But now... I..."

Her words stall. Mine don't. "Just like you do with your family, be open, honest, and say what's on your mind."

She swallows. "After touching each other, does that

mean we are still faking it, or are we something more? If we are, I want to know all about this device."

"Noelle," I say, skimming her arm with my fingertips. "You're an incredible woman."

"I hear a *but* coming."

I close my eyes, expelling a heavy breath. "But... this is complicated in so many ways. Let's just take it one day at a time. As far as everyone is concerned, we're faking it. But obviously, I'm not faking my attraction to you. There's a boatload of cum all over the bed to prove it."

She tips her head, staring up at me with a bashful smile. I tuck my knuckle under her chin, placing a slow, close-lipped kiss on her mouth. When we break, I turn on my side so we're facing each other. "I have diabetes, and this is my trusted companion, the glucose monitor." I let out a half-laugh.

"I thought so, but I've had friends with diabetes who just take a pill. But you... jab yourself."

"Yeah, mine's worse than that. It tells me when my sugar is too high or too low. So, when you're making fun of me for drinking protein shakes and not eating cupcakes and cookies, this is why."

"No sweets. That must be awful."

"Not anymore." I slide down her body until I can throw one leg over my shoulder, place succulent kisses on her inner thighs, and move to her center, licking. On instinct, her knees snap to my ears.

"Relax. I don't need sugar when I have all the sweetness a man could want right here."

And rather than ruin the moment talking about my illness, I lose myself in her slippery, sugary folds and nibble on her bundle of nerves. And it's music to my ears when I hear her moaning my name. Her flesh shimmers with sweat and desire. And when she tugs my hair, burying my face between her legs, I feel like I'm in a candyland with all the sweetness I'll ever need.

She cheers, "Yes, yes," until her whole body trembles. Her hands clench my skull, keeping me right where she needs me to be.

I don't give in until she detonates, covering my mouth and chin in her juices. Pulling back enough to see her, she's pink-cheeked and starry-eyed and so beautiful it hurts. "Still with me?"

"Matt?" she asks, my name nearly two syllables.

"Yeah." I scoot back up the bed.

"I feel... different." Her voice sounds wrecked in the best possible way.

"How?" My thumb draws lazy circles on her hipbone, the same place she reacted to first.

"Like I finally tuned in to the right radio station," she says, and I smile because she just stole my thought.

SEVENTEEN
NOELLE

Morning finds me in the same hotel bed, same sheets, but in an entirely different universe.

I lie very still and listen: the air conditioning vent whirs, footsteps thud above us, ice clatters in a hallway bucket. Matt's inked arm is solid over my waist, his breath steady at the back of my neck, teaching my jittery body a calmer song. Last night's surprising events play behind my closed lids. The whole night in soft-focus frames—his patience, his voice, the way he asked and waited, the way I answered and didn't feel wrong for once.

A mixture of desire and disbelief washes through me. I can't believe that happened. I can't believe it could feel like that without the panic of performing. I can't believe I got to be...with him.

The phone alarm nudges us out of the dream. Matt groans into the pillow like the world has personally offended him.

"Is it already time to wake up?" I ask.

He rumbles, "Not for you."

"I have rookie camp at nine," I say, though my voice doesn't sound convincing. "ESPN expects me to look presentable and be prepared."

"I can't help with being prepared. Well, I could, but this is your career." He peels his arm away and props himself on an elbow, studying me like he's checking for fractures. "But you may need a shower. You smell—"

"Rude." I smile anyway. He kisses me once, slow and unhurried, then another time for luck. The second one makes me forget my name for a second.

"I was going to say you smell like a dream."

There's a softness to Matt, a contradiction to the inked coach shouting and correcting players. I always knew it was there, but my main interaction with him has always been with my family. And with my brothers, if you're not cocky, they think something is wrong with you. They like being surrounded by people with confidence. And Matt has those qualities, but today I'm realizing there is more to him than a former football player and now a coach. He's more than Greyson's best friend. More than one of J.D.'s assistant coaches. He's quick-witted and caring.

Ripping off the tangled sheets, Matt's naked body twists, and that little round monitor catches my eye. He walks into the bathroom. I sit up, leaning where I can admire him in the mirror's reflection. He takes a needle and jabs it into his side, then places his palms on the counter and closes his eyes. His shoulders fall as he releases a quick breath.

Something is wrong. He's regretting what we did. It's not like we had sex. But in all honesty, this oral sex was a million times better than the full sex I had with Brooks. It was every-thing I had imagined but didn't think existed. Trusting someone else to let me find out what I enjoy. And I had orgasms, not pretending I was satisfied.

The shower turns on, and I gather our clothes and make separate piles on the other bed. He's out in five minutes. "All yours."

Does he mean his body is all mine? Or the shower?

I look in the mirror and somehow seem surprisingly rested, even though it was less than four hours of sleep. It's the post-non-sex glow. The veil of satisfaction. Being touched, almost worshipped, feels fantastic. The only thing bothering me is Matt poking himself with needles.

"I'm ready."

Matt's gaze travels the length of me. "I don't like it."

Dang, he can be grumpy. "Why?" I look down at my outfit.

"Because Brooks doesn't need to see your legs." There's a bite behind his words.

"Possessive much?"

He twists his lips and runs his hand over his stubble. "Let's call it protective."

"Whatever you say, Coach."

"Not your coach."

I skim my fingers over his cheeks. "What would you call last night?" I want to make sure he remembers how good we feel together and doesn't start reconsidering our fake-but-not-so-fake dating. "Pretty sure you were coaching me."

He raises a crooked brow, places his hand on my back, and leads me out of the hotel room.

At the facility, New Orleans is already roaring. Rookies swarm like bees, coaches clap, and whistles slice the heat. I'm back in my reporter skin—hair up, mic in hand, questions ready. I can do this. I can hold last night like a secret under my ribs and still ask questions. Today, I hope to find a story to work on and pitch to my producers, something other than, "How do you feel?" or "Is it harder than you expected?"

After interviewing one of the rookie linebackers, I have a story—a real one. A tearjerker. I'm pitching it to my producer when Brooks pops up like a bad memory. Helmet off, sweat beading at his temples, his smile turned to maximum wattage.

"Hey, stranger," he says, his voice pitched for me and the nearest camera. "Are you highlighting me tonight? I was surprised you gave the kicker all that airtime last night."

"It's about stories, not just stats. And after nearly two years together, I can't think of anything interesting to say about you." I keep my reporter smile in place.

He chuckles, knowing he's getting to me. "Late night?" His gaze flicks down and back up, a move I used to miss. But it reminds me of all the times he looked at other women in the exact same way.

"I slept." The lie tastes like chalk because I would rather scream, *"Matt gave me multiple orgasms, which you never did."*

He leans closer, too close, like we're sharing a joke. "Or did you?" His grin sharpens. He knows how I look without sleep, but for many different reasons. Parties that lingered into the wee morning hours or traveling on a bus from an away game. "Did you have to wait for the old man to take his little blue pill?"

I step back. "Don't," I warn, my eyes pinching in the sun, but I wobble. Something's not right.

He shrugs, catching my arm. "Relax. I'm kidding." Then he cocks his head like he's the lead role in his own movie. "Unless you're...knocked up with your old man's baby?"

The air evaporates. I'm certain the ground tilts. One time with Brooks. I see a calendar flipped open in my head with a big red circle around a date I've been pretending isn't important. I hate that my hand flies, traitor, to my stomach.

No.

Brooks sees it. Of course, he does. He smirks like he's scored.

"Back off, Brooks," I bite out. "I'm here to work. And you're here to learn how not to be a liability."

"Liability, huh? That's hilarious. I'm going to save New Orleans, and you know it."

His eyebrows shoot up; the smirk slides. A coach's whistle blasts nearby. The special teams assistant sprints over. "You okay?" he asks, already scanning my face like it's his job. "Take five. Get some shade."

"I'm fine," I say, since that's the script I memorized in childhood. If you say you're fine or okay, people quit asking questions.

When Mom died, I was asked, *"Honey, are you okay? Honey, can I get you anything?"* a dozen times a day. I'm well versed in the art of getting people to believe me.

He ignores me and scans Brooks's face. I'm sure he knows we were college sweethearts. "Take five," he repeats, firmer. Then to another staffer, "Grab her water." To me, lower, "Want me to call Stricker?"

"No," I say, too fast.

My producer says, "We've got enough film and spotlights. Let's talk more about that story later."

A cautious smile spreads across my face. "Okay." Then I tell the assistant coach, "I'll call Coach Stricker. Just give me a few minutes and I'll be okay."

He nods once and peels away. Brooks opens his mouth

like he's going to say something else, and I slice him with a look I learned from my mother when she meant business—*put your toys in their place when you're finished playing.*

"Go," I say again, and this time he listens.

I make it to the tunnel, flipping from sticky heat to cool shade. I sit against the concrete, and my stomach bubbles and sweat covers my face. I brace my hands on my knees and suck in air through my nose the way Matt told me.

Someone must have called Matt because he is by my side within minutes. He doesn't ask if I'm okay first. He presses a cold bottle into my hand, pops two stomach-calming tablets into the other, and takes my mic so I can swallow them.

"Talk to me," he orders, softer than the word sounds. He crouches in front of me, all heat and worry, and I see his mind working overtime.

"I'm okay," I say, because my mouth is stubborn. "It's just the heat."

"You were sick in Oklahoma," he says carefully. "And then yesterday in the car, you got quiet and breathed weird for twenty miles. And now today you look like the world is a carousel spinning faster than you can handle."

"It's not...I'm fine." My eyes sting, traitors. I blink hard. "He just said something disgusting."

"What did he say?" The temperature of his voice drops ten degrees.

"That I might be... that I might be pregnant with my 'old man's baby.'" I try to put air quotes around it, but my hands shake. I laugh, a brittle little sound, because the alternative is sobbing. "Hilarious, right?"

Matt doesn't laugh. Something moves behind his eyes that I can't name. He takes my free hand, his thumb pressing the map of my knuckles.

"We're not going to let him get in your head," he says. "You hear me?"

The part I don't say is the part that explodes quietly in my chest anyway. If I'm pregnant, there's only one possibility. The one time with Brooks, six weeks ago, when I convinced myself it meant we were fixing things. When I thought scraps counted as dinner. I feel sick for a different reason now.

I shove that thought into a box and hammer nails into the lid. Right now, I have a job. Right now, I will not fall apart on the sidelines for Brooks to enjoy.

"Hey," Matt says, like he can see the box and the nails and the way I'm holding the hammer too tight. "You want to call it for the morning? I can walk you back."

I shake my head. "I want to finish. I won't let him win. I want to be good at this."

A slow nod. "Okay. Then we finish." He leans in and touches his forehead to mine for a second, just long enough to transfer the steady from his body to mine. "You're not alone."

I breathe him in. "I know."

I make it through the rest of the morning. I get clean quotes. I take notes that aren't just about football—tiny things I like to fold into highlights: the punter with the lucky shoelace, the tight end who learned sign language for his sister, and the head trainer who keeps peppermints in her pocket for queasy rookies. She even offers me one. "You're a rookie reporter, after all."

"Can you tell?"

She says, "No, but everyone knows the O'Ryan family. And of course, Brooks has told everyone that will listen that he's going to win you back. Told us you were meant to be."

"Hah! He had his chance and blew it many times, and I'm happy now."

"With Coach Stricker?"

It throws me a little, knowing our relationship is a balancing act between fake and real, between my brothers and what I want. "Yeah. He's... a great guy."

I can handle my brothers if only I knew Matt's feelings.

She touches my elbow. "A word of advice from a woman who lives in a man's world the same as you. Make sure you know their demons. Most every man at this level has some. Heck, maybe us women do, too."

Demons? Like our mom dying.

What would Matt's be? Does it have to do with that little monitor? He always seems grumpy or mad when I bring it up. He tries to brush it off, but I see the mask he wears.

I wave to the New Orleans coach, and he gives me a little salute like we're on the same team. By the look on his face, he's proud that I pushed through and got back in the game, so to speak.

Brooks stays far away. Good.

Later, my phone lights up with a text from Birdie, then three missed calls, and then another text from J.D. I step into the shade to listen to the voicemail, but J.D. calls back first, breathless and happy and a little terrified. "The baby girl's coming," he says. "Sutton is in labor. Greyson's a mess. I'm pretending not to be. I'm going to be an uncle."

"You're already a dad." Excitement crashes through my body. "Oh my God."

"Can you get back?" he asks. "We know you're on assignment, so don't you dare feel guilty if you can't, but if you—"

"I can." It's out before I even glance at Matt talking to the female trainer just outside the end zone. "We'll be there."

"We?"

I turn. Matt's already walking toward me, like his bones felt my name. "Me and Matt."

There's a tiny beat on the line, and I fill the void with something harmless. "You know he's here with me because of Brooks," I add, which isn't a lie.

J.D. exhales. "Okay. Drive safe." His voice goes soft. "Love you."

"Love you, too."

Steam rises off the Texas highway.

Feet propped up on the dashboard. George Strait sings on the radio. The station I finally found. Inwardly, my body temperature rises just thinking about his low, sexy voice and his wicked fingers and tongue.

"Feet off the dash," he says automatically while staring at my legs.

"I'm soothing my nausea," I counter.

He flicks me a look. "That isn't a thing."

"It could be," I smirk, flirting.

We ride a few miles in comfortable nothing. The farther we get from New Orleans, the more my stomach unwinds. The more the memory of last night presses close again, warm and panty-melting.

I want his hand. I want it so badly my fingers twitch. There are no cameras now. No ex-boyfriends. No performance. If I reach for him, it's because I want to, not because I need to sell the story. Which is exactly why my hand stays in my lap.

"Thinking too much," he says, not taking his eyes off the road.

"Am not."

"You always are." He knocks his knuckles lightly against mine on the console. It counts. It's ridiculous that it counts, but it does. My chest loosens. "I'm worried about you."

Yeah, me too. What if I'm pregnant with Brooks's baby?

But I keep those thoughts to myself. It's a thought I'm not ready to entertain, so I close my eyes, faking sleep.

At the hospital, my big family is a small storm system in a waiting room—my dad pacing lines into the tile, Birdie with flowers in her hands, Greyson's daughter, Paulina, passing out gummy bears.

When Matt and I walk in together, the air shifts in that way it always does when you rearrange the dynamics of a family. Matt is supposed to be here as a best friend, not as my boyfriend. I just hope they can't see my evolving feelings for Matt. He's not just a fake revenge date anymore.

J.D. comes to me first. He smells like aftershave and anxiety. "You made it."

"Wouldn't miss it." I tuck myself into his side. "You okay?"

"I am pretending to be the calm center of this family," he says. "How am I doing?"

"You're vibrating," I say, and he laughs. "But you're hiding it well."

Over his shoulder, my dad is looking at Matt the way dads look at weather reports they don't trust. Matt goes into full coach mode—shoulders down, voice low and calm, one hand respectfully nowhere. "Sir," he says, nodding.

"Matt," my dad returns, skeptical of our fake-dating lie. It's not approval. It's not a warning either. It's a dad wanting to protect his daughter. What he doesn't understand is that Matt treats me a thousand times better than Brooks ever did.

Or maybe that's what he's afraid of.

My brother, Parker, slides in for a hug that leaves me smelling like masculine cologne. "You look tired," he says, which is college code for *were you knocking boots?*

"Brooks just gets under my skin, acting like he was good for me and that I should just forgive and forget."

"Promise me you won't get back with him. I'd rather you be with Matt than that cheating asshole," Parker says, knowing how it feels to be cheated on.

"Don't worry, that will never happen."

"Good."

Matt keeps his distance but brings me a water bottle and peanut M&M's. I don't remember ever telling him they're my favorite, but somehow, he knows. Or he just got lucky. "Here. But after the baby is born, you're getting something healthy."

My head jerks back. Does he think I'm pregnant? Then I realize he's talking about Greyson's baby. "Sure thing, Coach." I wink.

He shakes his head, drops his chin, and I'm willing to bet he's smiling inside.

An hour stretches, then two. We pass time in true O'Ryan fashion, competing. Witt, Parker, Dad, and I play Uno. J.D. and Matt dissect football players on the iPad. Birdie writes lyrics in a notebook. Then the door swings wide, and Greyson appears, hair in six directions, eyes shining like summertime.

"We have a little girl," he says, and the whole room exhales at once. My dad pretends it's allergies causing the tears. J.D. attempts cool and fails, glassy-eyed in two seconds.

Greyson lets out a ragged laugh. "She's perfect," he says. "Sutton's perfect. I'm... I don't have words."

"You never do," I say, which is a lie; Greyson is a fountain. He pulls me into a hug anyway, and I feel the tremor in his arms.

"Follow me."

We get a glimpse through glass—a tiny hat, even tinier fingers, Sutton's exhausted smile, Paulina bouncing, our family doubled by joy.

Once Greyson, Sutton, Paulina, and their new baby girl are settled in their hospital room, we take turns going in. "Have you named her yet?" I ask.

Greyson says, "Not yet. We wanted to talk to everyone about it." He grabs his phone, texts in the family group chat, and soon the whole O'Ryan clan is in the room, swooning over their baby girl.

Sutton's holding the baby; Greyson and Paulina sit on each side of her. With tears in his eyes, he holds Sutton's hand and she urges him on. "We want your permission to use Mom's name."

The room falls silent. Dad covers his mouth, and I don't know whether anyone is happy or mad. "Unbelievable," Witt says, shocked, and storms out of the room. For a moment, we all stare at each other. Dad says, "I'll go after him."

"No, let me," I say, and before I know it, Parker is following me following Witt.

Parker puts his hand on my shoulder. When we see Witt sitting slumped in a waiting room chair, we sit on each side of him. He's sensitive about Mom since she died giving birth to him. I place my hand on his knee. "Hey, what's wrong?"

Witt pinches the bridge of his nose, his eyes glimmering with tears, and softly bangs his head against the wall. Parker says, "Bro, we know babies are hard on you, but you have to get over this."

Witt lifts his head slowly and peers into Parker's eyes, and it's clear he has something to say, but instead he bites his bottom lip.

"Witt, what Parker means is that we all miss Mom, but we have to live with the hand life deals us."

He scoffs. "Miss Mom... I don't miss her. I didn't even know her. How can I miss someone I didn't know?"

But he does miss her. Her blood pumped through him. Her food fed and hydrated him.

Tonight isn't the night to take a deep dive into his feelings about our mom and what happened. He carries enough guilt to build a football stadium—or at least we think he does. Witt says a few sentences a day to any of us, and that's it. "Why did you storm out? You don't want them to name their beautiful baby after Mom? Because I think it's wonderful."

"She was your mom. You all decide whether you want her name to be used."

"Our mom."

"Whatever. Just go in there and say I was just being a dick."

"Well, that's not far from the truth," I tease.

Parker, ever the gentle giant, chimes in. "Mom would want you to be happy. I want you to be happy. I would love to have a relationship with you like J.D. and Greyson have." Parker folds his long fingers over Witt's shoulder, squeezing and shooting Witt a hopeful smile.

Witt doesn't respond but shakes his head. Mom's passing affected us all differently. I was six, Parker was five, Greyson sixteen, and John David almost eighteen, so Witt feels left out anytime the subject of Mom comes up.

"Be honest with Greyson and Sutton. They'll understand your point of view."

"I was being stupid."

"Okay, come on. Let's go back in and hold the baby."

When we come back, Dad grabs Witt, gives him a giant bear hug, and under his breath says, "I love you, son. I remember the day you were born. I laid you on her chest and she cried. She kept mumbling about how handsome and strong you were."

Witt leans into him but, again, stays silent.

Sutton asks Witt, "We decided we want to name her after you. Witley Suzanne."

"Oh my God, I love it!" I clap and bounce on my toes.

His eyes go wide. "Witley. After me?"

Greyson says, "When Mom was pregnant with you, she always said you were going to be an MMA fighter since you were always kicking. We want our baby girl to be a fighter like you."

Witt acts unconcerned and finally says, "It's your baby."

Greyson says to Witt, "We want you to be the first to hold her. Say hello to Witley Suzanne O'Ryan. Now sit so you don't drop her." The last part is more of a command.

I'm not sure if Witt is acting repulsed or if he really is, but in our family, it's an enormous honor to be the first one to hold a newborn. Greyson chose Witt, not Dad or J.D. or even me. He wants Witt to feel special, the way Mom made the rest of us feel.

Suddenly, I'm crying like a baby. "She's so beautiful." I stroke her soft little head while my little brother holds her, wondering if I'm carrying a baby.

NINETEEN
MATT

"Can you take me to the store?" Noelle asks as we're leaving the hospital. "I want to get the house ready for when they come home. Meals, decorations, the works."

"You have a broadcast meeting in the morning."

"Then we'll be fast, please?" Her mouth tilts, full of hope and happiness.

"It's almost midnight. I can't believe the nurses let us stay," I say as I pull the handle on the truck door, and it takes three times before it unlatches. Maybe *Holly* is ready for retirement.

"That's not a no."

What do I do? I drive to a twenty-four-hour store like we're planning a heist. Paper goods, freezer pans, foil, balloons, string, and enough food to feed an army or a football team. Everyone will come to see the golden couple's baby girl. They love Greyson, but the players and their families adore Sutton. She listens and always finds a way to move season ticket holders around to give extended family an opportunity to come see the Armadillos up close.

I come to a stoplight and need to break the tie in my head. Do I take her to my condo near here? Or do I take her to her home? My thumbs strum on the steering wheel when the light turns green.

"It's green."

"I know," I say, glancing at her smiling from ear to ear. "My place is closer, so the freezer food won't melt, and it's close to the network for you in the morning." My voice trails off, sounding like I'm making excuses to take her to my place.

"Coach Stricker, are you inviting me to your house? To spend the night?"

A humorless breath escapes because wanting her feels like both the best and worst idea I've ever had. Guess what I do?

"It's been a long drive. I need some rest," I explain. It's not a lie, but I want one more night with her. A night when her family won't stop by or call because they're exhausted too.

I see her smile as we pass under the city lights. "Right? Rest."

"I guess that means you're willing?" I ask.

"Willing? Yeah, I'm willing. But we have to go to Greyson's tomorrow to stock their fridge and decorate."

Noelle wears her emotions on her face and in her voice, which is why I'm scared her family is going to catch on to us coming close to *knocking boots*, as true Texans say.

After we park, unload the truck, take the elevator up to my condo, and put the fridge and freezer food away, I say, "I need a shower. The guest room is the last room on the right. Or if you need to unwind," I go to the den and pick up the remote. "Feel free to...unwind."

God, I sound like it's the first woman I've had over. I promise it's not, but it has been a while.

"Thanks. Now go shower. I'm going to go over my notes for the story and type them up."

"Okay, I'll just head to bed after."

She frowns, her shoulders slumping before she quickly recovers and pulls out her laptop.

The shower seems to take too long, needing to be back out there with her. The problem is I don't want her to know it. I wrap the towel around my waist and look at my reflection. The person staring back at me looks disappointed too, seemingly saying, *"Why did you bring her back here?"*

Good question. One I know the answer to, but I'm trying hard to resist the butterfly puttering around my house.

When I'm ready to brush my teeth, I realize that I dropped my overnight bag in the den. I step out of my bedroom, and I see her prancing around the kitchen in my T-shirt. I can't help but remember her tits. The way they pushed into my mouth. Rosy nipples screaming for relief.

I attempt to sneak past her, tiptoeing, but I'm a two-hundred-and-twenty-five-pound former football player. She turns, the shirt hitting her upper thighs. Her gaze travels the length of me.

She mouths a curse word that's meant only for her, but I hear it. Or maybe I'm hearing what I want to hear. But then she says, soft and determined, "Teach me."

Everything in me wants to undress her and fuck her on the kitchen island. There's no coming back from full-blown sex with Noelle. Do I walk away?

No. I drop my bag.

Stride into her personal space.

Back her into the island.

"What do you want to learn?" My voice is raw and rough.

"How to make you want me." She presses her hands on my chest.

Fuck me. I already do. So. Fucking. Bad.

Without thinking, I lift her onto the slate countertop, spreading her knees like a butterfly. She's my butterfly. Sweet, light. Spotted with pain and striped with scars.

"Me want you?"

It must come out harsh because she asks, "Can you at least pretend and teach me how to make a man feel good?"

"Yeah, I can do that. But when we're done with lessons, this is over." Before the words are even all the way out, I'm moving her thumbs over my nipples as I kiss below her ear, a spot she loved last night. "Move your hands and nails down. Slow...tease me."

She's a quick learner. Fire consumes my body from her silky touch and the slow drag of her nails.

"Take off my towel. Grip me." I slide my lips down her neck. She's panting from going slow, and I can already feel my core tightening.

"How can it be so hard and soft at the same time?" She floats her finger over the head, then pumps it a few times.

"Rub the precum over my dick."

"Why?"

"Your hand will slide easier."

"Don't you want to fuck me?"

I choke. "Yeah, Butterfly, I do, but this is coaching."

"No, I want to be fucked like you can't get enough of me."

"Well, that's lesson three. Tell the man how much you want him inside you. It will drive him crazy."

She looks down at my shaft, hard and throbbing, then her eyes travel to mine. Without hesitation but with wispy breaths, she says it back to me. "I want you to be inside me."

Jesus. She's the whole package.

Pushing my shirt up her body and over her head, I move her hand and fist a handful of her hair, pulling gently. Rough and needy, I suck on her neck until she's lying back on the cold, gray slate. I suck her tits while keeping a grip on her hair, biting just above her pelvic bone and then the inside of her thighs, until I slip off her panties and open her wings wide.

Running my fingers through her folds, she gasps and arches with each touch. Unable to stop myself, I spread the lips with my fingers and after admiring the plump, pink, sparkling flesh, I put my tongue to work, licking with the flat of my tongue, then with the tip, alternating until she's a complete mess. I mumble, "I'm going to hell for this, but your pussy is worth the sin."

She laughs, breathless, and pants out, "Hell probably isn't any hotter than Texas."

Christ, she makes me smile. Sharp and sarcastic. And so sexy.

Her back lifts off the counter when she can't handle one more second, and then she comes hard. Her body stiffens and her legs try to squeeze my ears, but I hold her knees apart. I want to see how her arousal flows from her body before I lick every last drop. She mixes my name with God's, and it feels damn good.

When her body finally softens, I stand and scoot her ass as close to the edge as I can get. "Tell me what you enjoyed most."

She shrugs, her face flushed.

"It turns me on. Probably all guys, if you say what you like. Encourage a guy when he gives you what you want. Or maybe I didn't give you what you wanted." I lift a brow. "Did I?" She has me second-guessing that earthquake that just took place in her body.

With a sated, lazy smile, she admits, "It was perfect. But do you like it?"

"Better than beignets."

Her smile widens, this time showing teeth. "Those *are* delicious."

"They are. But I can't eat them." I run my finger along her outer thigh. Gently sucking her neck, I whisper, "Will you be my dessert?"

She shivers and I pick her up in my arms and carry her into my room with her legs anchored around my waist, our eyes locked together in expectation. Noelle doesn't answer, lost in the moment. I press a knee to the mattress and dip her until her back hits the comforter. She covers her breast and I move her hand. "If we're doing this, you have to be open."

"Okay, Coach."

Damn, she can be sassy. "Noelle, spread your legs and stroke me." Her fingers wrap around my shaft, and her hand pumps slowly and methodically. "Fuck yeah. That's it, Butterfly." I sit up on my knees, and she comes up with me.

She takes me into her mouth. It doesn't take much until I'm fucking her mouth, pistoning my hips hard and fast into her face.

She makes little moans and pops off, licking her lips and catching her breath. "You're perfect."

Nowhere close, but good to hear when she's giving me oral.

She slides back on and I tip her chin so I can see her

watery eyes. "I'm going to fuck you now." My voice is a low baritone. Her shoulders do a little dance, and her lips release my dick.

"Okay. I like your dirty talk."

"Do you want me on top?" I ask.

To my surprise, she shakes her head no and explains, "I don't want to just lie there."

"Butterfly, you won't."

"That's what I did with..."

"Don't you say his fucking name after my cock was just in your mouth," I growl. "He didn't care about you getting off. I'll tell you what I like in this position, and you do the same."

I crawl forward, forcing her to lie back. Her hair falls to the side, decorating my light gray pillows. "I'm going to get you ready." I slide my dick between her folds. The outside is already producing a sheen of arousal, and I slide easily, making sure my tip teases her clit.

She mutters, "Yes."

"Butterfly, I want your hands all over me: my ass, my back, my shoulders. Just touch me." She hesitates but then skims her hands down my shoulders and wanders down my back, landing on my ass cheeks.

She massages my ass as she tries to get me inside her. Teasing her and hearing the uneven breaths she takes just makes me harder, so I nudge my tip against her, pushing in.

A pained expression crosses her face. Worry lines on her forehead, lips pinched. "It... hurts."

"Do you want to stop?"

"No."

I grab my length and pull the head out, fingering her

instead. Her chest relaxes, so I scissor my fingers inside her, stretching the opening. "Is that better?"

"Yes."

"Thanks for telling me. Are you ready to try again?"

Nodding, she says, "Be easy."

"I'll do my best. It's hard when your body is so tight, like a fucking goddess." My words cause her to blush and look away. "Oh no, you're going to learn how to take a compliment."

Instead of pushing right back in, I place a soft, open-lipped kiss on her lips, alternating between her bottom lip and the top. She moans into my mouth, and I push my head back in.

"Oh... oh." She gasps.

Swirling my hips, it stretches her enough that she grabs my ass and just shoves me deep inside her. Both of us still. I'm inside Noelle, feeling the blood pumping through her inner walls. How they contract and tighten around me.

"Damn, Noelle. This feels too fucking good," I say low into her ear. Slowly, I start moving, sliding halfway out then back in. She lets out a little mewl then, and it creates a monster inside of me.

But when I pull out completely, she begs, "No, no, no."

"Wrong words. Yes is much better."

"But it's too much."

I tuck a tendril behind her ear and remind her, "It's the anticipation. Close your eyes and rock with me."

For a few minutes that's what we do, but then with my knees, I spread her legs out a little and twist so that I'm at an angle when I plunge into her, playing with the nerves under her hood. "Yes."

It's a good thing I'm a master at one-armed push-ups because I plunge into her repeatedly while she pants, "Matt. Yes. Oh. Oh. Yes."

"You're so tight, Butterfly. Perfection."

Noelle occasionally lifts her body to suck on my chest but always has the tips of her fingers running over my abs or back. I feel my core tighten and I know I could go off in a hot second, so I pump faster. At the same time, my fingers erratically stroke and pinch her clit.

"Matt, Matt, I...."

Her legs are strong, and she tightens them on me, trying her best to close her legs, but as she does, it's tighter, and I love how she's clamped down on me. Clawing at my back, she's bucking, chasing euphoria. Then she lets out a scream of ecstasy. "Yeeeessss."

I literally feel her juices gushing from her sweet bottom lips. When she's caught her breath, I sit back up on my heels and push her knees into her chest.

"What? What are you doing?"

"Teaching you. That's what you want, right?"

"Okay."

"Noelle, I need to be as deep inside you as possible. I just can't get enough of you. This angle..." I push in and she yelps. "It may be a little bit of hell before we get to heaven."

"I'd rather go to heaven than hell." She screams as I push inside. Her nails bite into my skin. Sweat drips from my body to hers.

I pound into her until it becomes sloppy. I'm all out of control when she has her third orgasm, gasping for air. My toes curl, and this orgasm races through me like a semi-truck driving at top speed down a fucking mountain.

Erratic, I nearly black out, cum pumping like an oil well as I pull from her body. Noelle wraps her fingers around my shaft and pumps me until I'm empty. And when she releases me, she smears it onto her stomach.

Collapsing on top of her, she absorbs my weight. "Sorry," I whisper.

"For what? For being with me?" her voice sounds small, with a hint of surprise.

Rolling off her and to the opposite arm, I joke, "No, for not lasting longer. You're just..."

"Don't say I'm just too young. I'm a woman."

I pull her head to my mouth and kiss her temple. "Every ounce of you is a woman. I was going to say you're just too fucking sexy and that we should have used a condom."

Now I'm thinking about her and Brooks and how she's been sick. An internal reminder that I can't really have Noelle. Maybe this once, but not long-term.

She pops up, half lying on my chest and half on the bed. "No one's ever called me sexy until you."

"Everyone can see it except you. Lean into it. It'll make you feel more confident to do whatever you want to me," I chuckle.

"Once you teach me everything you know, I'll do them all to you."

All I know? That could take weeks. Months.

I find myself grinning, but there's no way we can keep up this fake dating for her family. They want this done as soon as possible. Rookie camp is over, so there's really no need to fake a relationship now.

Of course, her family has no idea that I've tasted, fingered, and fucked Noelle. If I'm honest with myself, she's the woman I would want if I wasn't sick. So, as long as we have a reason to fake it, I'll keep coaching her.

But in the long run, she needs a man that will be around.

And I won't be.

TWENTY

NOELLE

Cloud nine? I'm on cloud ninety-nine.

Feeling desired. Complete. Satisfied. I sure hope heaven feels just like this. Waking up. Going to work and then spending the afternoon with Matt picking out a few items we missed last night.

"You bought too much cheese," he says, staring into the cart like it's a playbook.

"There is no such thing," I inform him. "Cheese is the duct tape of food." I eye the ingredients. "But I'm most excited about making a Cherry Surprise."

He grunts, grumpy on principle, tossing another bag into the back. "I'm not eating anything with the word *surprise* in it."

"Are you saying that you won't eat my momma's Cherry Surprise?" I ask, elbowing him in the side.

"Nope."

Rising to my toes, I kiss his cheek. "Please."

"Can't eat sweets, remember?"

My lips press into a thin line, thinking about all the

amazing foods he can't eat. I wonder if it would be easier if I had never tasted a chocolate chip cookie or a beignet or if he's just that strong-minded that it doesn't bother him. It will take every ounce of my will plus some prayers not to have a brownie that's sitting in front of me.

We get to Greyson and Sutton's house with a dozen bags and a shared mission, ready to cook, decorate, and celebrate Witley Suzanne's homecoming. He unlocks the door, dumps the bags while I inflate balloons until my veins almost pop out of my neck.

I hand Matt the "Welcome Home Baby" banner to tape across the mantel. "Higher. No—now it's crooked."

"Dictator," he mutters, but he fixes it and then tilts his head. "Better?"

"Perfect." I balance on the couch arm to tie a ribbon and nearly fall. Of course, Matt catches me by the waist with an annoyed sigh that is ninety percent dedication.

"Feet on solid ground," he commands, setting me down like I'm a piece of Waterford crystal. "I don't need you spraining an ankle two days before media day."

"Careful," I tell him. "The way you fuss is cute."

He scowls on purpose. "I do not fuss."

"You fuss."

"I coach."

"Same thing." I jump onto his back because I never learn. He groans like I weigh as much as a bull and reaches back to hook his hands under my knees without thinking, which makes something unreliable flutter in my throat. I kiss his neck on impulse—just a brush, a thank-you—and he goes still like I unplugged him.

"Butterfly," he says, a warning that doesn't want to be one.

"Sorry," I say, not sorry at all. Not here. I know.

In the kitchen, we attack meal prep like a competition show. He chops; I stir. He seasons while I write out the food labels. I write "Cherry Surprise" and "Cheese Mountain" and "Soup for Sleep-Deprived Humans." He snorts at the last one and tries to swap my neat all-caps for his blocky coach scrawl, writing "Pasta" under Cheese Mountain and "Potato Soup" under Sleep-Deprived.

"Your handwriting looks like it got tackled," I observe.

"Function over form," he says, bumping my hip with his. We move around each other like we've done this a hundred times, like kitchens live in our bones.

When the casseroles cool, we slide them into the fridge and freezer, neat rows of future comfort. We stand there shoulder to shoulder, doors open, admiring our creations.

"This is a ridiculous amount of pasta," he says.

"You know the whole team will visit and Sutton will insist on feeding them," I say.

Greyson and Sutton are Austin's version of a prince and princess. And the Armadillos love them.

He considers it. "Fair."

The house is quiet, and unused labels are scattered across the counter. I turn, leaning my hips against it. "Come here," I say, and he does. The kiss is easy and sweet and somehow still wrecks me. His hand finds the small of my back; mine finds the side of his neck. When we part, we're both smiling like idiots.

I tape a grid to the fridge—meals with dates and notes and hearts—and step back, satisfied.

He watches me, something tight and fond pulling at his mouth. "You weaponized a spreadsheet," he says. "On a refrigerator."

"I'm multi-talented."

He sobers a little. "I'm worried about you."

The sentence lands like a stone in a pond, ripples widening. "I'm fine," I say, too fast.

"You were sick in Oklahoma City last week," he says, counting on his fingers like he's reviewing game film. "You were queasy in New Orleans. Today you went gray on me. That's a pattern. I think we should get you checked out."

The blood roars in my ears. The box in my chest rattles its nailed lid. I step sideways into humor because it's my safest hallway.

"Are you trying to get rid of me by dropping me off at urgent care for a day?" I deflect.

"Funny," he says, not smiling. He reaches for my wrist, not to trap—just to anchor. "I'm serious."

"I know." I tug free gently and busy my hands with the marker caps, making sure the correct ones are on the markers. "We've got Sutton and the baby to worry about. Don't worry about me."

He studies me for a beat that feels longer than a beat. "Okay," he says finally, though I hear the part where he wants to press. He takes the step I was hoping for and the step that disappoints me at the same time—he lets me have my no. "If you're sick tomorrow..."

"Got it, Coach. I'll review the play." I echo, relief and guilt colliding in my ribs.

"Are you staying until they get home? I have an appointment, so I need to bounce."

"I thought you didn't have to work for a few weeks."

"I have an eye appointment. Can't coach if I can't see."

"Oh, you can coach. I could use a little more coaching so I can make you happy."

Behind me, he sighs as he throws the nails, hammer, and tape into a box and clamps the lid closed. Then he says, "Noelle, the point of coaching you is to make yourself happy. So you know what you like and can tell your future.... Just quit worrying about everyone else."

He holds up a ridiculous stuffed armadillo that Sutton bought Greyson. It wears a tiny helmet and a scowl matching his own.

Got it. He doesn't want me snooping in his business even though he's completely okay with making sure I find out why I've been nauseated.

We turn off the lights. We lock the door. We walk out into the muggy afternoon and the sound of hay being baled. His fingertips press against my back, helping me into the truck.

He seems as if he's in another world.

I'm worried about why he's driving if he can't see. And my stomach turns at the thought of what might be happening inside my body.

TWENTY-ONE
MATT

Rookie camp.

The smell of freshly painted white lines and cut grass. The pristine look of the various position rooms. But it's the sound that gets me. Cleats grinding into turf. Whistles snapping sharp enough to raise the dead. Twenty-two-year-old men trying to prove they belong before anyone can tell them otherwise. It's football stripped down to its bones. They're here to show their speed, agility, and ability to learn fast and make decisions even faster.

I love it here.

Which is probably why I don't love that my head feels like it's concussed.

I blink hard, adjusting my cap as I watch two new rookie quarterbacks cycle through drills. Footwork. Release. Timing. Muscle memory built one rep at a time. I bark a correction, clap my hands once, and force my body to fall back into the rhythm I've lived in most of my adult life.

"Again," I call out. "Quicker feet. You're late."

The kid nods like his life depends on it. Because right

now, it kind of does. These aren't first-round draft picks. We signed them as free agents to the scout team, where they'll stay for now unless we need them. Fighting for a spot on the fifty-two-man roster starts today.

Greyson says something to number one, pats his shoulder, and walks toward me.

Shaking my head, I say, "Number one. I hate guys who pick number one. I already know they've been coddled from an early age, told they're the best, just as the number implies."

"Stricker, he has talent. Give him a chance. I won't be around forever to make you look good," he smirks.

"I corrected him, and he did the same damn thing over again."

"Everyone can't be me," Greyson lifts his palms into the air, which makes me glance behind him to the sideline. Sometimes I wonder how he's my best friend in Austin.

Noelle stands just past the numbers, microphone crooked, notepad tucked under one arm. She's all business today—neutral clothes, hair pulled back, posture straight like she's daring the world to underestimate her. She's talking to a rookie receiver, nodding, smiling, and asking questions that don't sound like fluff.

Good.

She's doing exactly what she said she would. Staying away from O'Ryan territory. Free from her brothers and charting her own course. And I just need to make her steer clear of me.

My chest tightens anyway, watching how she's confident in her abilities here but not in the bedroom.

"She's good," Greyson says beside me, his voice casual but proud as hell.

I don't look at him. "She's always been."

Greyson snorts. "I wasn't disagreeing."

He shifts, hands on his hips, scanning the field like he still belongs out there throwing passes instead of managing them. He looks wrecked in the way only new fathers do—dark circles under his eyes, shoulders slumped—but there's something lighter about him too. Happier. Softer around the edges.

"How's Witley?" I ask.

His whole face changes. "Three days old and already running the house. Sutton hasn't slept. I haven't slept. Even Paulina is in dire need of some shut-eye. Pretty sure I cried during a diaper change this morning."

"Is that because you're sentimental or because you forgot how gross babies are?"

Greyson grins. "Both. Why do babies look like Winston Churchill when they frown? But Witley is worth it."

I chuckle, even as something twists low in my gut. Greyson gets all of this. A family. A future measured in birthdays and first steps.

Me? I get a timeline based on lab results.

"You look tired," I say.

He scoffs. "You're one to talk."

"Fair."

We watch another drill in silence, the air thick with heat and noise. My vision blurs at the edges when I turn too fast, and I have to pause longer than I want to let the dizziness pass.

Greyson notices, like the best friend he is. Our relationship started out rocky, but he's the one person in Texas that I tell my secrets, except for how I feel about Noelle. "Hey," he says quietly. "You sure you're ready to be back?"

Ready? Yes. Should I be? Probably not.

I keep my eyes on the field. "What, you think rookie camp's too much for me?"

"I think you almost walked into a tackling dummy."

I sigh, rubbing a hand over my face. "The sun's bright."

"That's not what I asked." He lowers his voice. "How are your eyes?"

I hesitate, then shrug. "After Noelle and I cooked and decorated, the doctor stuck a four-inch needle straight into my eyeball."

Greyson winces. "Jesus Christ."

"Fun party trick," I add. "I don't recommend it."

"Matt."

"I'm fine," I say, sounding like a rehearsed line. "Pressure was up. They drained it. Adjusted meds."

"And the rest of it?" he presses. "The stuff you keep dodging."

I glance at Noelle again without meaning to. She laughs at something the receiver says, throws her head back just a little. Looks alive. Focused. Free.

I swallow. "They want me to start dialysis," I say. "Sooner rather than later."

Greyson's jaw tightens. "And?"

"And I'm on the transplant list for a kidney." I roll my shoulders like I'm shaking off a bad hit. "Not exactly breaking news."

"That's not nothing," he says sharply.

"I know." I force a half-smile. "But it's manageable. I've been dealing with this my whole life."

"Managing and pretending it's no big deal aren't the same thing."

I twist my lips and say, "The clock's ticking, Grey. I get it."

The words hang there, heavier than they should. I don't like the look in his eyes—too knowing, too worried.

He exhales slowly. "When can you have a transplant?"

"When someone who matches all the markers dies, is a donor, and lives close enough to Austin for a helicopter to fly it in within an hour or two."

"So, you don't know."

"Maybe soon. Maybe never."

Grey takes his helmet off, letting it fall beside his leg. "What if you have a live donor?"

I shrug.

"Shrugging is not an answer, Stricker."

"Neither is hovering," I shoot back, then soften.

Greyson studies me for a long beat, then nods once. "All right. But don't freeze me out. You don't get to go through this alone."

I don't trust my voice to stay steady, so I leave it.

As I blow the whistle, the two rookie QBs run to us. "Five-minute break, then we're running with the receivers."

They jog to the Gatorade, dangerously close to Noelle. Any man in her proximity brings out the possessiveness inside me. I guess my focus stays on her a little longer than needed.

Greyson clears his throat. "So."

Here we go.

"So," I echo.

He glances toward Noelle again, then back to me. "Fake-dating my sister. That's... done now, right?"

My chest tightens. "She can't stop talking about Witley," I blurt out, which has nothing to do with his comment.

"Witley is adorable, but I'm talking about Noelle." He keeps his tone even. Careful. "She went to New Orleans. She's not going to be around Brooks for a while. Seems like time for a clean break from him and this ridiculous fake relationship."

Clean.

Nothing about this has been. I want her more than she can ever know.

I nod slowly. "That was always the plan."

There was a fork in the road, and we took the forbidden path.

Greyson watches me like he's trying to read something I'm not saying. "Good."

"You don't sound convinced."

"I just don't want her hurt," he says simply. "She's been through enough."

I think about Noelle in that bathroom stall. On my couch. In my arms. About the way she looks at me like I'm something solid she can lean on.

I think about dialysis rooms and transplant lists and the math I do in my head when I can't sleep.

"Me neither," I say quietly.

Greyson claps my shoulder once, firm. "All right. Let's survive rookie camp without anyone tearing an ACL." He heads back toward the field, barking orders, already shifting gears.

I stay where I am for a second longer, watching Noelle scribble something down, completely unaware of the way my life feels like it's narrowing to a single point.

Fake-dating should be over.

That's what we agreed on.

But standing here, with the Texas sun blazing and the

clock ticking louder in my head than any whistle, all I can think is how much I want one more day. One more conversation. One more chance to pretend that timelines don't matter.

I adjust my cap, force my focus back to the quarterbacks and wide receivers who are anxiously waiting to show me their mad skills, and blow the whistle.

"Blue 42, Cinderella," I call out. "You ladies did read up on the playbook, right?"

Because if there's one thing football taught me, it's how to keep playing even when you know the hit is coming.

This isn't the kind of meeting that happens in a cramped office with a dusty window.

This one takes place in a glass conference room overlooking downtown, my name printed neatly on an agenda that feels far too official for someone who still triple-checks her mascara in the rearview mirror. Three producers. One executive. Coffee cups lined up like witnesses. Danishes in the center of the table, untouched, like they know this isn't a social call. I think about how long it's been since Matt had one.

I'm jarred from my thoughts when my boss leans back in his chair and says, "Your name got you in the door. But your skills? Those will make you a star on this network."

A star. Me? Relief travels through me. Not just relief. Validation. I don't have to be anyone's sister or daughter to belong on the sidelines or at this table.

"We're getting more texts and emails than ever about Noelle O'Ryan, the gorgeous reporter who knows her football. You're our rookie sensation." He pauses, fiddling with the agenda. "Rookie camps are over, so training camp begins, and you'll make the same rounds as before."

"When?"

"Starting this weekend."

I was planning on taking a pregnancy test since I'm still sick to my stomach every morning, and I worry if all the pink tablets I'm taking will affect the baby, if there is one.

"Thank you, sir, but can someone else go to New Orleans? I know it's horrible of me to ask since I haven't been working here that long."

The producers hold their breath like I'm asking for a month-long, all-expenses-paid trip to Greece.

My boss taps his fingers against the black lacquered table. "Noelle. This is your career, and even though I've been told about how your ex acted during rookie camp, you need to do this not just for us but for yourself."

"Yes, sir." I smile, nod, and thank them like a professional, but I dread seeing Brooks again, especially if I'm pregnant. "I'll be there."

By the time I hit the sidewalk, the Texas heat wraps around me, feeling like someone squeezing me too hard or too long.

My phone buzzes with a calendar reminder about the Canadian league championship game I just covered. The assignment was last-minute. The reporter originally scheduled for it landed in the hospital with the flu. It was a great distraction from the two things on my mind: pregnancy and Matt Stricker.

Being busy is a gift of distraction.

Busy keeps me from overanalyzing my feelings about my love life.

Matt's been busy too. I noticed he went back to work

early. Pretended I didn't. Told myself it was fine we hadn't connected because I'd been on planes, in stadiums, chasing stories with a headset pressed to my ear and adrenaline pumping through my veins.

We haven't really talked in days. A text here and there. But now I'm home. Alone with my thoughts for the first time in too long.

Desperately needing cover from the heat, that's when I see it—the library.

Not the familiar brick building I grew up going to on school field trips or the one on Dad's campus when the boys were busy and I had to tag along.

This one is massive. All glass and steel and quiet confidence, like it knows it holds answers whether you're ready for them or not.

The doors slide open, and the cool air causes my bare arms to pimple. Sunlight spills across long tables in the enormous lobby. People are tucked into corners of their own worlds. Some reading. Some on laptops. Others wander around, in just as much awe as me.

Without a plan, I roam the first floor. History. Architecture. Travel. I take the escalator to the second floor, hoping I can find the sports section. I've never been one to ask for help. I'm an O'Ryan, and we are wired to figure it out.

Then I freeze. Parenting. A section much larger than I would have ever anticipated. I've never thought about babies other than J.D. and Greyson having children of their own.

My stomach flips, sharp and sudden, like my body's trying to tell me something my brain isn't ready to hear. I tell myself it's curiosity. Curiosity is normal. I'm a journalist, and journalists tell stories. Stories need context.

I reach for a book before I can talk myself out of it. *First

Trimester Basics*. I stare at the cover with a grape inside a cartoon belly.

"You know those don't bite," a voice says gently.

I jump.

The girl beside me smiles, pushing her glasses to the bridge of her nose. "You wouldn't believe how many women just stare."

I laugh, a little breathless, unsure of why I'm here.

She tilts her head. "Research?"

"Something like that," I say. "I just stumbled in here to get out of the heat."

She hums like she doesn't entirely buy it but won't press. "I'm Clara."

"Noelle."

Clara isn't like any of my so-called friends. She talks quietly, lacking confidence. Her skirt hits mid-calf and makes her look frumpy, but her brown hair is thick and shiny. I tell her I'm a reporter and one of the stories I'm working on is about a football player learning his ex-girlfriend is pregnant. She nods her head and confides she comes here when the world feels loud.

It makes me wonder what feels loud. What is she going through? Because most of us are just trying to keep our heads above water. One minute you feel like your world is upright, and the next minute it's upended. Just a couple of weeks ago I was in a daydream with Matt, and now something has shifted between us. Men suck.

"If you're ever here again, I'm usually in the thriller section. Sometimes romance."

"My work is just around the corner, so if I'm here, I'll look for you."

When we part ways, I stare at the enormity of parenting

books. I find the sports section, and, of course, there are two books facing forward about the Austin Armadillos. One features G and the other J.D. I check them both out to see what this writer has to say about my family.

Outside again, the sun feels warmer. Heavier.

I check my phone. No missed calls or messages, and I tell myself not to read into Matt's silence.

Easier said than done.

By the time I get home, the silence presses in. My room-mates are nowhere to be found. I drop my bag, kick off my shoes, and wander from room to room, pacing back and forth.

Fake dating was supposed to be armor. Something sharp and temporary to get me through the fallout. But somewhere between pretending and surviving, it became the place I felt comforted and most alive.

I'm a woman, and I don't have to wait for Matt to call. If something is wrong, I need to know. My thumb hovers over his name until I hit call. It rings long enough that I'm already bracing for voicemail, for the hollow click and the ridiculous sting of pretending I'm fine with it.

"Hey," he says finally, his voice low and worn down—familiar enough to loosen something tight in my chest.

Relief hits first. Then nerves. "Hey," I reply, suddenly hyperaware of how fast my heart is beating. "Are you busy?"

There's a pause. Not long—but long enough to feel loaded. The kind that carries everything he isn't saying. He's not into me anymore. He had his taste and is ready to move on.

"I'm still at the facility," he admits.

Of course he is. I imagine him there, refusing to slow down, choosing motion over stillness because stopping would mean thinking, same as me. "You weren't supposed to be," I say lightly, even though the words aren't a joke and we both know it.

"I know."

I lean against the pantry cabinet, staring at nothing. "I just got back into town."

"Yeah?"

"I had a meeting today." I wait, then add, "The boss said I'm going to be the star of the network."

"I never had a doubt," he says, and I can hear the smile he's not letting fully form.

My heart ticks faster, unsure of whether to ask given how tired he is. "I was wondering... if maybe I could see you?"

There's another silence, heavier than the last. His breath changes. I hear it through the line.

"Noelle—"

"I know you've been busy," I barrel on, hearing the breakup tone in his voice. "And I have too. Canada was insane, and rookie camp, and everything just kept moving, and I didn't want to be... I don't know. A distraction."

"You're not," he says immediately.

I close my eyes. "Then can I come by? Just for a bit. It's important."

Another pause. Longer this time.

"I'm not great company right now," he says carefully.

"I didn't ask for great. I asked for you."

Silence stretches, tight and fragile.

Finally, he exhales. "Yeah," he says. "Okay. You can come by. I'll be home in an hour."

Relief rushes through me so fast it almost knocks me over. "I'll see you soon." My nerves are shot, and he's the only one who can calm them.

"Yeah," he repeats, quieter. "I'll see you."

The line goes dead, and I stand there, phone pressed to my chest, knowing—without any dramatic reveal or gut-punch moment—that something has shifted. He's pushing me away.

Being busy with my new career has protected me. But now? I'm walking straight toward the truth.

And for the first time, I'm not sure I'm ready for what I might find waiting for me on the other side of Matt's door.

Man cave chair, except it's not.

A recliner is supposed to be every man's go-to chair, but this one whirs beneath me. Too mechanical. Almost like it wants to remind me of why I'm here.

I hate that about it.

A nurse tightens the cuff around my arm—efficient, kind, already bored with my discomfort. I look away when the needle slides in—thick, unforgiving, no room for denial. Blood leaves my body in a slow, steady line, disappearing into tubing that promises to clean it and give it back better than before.

Funny how much faith we put in machines.

"You doing okay?" she asks, adjusting the monitor.

"Been hit harder on third down," I mutter. "Weird that getting hit seems like the glory days."

She smiles like she's heard every version of that joke. "Try not to move too much."

As if I could.

"Former football player? Are you still playing?" she asks.

"No, I'm a coach for the Armadillos."

She hums a tune that I remember Noelle singing, and it hits me that they're probably the same age. I can't get that woman out of my head, and last night didn't help.

My body's here, but my head? My head is still with her.

"Relax," I'd told Noelle last night, my hands steady even though everything inside me wasn't. "Let me show you. You don't have to rush it."

She'd laughed—soft, breathless, trusting. *"You're bossy."*

"Only when it matters."

I squeeze my eyes shut, replaying her soft body in my arms. Her lips swollen from kissing.

I shouldn't have touched her like that. Shouldn't have taken my time, shouldn't have taught her anything that I don't want her doing with another man. And yet, I memorized every sound she made like it was something sacred. Like I wasn't already crossing lines I swore I'd never step over.

No self-control. Not with her.

The machine beeps, reminding me where I am. Who I am. A guy with a failing kidney, blood cycling through plastic tubes, pretending this is temporary when it might not be.

I stare at the ceiling and think about my life—football fields, locker rooms, rules, discipline. Decades of control. Of choosing to take the hits. Yet it's not football that is taking my life—it's damn sugar and my body's inability to process it correctly.

I left Logan and the Louisville Heavyweights to take the QB coach position with the Austin Armadillos so I could be treated by the best kidney transplant doctor in America.

This has been my plight for a long time, and I never

cared, even after the first kidney transplant. Sure, I eat right. Work out. But I never let a woman get too close. At least not recently, when I knew my health was declining.

Until Noelle.

Is it because she's forbidden? My best friend's sister. Too young. Too good. Or is it because she looks at me like I'm not broken? Like I'm not a risk assessment waiting to happen? I should have told her last night that I was starting dialysis today. But I wanted one more night with her, feeling like I was the strong one.

The nurse checks my vitals, scribbles something down. "The first session's always the hardest."

"Yeah?" I ask.

She nods. "Your body adjusts. The mind just takes longer."

My grin is weak, but it's there. It's all I can muster right now because I don't know if I'll ever adjust to dialysis.

Last night, with no sugarcoating, I told Noelle, *"You need to take a pregnancy test."*

She'd rolled her eyes, brushing it off like she always does when she's scared. *"I'm fine. I feel better today."*

I think she knows she is and just isn't ready to admit it to herself. And no one understands that better than me... so I let it slide.

The machine hums softly, cleaning me out, buying me time I don't know how to spend. Do I retire? Step back before I become a liability—on the field, in her life? Or do I do what I've always done when the clock's running out?

Go down throwing the Hail Mary pass.

The nurse interrupts my thoughts after four hours, and as she unhooks me, she says, "See ya in a couple of days."

Her voice is light and her smile is bright. She has her whole life in front of her, just like Noelle.

I glance at my phone resting on the tray beside me. No new messages. No missed calls.

Good.

Or maybe not.

When I drive away, I try to figure out how the hell a man who set firm dating rules has fallen for a girl he shouldn't. A girl that needs a man to be there for her, not someone she feels the need to take care of.

The problem?

I'd do it again without hesitation. In case I don't go to heaven, I'll have experienced it firsthand with Noelle.

TWENTY-FOUR
NOELLE

The pregnancy test sits in my hand like it's judging me.

It's small. The drugstore is too quiet. The box is too capable of changing everything.

Acting as if it's any other errand, I buy it like I would milk, bread, or tampons. Oh, Lord, if I'm pregnant, I won't be buying any of those. The cashier doesn't look twice at me, and I'm grateful. I don't want witnesses to this moment where I feel like a teenager instead of a grown woman with a career.

At home, the bathroom is bright as I tear open the box and read the instructions. I'm looking for one line. Not pregnant. I follow the directions, which are self-explanatory, but I feel like they're schematics for a flying car. All the numbers with lines point to the cap, to the tip, to the little window that will reveal my fate. After peeing on the stick, I lay it on the lip of the tub, then perch myself on the edge. Sitting there with my elbows on my knees, hands covering my eyes, my breathing is shallow, as if I can avoid the truth by not fully inhaling.

My knee bounces rapidly until the alarm on my phone rings out, and I look.

Two lines. I'm pregnant.

The word doesn't knock the air out of me. It settles instead. Heavy. Real. Permanent. And the first person I think to call is Matt.

Of course, it is. Because I trust him.

Why not call Brooks? It's his child.

Last night flashes through me without warning.

"You like it this way," he murmured, his voice low and steady. "I've got you. Tell me what feels good."

The memory twists, sharp and warm all at once. The care. The patience. The way he made me feel chosen.

I don't text him. I don't call. I just go.

Practice is winding down when I get to the facility, the sounds of football echoing across the field—whistles, shouts, collisions. Normal life continues while mine fractures.

Matt looks exhausted. Not just tired—drained. His shoulders are tight, his movements clipped, like he's holding himself together by sheer will.

Do I give him space? No. Because I'm freaking out. So, I follow behind him at a safe distance to his office, where I've never been before. I've been in J.D.'s office, Sutton's, and even the quarterback film room, but never Matt's.

As I tap two knuckles on the door, he snaps, "What are you doing here?"

The edge in his voice makes my stomach drop. *This isn't how I imagined this.*

"I need to talk to you."

"Not now."

"Yes. Now. Please, it's urgent." I close the door behind me, my palms damp. My heart is pounding so hard I'm afraid he can hear it. If I thought I had morning sickness, it's nothing compared to right now. My stomach is in my throat. Matt busies himself by tossing his clipboard onto the desk and opening his computer. "I took a pregnancy test."

He stills. "And?"

"I'm pregnant." The words feel fragile, hanging in the air between us.

He stares at me like I've spoken in another language. Then his jaw tightens. The dismissal hurts more than I can digest. "I came to you," my voice is barely above a whisper.

"Why?" His voice is rough. "What do I know about this? Why aren't you talking to Sutton? Or Birdie?"

"My mom is dead," I say before I can stop myself. The words come out sharp, defensive. He flinches, and for a second, I feel terrible. Then the hurt floods back in, both for how he's being and for not having a mom I can turn to, who can hold me and tell me that everything will work out.

"This isn't my place, Noelle," he says.

Then why did you make it feel like it was last night?

"You didn't seem to think that when your hands were on me," I say, sucking in tears.

His jaw locks. "That was different."

Was it?

Because it didn't feel different to me.

"This is Brooks's baby," he says finally.

The words land like a slap.

"I know that," I say, my voice shaking. "He cheated on me. Over and over. But he doesn't get to control my life anymore."

"That doesn't change biology," Matt snaps. "And it doesn't make this my decision."

"I'm not asking you to decide," I say. "I'm asking you what to do or to hold me..."

He scrubs a hand over his face, and as it drops to his side, he lets out an exasperated sigh. "You tell him. When you see him this weekend. That's what you do."

The finality in his tone hurts worse than anger would have.

"You don't get to talk to me like this," I whisper.

"And you don't get to drag me into something that isn't mine," he fires back.

That's when I realize he's already stepping away, already drawing the line I didn't want to see. I leave before I can beg him to look at me the way he did last night, before I can ask why the man who taught me how to trust my body won't just take me in his arms and let me cry it out.

Tears start to stream down my face. It's all too much. As I jog down the Armadillo hallway, G yells, "Sis, wait up."

I wave him off, rushing out the door and into the blinding light and smothering heat. My world has spun off its axis. No fake boyfriend. No mom. No one.

Once I'm home, I go straight to my room and lock the door. My roommates are in the backyard laughing, and I'm not in the mood to party or explain why I'm an emotional wreck.

Sleep never comes. My thoughts spiral. The baby. I'm having a baby. With Brooks.

Matt: I'm sorry I was an ass today. I'm going through some stuff myself.

Matt: But you really need to talk to Brooks.

I stare at the screen, chest aching. I realize I have fallen in love with my brother's best friend.

You don't get to be gentle with my body and brutal with my heart. The reverse would be preferable.

I turn the phone facedown and let the tears come, knowing—too late—that loving Matt doesn't protect me from losing him.

Dialysis is easier the second time.

I know what to expect. My nurse eyes my tattoos as she hooks me up to the machine, but her shy, understated manner puts me at ease. She wears thick, Coke-bottle glasses and Pokémon scrubs and has a smattering of freckles. It's a nerdy look, but maybe she has kids that love anime.

Kids. Noelle. Baby.

I've checked my phone at least two hundred times since I sent her the apology text, and she hasn't responded. Part of me thinks, "*Good for her. Don't take shit off any guy.*" The other part is desperate to hear her voice. I should have just told her about my eye injection, dialysis, and needing a kidney within the year. But I'm an asshole, which is why I haven't dated recently—until her.

Okay, I know it started out as fake, but Noelle has not only wrapped her legs around my waist but also spread her butterfly wings around my heart. Our relationship isn't fair to her. I have to cut it off permanently. The problem is I don't want to. Or maybe I already did without saying it. Maybe that's why she didn't answer my text.

The nurse comes by to check in and hands me the television remote. "Thought you might want to watch the spelling bee," she jokes, turning my frown into a smile.

"What gave it away?"

"I did a little research and figured you would want to watch the sports network." She grins and makes her way to another patient.

My smile curls upward. This is how I should have talked with Noelle. Been supportive and brought some levity to her situation. I look at the remote, tap Guide, and scroll down to the network Noelle works for.

To my surprise, after only fifteen minutes, they go live from the New Orleans training camp. Her hair is down, falling over her shoulders in waves, with a microphone in hand. "Thanks, Joel. New Orleans linebacker Stu Johnson has had a rough off-season. His little girl was diagnosed with Usher syndrome, causing hearing loss. Johnson has worked tirelessly to raise money for other kids with the disease, but he and his wife have also spent time learning sign language so they can communicate with their daughter. Watch the excerpt, then tune in tomorrow for the entire documentary."

I know Stu. He played on the defense for the Kentucky Stallions when I was a quarterback coach there. He's one of the nicest guys you'll ever meet. I make a mental note to watch the full version as I look up Usher syndrome. Sometimes we think we're the only ones with problems, but everyone has something they need to deal with, and it makes me want to rip these tubes out, fly to New Orleans, and apologize to Noelle in person—especially when I read that Usher syndrome may be genetic and if both parents have the gene, the result is one in four pregnancies will have the disease.

That must have been hard for Noelle to hear and process, knowing she's pregnant and wondering what all could go wrong.

I put on my big-boy pants and call her, but it goes to voicemail. I don't leave a message, but after the third time, I do.

"Noelle, um... hey. I'm sorry about my reaction when you told me about the baby. I don't want to leave it... I mean us. I don't want to leave us the way we did. Have you told Brooks yet? I'm here if you need a shoulder to cry on or a person to yell at. God knows, I deserve it."

I sit for a moment, wanting to say more, like *I realized I'm falling for you*, but that's not fair to her. Finally, I hang up, finish my treatment, and head back to the facility. J.D. catches me and asks how dialysis is going and says that he told Sutton. "She's the boss and needed to know."

"I know. I'll talk to her. I'm headed to Greyson's house on Sunday."

"Good. If you need anything, don't hesitate to ask. Oh, and G said the fake dating situation with Noelle is over. That's good too."

Good for whom? You? Greyson? Their dad?

I nod ever so slightly. Because the fake part is way over. But is the relationship? It should be, but I'm so damn selfish that I've found a person so caring, so fun-loving, so stunning, that I'm having a hard time letting her go.

TWENTY-SIX
NOELLE

Sound bites. That's how I'm judged.

Finding that story that may be thirty minutes long and breaking it into a sound bite that will hook viewers in an instant. Then they'll come back to view the whole story.

Stu Johnson sits across from me on a folding chair in the locker room, helmet resting at his feet, sweat darkening the collar of his jersey. There's nothing flashy about him. No nerves. No performance. Just the calm steadiness of a man who's been doing this long enough to know what matters and what doesn't.

When I ask about longevity—what keeps him grinding through another season—something shifts.

His expression softens, his eyes dropping for just a second before he looks back up at me.

"My daughter's sick," he says quietly.

My stomach tightens before my brain can catch up.

"She's six. It's called Usher syndrome Type 3," he continues, his voice even, practiced. "It affects both hearing and vision. Her vision is okay right now. She wears glasses but she can see. In the last year, she lost all her hearing, and her vision will go at some point."

Words like genetic, progressive, and permanent weigh heavily in my chest. Too heavy. My hand curls tighter around the side of my notepad.

Stu tells me how he and his wife learned sign language together. How they practice as a family every night at the kitchen table. How they narrate the world for her—colors, expressions, everything she won't always be able to see clearly. He doesn't dramatize it. He doesn't ask for pity.

"We don't know how fast it'll progress," he says. "So, we focus on what she can do now. We want our baby girl to experience and see everything she can, so in the future, when she can't see, she'll know. She'll be able to imagine what the rest of us see clearly and take for granted."

I nod, professional on the outside, unraveling just a little on the inside. My pulse stutters, my thoughts skidding into places I don't want them to go.

What if? What if something goes wrong with my baby? What if love isn't enough to protect a child from the things you can't control?

I force myself back into the moment, back into my role. I ask the right follow-up questions. I thank him. I keep my voice steady.

But fear has already found its way in. What I learn from Stu is *love is blind.* It doesn't matter what body part fails when you love someone. You do what you need to do to make that person feel loved and connected. Genetics give us hair and eye color but also things that require medical intervention.

The cameraman and my female producer give me the

wrap signal. I thank Johnson for his openness and ask him to let me know if they need anything. And all the while, my hand rests unconsciously over my stomach, as if instinct already knows what my heart hasn't fully accepted yet.

After camp concludes, I sit in my rental car longer than necessary, hands gripping the steering wheel while the sun dips lower. I pull out my phone and stare at Brooks's name.

I hate that my stomach still reacts.

> Me: Can we meet for dinner after camp?

The reply comes almost instantly.

> Brooks: Thought you'd never ask.

Trademark Brooks.

He shows up cocky in text form too—assumes this is me circling back, realizing my mistake, missing the crumbs he offers. I let him think that. Let the arrogance sit between us unchallenged while we settle on a local dive just outside town.

Before I go inside, my phone buzzes again.

A voicemail from Matt. I step back into the quiet of my rental car and listen. He sounds tired. Regret laces every word.

"Noelle, umm... hey. I'm sorry about my reaction when you told me about the baby. I don't want to leave it... I mean us. I don't want to leave us the way we did. Have you told Brooks yet? I'm here if you need a shoulder to cry on or a person to yell at. God knows, I deserve it."

He shouldn't have snapped at me and been so curt. It cut me deeply when it was the last thing on earth I needed. The knot in my chest loosens a fraction, so I text him back before I can overthink it.

> Me: Meeting Brooks tonight. I'm telling him.

Three dots appear. Disappear. Then:

> Matt: Be careful. I'm here if you need me.

I tuck my phone away and open the door.

The bar smells like fried food and old beer. Neon signs hum softly, casting everything in a hazy glow. Low lighting. Sticky floors. The kind of place where secrets blend into the background noise. Brooks is already here, lounging like he owns the place, a drink in hand, his grin firmly in place.

It feels fitting.

I slide into the booth across from him, my heart hammering so loud I swear he can hear it.

He talks. I barely listen. Something about how we can still be together when I'm in town and have some fun.

What? No.

I watch the door. The clock. My hands twist together in my lap.

Just say it.

Don't back out now.

When he finally pauses, smirking as if he's waiting for me to grovel, the anxiety spikes so hard it's almost physical.

"I'm pregnant," I say. The words tumble out before I can soften them.

For a second, he just stares. His face shifts—confusion first, then calculation. His jaw tightens, eyes narrowing as he decides how this affects him.

"If this is some ploy to get back together," he says slowly, "it's not happening. I need to share this." His gaze travels down his chest to his groin area.

Disbelief flashes hot and sharp. "Of course I don't want to get back together. I won't be one of your side pieces."

His brows lift, offended. "Then why—"

"It's yours," I blurt.

That's when it hits him.

Color drains from his face. His mouth opens, then closes. He leans back hard, as if the booth might tip, running a hand through his hair. Anger flares next—his breathing labored. "I want proof," he snaps.

"You'll get it," I say calmly, surprised by my own steadiness. "But don't worry. I don't want you to be part of his or her life."

That stops him.

I press on before he can interrupt. "I don't want anything from you. But I thought you should know."

He gives a harsh, single laugh. "If you're here for money, it's not happening."

"I didn't ask," I say quietly. "I just wanted you to know that I'm raising this baby on my own."

Silence stretches, thick and ugly.

Then he squints at me, his lips curling. "So...what? You and the old man parted ways?"

The insult lands, but it doesn't stick.

Because now, I realize something with startling clarity: Brooks doesn't see people. He only sees how he can gain an advantage. How in the world did I not see this for over a year? Back then, I didn't listen to my intuition.

I stand, shoulders back, heart still racing—but lighter.

"No," I say. "We didn't."

Did we?

I leave him sitting there, off-kilter, tapping his drink against the table, while I walk out feeling proud of myself for standing my ground and knowing one thing for sure.

I can do this. The O'Ryan family may be messy and loud, but we are loyal, and I know I'll never be in this alone.

Witley fits perfectly in my arms.

Greyson places her there carefully, his hands hovering even after he lets go. His eyes sparkle even though he has dark circles under them. Her fingers curl around my thumb, impossibly small but tight.

The first thing that hits me when Greyson places her in my arms is how something so light can carry so much gravity. Meaning. How a baby makes a family. Even if it's a single mom, like Noelle.

"She's got a grip," he says, proud as a peacock.

"She knows what she wants," Sutton adds from the couch, exhaustion and pride tangling in her voice.

Witley, cute as a bug in the ruffled pink sleeper I bought her, gets passed around next—Mr. O'Ryan, Parker, Paulina— each of them tracing her tiny fingers, murmuring soft nonsense like it's instinct. When Noelle holds her, she stills completely, her thumb brushing over Witley's knuckles with a tenderness that makes my chest ache.

Noelle holds her through dinner like a pro, and afterward, Greyson lays her down in the bassinet.

"She'll sleep two to three hours," Greyson says. "Let's eat and maybe get a ping-pong game in before she proves us wrong. I need to feel like a human."

Paulina shoots her hand into the air. "I play first—because if Witley wakes up, I want to feed her."

Sutton laughs. "I'm breastfeeding for a few months, but you'll get your chance soon."

Paulina groans. "Tragic."

Teenagers think not feeding a baby is tragic. Typical.

She points toward the basement. "Uncle J.D., first game."

"Prepare to lose," J.D. says, fist-bumping Paulina.

Birdie stretches out beside Sutton on the couch, content to watch instead of competing. The house fills with movement—laughter, plates clinking, footsteps heading downstairs.

Normal for the O'Ryan household.

My chest feels tight as I hope I can make things right with Noelle. So when a text comes from my sister, it offers the distraction I need.

Sis: How did the second time go?

Me: Fine. Can I call you later?

Sis: Sure, but don't forget. I hate that I'm not with you.

Me: I'm an adult.

Sis: I know, but no one loves you like I do.

Our mom may beg to differ.

At that exact moment, I spot Noelle, hands wrapped around a glass of something she hasn't touched. She looks scared and full of doubt. She's rarely like that, especially when she's with her family.

I don't think. I just move.

"Hey," I say softly. "Can we take a walk?"

The room pauses. Greyson looks up. Sutton tracks the shift instantly. Noelle meets my eyes, then nods.

Outside, the night air is cool and quiet, the sounds of the house muffled behind us. We walk down the driveway, gravel crunching under our feet.

"Did you talk to Brooks?" I ask.

She exhales. "Yeah."

That one word tells me enough. She's upset. "Why didn't you call me?" I ask. She raises her brows. I stop and turn to her. "You don't owe him anything." I shake my head, heart thudding. "How did it go?"

She exhales slowly. "About as badly as you'd expect."

That tracks.

"I'm sorry," I say. It feels inadequate.

She shrugs, but the movement is brittle. "Thank you. But you don't get off that easy. And... and I needed time to take in what he said, how I feel. It's his baby."

She looks up at me with a film of water over her eyes, searching my face like she's afraid to hope. Something in my chest gives.

"I'm here for you," I say. "Whatever you need."

Her shoulders drop, and she steps into me, not answering with words.

Words aren't enough.

The kiss is soft at first, but the second her hands curl into my jacket, restraint shatters. I kiss her back, deeper now, forgetting where I'm at and who might see. My hand comes up to cradle the back of her head as muscle memory takes over.

For a moment, everything else disappears. The baby she's having. The medical issues. It's just us.

From behind us, I hear, "You have got to be kidding me!"

We jerk apart, heat replaced by panic.

Greyson and Sutton stand a few feet away, having just stepped outside. Greyson looks stunned, eyes flicking between us as if he's trying to make sense of what he's seeing.

Sutton claps once, grinning. "This is almost as sweet as having a baby."

Greyson doesn't laugh.

Instead, he steps closer and grips my arm—right where the skin is still tender, where the port sits beneath the surface. The pressure is light but deliberate.

"I thought this fake dating thing was over," he says. It sounds more like a question than a statement.

I don't pull away. "This is between Noelle and me," I say evenly.

Greyson's jaw tightens. "The hell it is." His voice drops. "I thought I could trust you."

The words land heavy.

Noelle stiffens beside me, but I don't let go of her hand. She opens her mouth, but instead of saying she gets to decide who she dates, she blurts out, "I'm pregnant."

Time slows down as I feel Greyson's fist connect with my jaw. Soon the whole family gathers to witness the commotion. J.D. pulls Greyson away from me. "G, G! Stop! What's going on?"

"My best friend is fucking our sister. That's what's going on," he says.

A collective gasp comes from the O'Ryan crew. "And she's pregnant," he adds. An even louder gasp.

Then silence.

Not even a late-summer cricket chirps.

TWENTY-EIGHT
NOELLE

My pulse races.

My words are measured as I step into Greyson's personal space. "Congratulations. Paulina and Witley officially have an asshole for a father."

I push past him, brushing my shoulder against his arm. Sutton reaches out, but I shake her off, humiliated. How could Greyson tell everyone I'm pregnant? When I told him, I thought it would be in confidence. He's always been the one I confided in. Suddenly, I'm running up the stairs to get away from everyone in this family. When I reach the landing, my feet give way, and I crumble to the ground.

Crying.

Dad appears and sits beside me, stroking my hair while saying, "Shh... everything is okay."

Growing up, he had to play both mom and dad. Sutton and Birdie have taken over the role of mom when needed. They both have that motherly instinct, but Dad always knows how to find the right moment to be soft when he usually has a rough, more direct nature.

He tucks me under his arm, my head falling onto his chest. "Are you ashamed of me?" I slurp up my tears, and my voice shakes.

"Never in a million years would I use that word about you. You've always been the light of my life. The little girl who helped me become a real man. A real man braids a little girl's hair and sings Taylor Swift songs. Do you think Matt will do that?" His words trail off, but I heard them.

I lift my chin, and my dad wipes a tear away, even though they keep falling. "What do you mean?"

"You're pregnant. Will Matt be the man you need?"

My lids fall closed. Ashamed is the word to describe how I feel. Not because of dating Matt, if that's even what we're doing. But ashamed that I had sex with a man I knew I shouldn't have—Brooks.

"It's not Matt's baby. God, I wish it was. The baby is Brooks'."

"Are you sure?" he asks, pressing a soft kiss to the top of my head.

Nodding, I say, "Yeah, the symptoms started before things changed with Matt and me."

"Well, if there's one thing I know with one hundred percent certainty, it's that you'll be a terrific mom. You have your mother's blood flowing through you, and there was no one better at mothering than your mom."

We sit quietly for a few minutes before I hear footsteps coming. Dad stands me up and moves us into the den as my family converges on me. J.D. and Birdie hug me. "We'll help you. You know that."

Paulina, who is almost as tall as me, flings her arms around me. "I'll babysit."

"Thank you," I whisper in her ear.

Witt says nothing but pats my shoulder with a slight grin on his face.

Parker says, "How much do daycare workers get paid?"

I snort. "Not as much as the NIL money you're getting."

Sutton gives me a nurturing, long hug and whispers, "I think it's fantastic that we'll all have kids growing up together. Congratulations. Now I need to rest while Witley is asleep."

Shooting her a close-lipped grin, I see Greyson is just behind her. He reaches for my hand, but I want to jerk it away. I don't. I can't afford to. He's always been my rock. The one to tell me that I can be a tomboy and play softball and still dress in pink. I can cheer on my team and still have insane athletic ability, able to be tossed up and do a double tuck in the air.

"Sis. I'm sorry."

I cross my arms. Defiant. "For what?" There's a softness in my tone even while I'm trying to act like a badass.

"For not being happy for you. This thing with Matt... it clouds my judgment. The baby is Brooks'?"

"Yes. I told him I was raising the baby on my own, that I don't want anything from him. And he doesn't want anything to do with this baby." Looking down, I didn't realize my hand was cradling my stomach. "Even though before I told him, he was still thinking I was there to grovel for him to take me back."

"I never liked the way he treated you and dismissed you. Even at our family functions, he would ignore you."

Matt interjects, "Like at your wedding. He danced with every girl there except Noelle." Matt takes cautious steps toward me and says to Greyson, "We need to have a conversation."

I point my finger toward my chest, and he shakes his head no. Gathering myself, I say, "No. We need to have a conversation before you have one with my brother."

Greyson smiles. "I love you."

"I love you too. I'm heading out. I just need a little time before being bombarded with questions."

"I haven't had any sleep, and I'm sorry," Greyson says, weary and worn.

Matt folds his lips over his teeth and just nods in appreciation for the apology. Our feet seem to be stuck in cement. No one moves.

"Okay. Leaving now. Matt, follow me to the diner?" I ask.

"How about we just go to my place?"

"Okay, then I'll follow you." Because if Matt doesn't say what I'm wishing for, then I'll need an escape plan.

We leave without saying goodbyes. It's better this way.

"Want a drink? Oh, uh. I have water and Diet Coke."

"I'm good."

I grab two water bottles out of the fridge, loosen the top on one, and hand it to her. "Sit. I have so much to say."

We sit the same way, half-turned to look at each other with one knee tucked under the other leg, making a diamond shape. Placing her hand in mine, I brush back and forth over her skin.

"There's only one thing I need to know. Are we in a real relationship or not? Because if the answer is no, we're not, then there's not much else to say."

I wish that was all that mattered.

"No, there's more that you need to know."

"I have six months or so to figure out how to be a mom. Just tell me if you want me."

Her words are brittle, like she might break if I say no. But sometimes life isn't easy, and we need to lay all of our cards on the table before decisions have to be made. She needs to know what I've been hiding from her.

"I'm on dialysis," I say plainly. No jokes. No deflection. "Started recently."

Her face drains of color. "Dialysis? Why?"

"Diabetes is a nasty disease, even when you do everything right. I'm on the kidney transplant list too," I continue. "They don't know when—or if—a match will come."

The silence stretches. Heavy. Fragile.

"That's why I tried putting a little distance between us. I didn't tell you because I didn't want to scare you," I admit. "I'm still getting used to it myself."

She scoots closer. "Matt..."

"You already have so much on your plate. I need you to worry about you and your baby's health, not mine."

"You don't get to decide that for me," she says, her voice quiet but rock-steady.

"You should walk away from me without regrets. I've loved every minute we've spent together, but..."

"Is that what you want? For me to walk away?" she asks, stressing the word *you*. "Because I'm asking you if you have real feelings for me. Not as a sex mentor or my brothers' little sister. But for me?"

I almost choke. "I do. I haven't attached myself to someone in a long time. One, no one interested me. Two, I can't give a girlfriend... you. What can I give you? A life of wondering when I'm going to die?"

She reaches for my hand and says, "Mom lived a short life. She was about your age when she passed away. Do you think my dad sits around and thinks he should have married someone else? Someone who wasn't going to die on him?" She pauses. "Of course, he doesn't. He thinks about all the things they did together, the life they lived. How hard they loved."

Noelle looks up at me with those big, round eyes. "Forget Greyson, the age difference, the baby, and your diabetes. Give us a chance."

My chest tightens. "I don't want to be a burden."

She shakes her head. "You're not."

I study her face and realize she's afraid. But she's still standing here. Still choosing this moment.

"I don't know what will happen next," I say.

"This is when you take me to bed or lose me forever."

"Top Gun. Were you even born then?" I chuckle as she playfully slaps my arm. When the laughter dies down, I take her hand in mine. Our relationship has shifted, and her fingers tremble just a little as they lace through mine.

Suddenly, my living room feels too large and exposed with the glow of all the city lights flickering through the floor-to-ceiling windows. It's a total bachelor pad. No warmth to this place at all.

My heart pounds, harder than it ever has. We're choosing to take a leap of faith that it will work out. Even with the life growing inside her that's not mine or the dialysis that will take four hours of my day three times a week. None of that matters now.

"Come with me," I murmur, my voice low and rough, pulling her gently toward the hallway. She follows without hesitation.

We step into my bedroom, the door clicking shut behind us like a promise sealed. The room is simple—a king-sized bed with crisp white sheets, a few books on the nightstand, and the faint scent of my cologne lingering in the air. I turn to her, cupping her face in my hands, my thumbs brushing her cheeks. God, she's beautiful—her hair cascading over her shoulders, her skin glowing in the soft light from the lamp, her eyes wide and wanting. I want to protect her, worship her, show her that this is real.

"Noelle," I breathe, leaning in to kiss her softly at first, savoring the hint of strawberries on her lips from dinner. Holding her upright and close, our bodies meld together, and our mouths dance in a rhythm that's both urgent and tender.

"What?" she asks, her words wispy and breathless, almost without edges.

"I... I..." The feeling is there, but I'm not sure I want to say the words I've not said in so long. So instead of finishing my sentence, I slide my hands down her neck, over her shoulders, tracing the curve of her back until I reach the hem of her shirt. "I need you." I lift the fabric slowly, exposing the smooth skin beneath. She raises her arms to help me, and when the fabric hits the floor, I step back enough to look at her.

To drink her in.

"You're incredible," I whisper, my voice cracking a little. I drop to my knees before her, pressing my lips to the taut skin just above her navel. She gasps, her fingers threading into my hair. I caress her stomach with both hands, palms flat and gentle, feeling the warmth and the faint shiver. "This... all of you... it's a miracle. And I want to be part of it. With you."

Noelle doesn't respond verbally, but tears glisten in her eyes as she looks down at me, and I rise slowly, kissing my way up her body—her sternum, her collarbone, back to her mouth. We undress each other with careful hands, no rush, every touch a declaration. Her skin is silk under my fingers, and when she's bare before me, I guide her to the bed, laying her down like she's the most precious thing in my world.

I join her, my body covering hers but careful not to press too hard, mindful that her breasts may be tender. Honestly, I know nothing about babies other than holding them. And I've only heard about breasts getting sore.

Our kisses grow deeper, hungrier, my hands exploring—cupping her breasts, my thumbs teasing her nipples until she arches into me with a soft moan. "Matt," she whispers, her nails grazing my back, sending shivers down my spine. I trail kisses down her neck, over her shoulders, lingering on her chest before moving lower again, lavishing attention on her stomach once more.

"You know how to make a woman feel special," she says.

"Only you. You're the only woman I want to make feel special."

I kiss every inch, my hands stroking her sides, feeling her breath hitch and her body respond.

When I finally settle between her thighs, it's with reverence. I taste her slowly, drawing out her pleasure, listening to her gasps and whimpers like they're music. She's wet and ready, her hips lifting to meet me, and I bring her to the edge with my mouth, my fingers, until she shatters, crying out my name. The sound of her coming undone is the most erotic sound I've ever heard—emotional, intimate, binding us closer.

I move up her body, positioning myself carefully, our eyes locked as I enter her inch by inch. It's exquisite agony, the way she envelops me, warm and tight. We move together, slowly at first, building a rhythm that's as much about connection as it is about release. My arms bracket her head, our foreheads touching, breaths mingling.

"I'm in love with you," I groan against her lips, the words spilling out like I've said them a thousand times.

Her eyes flutter open.

Her chest rises.

She sucks in a breath.

"You love me?"

"I didn't want to admit it. I thought it was a betrayal to Greyson, but I do. I love you."

She wraps her legs around me, pulling me deeper, her hands clutching my shoulders, and in a lustful breath, she says, "I love you too. I think I've loved you since you danced with me at Greyson's wedding. That you would protect me and save me from that asshole. From that moment, I have loved your heart. But now I love everything about you. Your tattoos, your little white box—your body speaks for itself."

She nibbles on my bottom lip, and we smile into a kiss.

Every thrust is laced with emotion—the fear of not being around for her, the joy of having her, the promise of a future we're building despite everything. I caress her stomach as we move, my hand splayed protectively over it, and she covers it with her own, our fingers intertwining. The intensity peaks, her body clenching around me, drawing me over the edge with her. We come together. It hits like high tide—sudden, unstoppable, and impossible to outrun.

And I'm done running.

I hold her close, our bodies slick and spent, my hand still on her stomach. Her head rests on my chest, listening to my heartbeat—the one that beats for her now. In this quiet, with the world outside forgotten, I know we've found something real, something worth every risk.

The dialysis center smells like disinfectant and burnt coffee.

I couldn't go on Monday due to work obligations, but today, I'm here to see for myself what my man is going through.

My man. Crazy.

Matt calls it a pit stop, like we're just pulling off the highway for snacks before heading back into real life, but watching his blood disappear into a machine and come back cleaner feels anything but casual. I sit beside him in a plastic chair that squeaks when I move, my fingers laced through his.

"Don't make that face," he murmurs, his eyes half-lidded but alert. "I'm still very charming."

"I'm not worried about your charm," I say. "I'm worried about the fact that you're attached to a robot."

He smirks. "You're just jealous. This one gives me all its attention."

"I'm serious. What if they're secretly cloning you?"

"Conspiracy theorist, huh?"

"Of the worst kind. In college, I would watch documentaries and then couldn't sleep, thinking about how the government may have conspired to kill Kennedy. Here. In Texas."

He throws his head back against the fake leather, laughing. "Did they have any actual evidence? Or was it just people's opinions?"

"Opinions mostly, but they were convincing. After my doctor's appointment, let's go to my house and watch it."

I snort despite myself, leaning in so my shoulder brushes his. He squeezes my hand, grounding me.

I tell myself this is normal.

This is manageable.

But my heart keeps whispering, *This is real and it isn't normal.*

Matt is the picture of health on the outside—a strong body, a six-pack of abs, and his endurance. Well, let's just say he can *go!* On the inside, his kidney is failing and wreaking havoc on other parts of his body, like his eyes.

His nurse is about my age, shy but professional. She unhooks him and says to me, "I'm glad he has someone to lean on. Dialysis is hard on the mind. Too much time sitting still."

"Thanks. Will you be his nurse all the time?"

"Most of the time. We're on the same schedule. See you next time."

Matt interrupts. "She won't be here often. My girlfriend is a sideline reporter and travels for her career." His eyes brighten and his smile widens. "Now let's get going before we're late for your doctor's appointment."

His nurse doesn't pry, and we drive straight to the obstetrician, the same one that delivered Witley. The doctor asks if Matt is the father, and he looks at me. I'm almost certain he wants to say yes, but then he shakes his head no. The nurse draws blood, returning a few minutes later and pointing out something on the screen.

"Noelle, you are eight weeks pregnant. The good news is the nausea usually goes away at twelve to fourteen weeks. Usually." She goes through a list of things that I should research: how I want to have the baby—by midwife, at the hospital, with or without pain meds, and more. "Are you ready to hear the heartbeat?"

"Yes." My voice goes up three octaves.

"First, we'll see if we can capture the fetus on an abdominal ultrasound. If we can't pick it up, we'll do a transvaginal one, if you want to."

I nod as she lays the exam chair back, lifts my shirt, and squirts jelly on my belly. Cold. Matt holds my hand while the doctor checks for a heartbeat. She moves it around until I hear it. My baby's heartbeat.

"It's so fast," I blurt out.

Matt calmly asks, "Is that normal?"

A smile slides onto the doctor's face. "Very normal. It's perfect."

By the time we get to the pizza place, I'm clinging to that truth like a lifeline.

Greyson rented the entire place out for Witley's first time at a restaurant, which feels both ridiculous and completely on-brand for the O'Ryans. The neon sign glows in the windows, and inside it's loud, warm, and chaotic—exactly what I expect when this many people who share blood and volume gather in one place.

Parker flags the waitress down, sitting back with his long legs stretched out, his hands behind his head. "I need something special... cheese," he says, flashing her a megawatt smile and a wink.

She rolls her eyes, and I admit he's become quite cocky over the last year. Working out with the Armadillos gave him a little too much swagger. "Special, non-dairy cheese? Chemically altered cheese? Because we are a local pizza joint that carries regular cheese."

"Just extra."

"Extra what?" She pops her hip.

"Extra cheese," he says seriously. "It's a lifestyle."

"Got it. Lots of cheese for the cheesy guy."

J.D. grins from across the table. "The waitress isn't taking any shit from Parker. I like it."

Birdie rolls her eyes. "I'm positive that he's your mini-me."

"Was. I left that all behind when I met you," he says, lifting a brow.

I slap Parker on the leg. "Are you flirting with her?"

"God, no. Did you see her? She's not my type."

"Because her skirt is too long and you can't see her vagina? She's not slutty enough?" This time it's me who lets my eyes roll back as far as they can go. "Men."

Matt squeezes my knee under the table. "Don't lump us all in together. Not fair."

Then Witt chimes in. "Oh, it's fair in this family."

Greyson chimes in. "Not anymore."

I know that hormones are flooding my body and I'm overly sensitive, but it reminds me of the way Brooks would flirt with me right beside him.

The waitress brings out the first round of food. Sutton sits with Witley tucked against her chest, eyes half-closed but glowing. "These fries are mine. If anyone touches them I'll... I'll... Well, I'll do something. I need some sleep."

Parker raises his hands. "Your fries are sacred. We know."

Dad clinks his glass. "I raised you all better than this."

Matt brushes my knee under the table. I feel him there—steady, warm, grounding me when the noise starts to feel too big. Maybe it's the baby. Maybe it's the pizza. Maybe it's the way Matt looks at me.

"I have something to say," I blurt.

Everyone goes quiet.

My heart pounds. "Matt and I... we're together. For real."

There's a half second of stunned silence. Then—

"Oh my God," Birdie squeals.

"I knew it!" Paulina shouts.

J.D. knocks his knuckles against the table, a grin on his face.

Sutton tears up.

Dad chews on his lip.

Witt says nothing.

Parker grabs my hand and says, "Since the dinner, we've all known."

"Well, it wasn't official then. Now it is."

Dad finally weighs in. It's his opinion that matters the most. Dad's, then Greyson's. It won't change my mind if they don't approve, but I'm afraid it might change Matt's. He's loyal like the O'Ryan clan. So, I'm keeping my fingers crossed.

"As long as you're happy, and I can see that Matt makes you happy." He stands, comes around the table, kisses me on the head, and shakes Matt's hand.

Greyson just stares at us. "What about the baby?" he asks, his voice calm but heavy.

The room stills again.

Matt clears his throat. "I have an idea. Noelle and I haven't talked about it yet."

My pulse jumps.

"I want Brooks to sign away his parental rights and a non-disclosure agreement," Matt says. "That way he can't use the baby or Noelle for publicity. Ever. It protects them. And if... if we ever got married, there's no risk of legal issues."

Married? He's thinking about marriage?

Silence spreads like ripples on the water. Calmly.

Sutton's hand flies to her mouth.

Birdie's eyes go wide.

Paulina whispers, "Oh, wow."

Even Dad looks shaken.

I feel all of it—the love, the fear, the weight of being seen too clearly.

"Okay," I say too fast. "Let's go."

Matt looks at me, startled. "Noelle—"

"I need air," I say. "Now."

He stands immediately, because he always does. As we walk out, the noise and warmth fade behind us, but I know one thing with startling clarity.

Whatever this is between us...

It's not pretend anymore.

And that's both the best and scariest thing that's ever happened to me.

THIRTY-ONE
MATT

Noelle stares out the window, neon lights from the restaurant streaking across the glass in a blur as we drive further away. Her family's laughter still echoes in my head, along with the weight of what I said in front of all of them.

I clear my throat. "I'm really sorry."

She turns slightly. "For what?"

"For not talking to you first. About Brooks. About the NDA." I keep my eyes on the road. "I didn't mean to ambush you in front of everyone."

"It felt like you were... planning my life," she says carefully. Not accusing. Just honest.

I nod. "I was."

She looks at me, shocked.

"I don't want Brooks anywhere near you or the baby," I say. "Not now. Not ever. And if something happened to me..." My voice tightens. "I need to know he couldn't swoop in and take advantage of you."

Her breath catches. "Matt..."

"I've already set things up," I admit quietly. "My insurance. My retirement. Everything. If I'm gone, it goes to you and the baby. Married or not."

The words sit heavy between us.

"I'm not trying to trap you," I add. "I just... refuse to leave you unprotected."

Her eyes shine, and for a second she can't speak.

"I don't plan on you going anywhere," she finally whispers.

"Neither do I." I glance at her. "But I plan for worst-case scenarios. It's a coach thing."

A soft laugh breaks through her emotion. "You and your game plans."

"I'm serious," I say. "You're not alone anymore. Not in this."

We stop at a red light. The city hums around us, but the moment feels small and private. I reach for her hand.

"I meant what I said," I tell her. "Whatever you need... I'm here."

She leans across the console and kisses me—hard, sudden, full of everything we're not saying out loud. I pull her closer, forgetting the street, the future, the world, until a car honks behind us and she laughs into my mouth.

"Okay," she breathes. "Before we get arrested..."

We pull apart, still smiling.

"Will you ask Brooks to give up his rights, legally—and sign an NDA?" I ask, forcing my voice to stay steady. "It's your decision."

I don't look at her right away. I'm afraid if I do, she'll see how much I need her to say yes—not for control, not for power, but because the thought of Brooks having any claim on her or the baby makes something primal twist in my chest.

She exhales, long and slow, and the sound of it feels like

a release. Like she's been holding her breath longer than either of us realized.

"Yes," she says. "I'll have Sutton ask the Armadillos' legal team to draw up a contract. Then I'll go see Brooks."

Relief hits me so fast it's almost dizzying.

"We can just overnight the documents to him," I offer, already thinking ten steps ahead. Distance is safer. Cleaner. Less room for manipulation.

She shakes her head. "Coach... this is Brooks's baby. He has a right to change his mind. I don't want him to, but..."

Her voice trails off, and I hear the conflict in it—the part of her that still wants to be fair even to someone who never was.

I turn to her then, needing her to understand. "Not your coach." I wink. "Your boyfriend."

The word feels dangerous in my mouth. Powerful. True.

"And he'd be crazy to give up this baby," I admit, even though every selfish part of me hopes he will. "But I still hope he does."

Because loving her means wanting to protect everything that belongs to her—even the parts that terrify me.

Then she presses a hand to her stomach. "I need deviled eggs."

"What?" I blink, my mouth falling open. I don't think I've ever heard that phrase uttered. Maybe on Thanksgiving. Maybe.

"Right now. I need deviled eggs." She nods firmly. "If I don't get deviled eggs, I might cry."

"Drama must run in the O'Ryan genes."

"This baby is dramatic," she says. "You stressed it out with legal talk."

I laugh. "Your baby is eight weeks old."

"And already very emotionally complex."

So, we head to her house instead of mine because she needs eggs like a desert needs water. Ten minutes later we're in her kitchen, boiling eggs like it's a crisis response. She's in my hoodie, hair up, pacing like she's waiting on lab results.

"How many eggs do you think is appropriate?" I ask.

"All of them."

I peel shells while she mixes yolks with mayo and mustard, focused as if this is the most important recipe of her life. Some of the filling ends up on her cheek.

"You've got—" I reach out, wiping it away, my thumb lingering longer than it should.

She looks at me the way she always does when things go quiet—like she's taking a snapshot she doesn't want to forget.

"Thank you," she says softly. Not for the eggs. For everything.

We eat deviled eggs straight off the counter, laughing when the filling falls out and lands on the floor. She adds pickle relish to the top, and I can't think of anything more disgusting. But at this moment, she's the cutest thing in Texas. She lights up my world, one that has been hiding depression for too long.

And for the first time all night, I stop worrying that I crossed a line. Because no matter how long I have on this earth, I plan to protect Noelle and the baby with everything I have. And all that I am.

Three weeks later, everything feels different.

Not easy. Not settled. Just... steadier. Like the ground stopped shifting quite so violently beneath my feet.

I'm beginning to show, my belly popping out ever so slightly.

I come straight from seeing Brooks. Sutton had the Armadillo Team plane take me to New Orleans so I wouldn't have to spend the night. My nerves are still zipping when I pull into the parking lot of Matt's high-rise. The papers are signed. The NDA. The relinquishment of rights. Black ink on white pages that somehow made everything both safer and scarier.

Matt opens the door before I can knock. "Well?" he asks, his eyes searching my face.

"He signed it."

The relief that washes over him is immediate and unguarded. He pulls me into his arms, his forehead dropping against mine like he's been holding his breath for weeks.

"Thank God," he murmurs. "One less thing we have to

worry about." He gives me a gentle peck on the lips. We don't say Brooks's name again. We don't need to.

"I've been thinking," Matt says after a moment, brushing his thumb over his lips. "You could move in here. If you want. No pressure."

The words hit deeper than he knows. "Are you serious?"

"Your roommates are never home. Professional cheerleaders must travel a lot, and I just want you here with me," he rambles, trying to throw out as many reasons as possible.

"I need to think about it," I say softly. "Is that okay? It's not just me anymore, and I..."

He nods, even though I see the hope flicker and retreat behind his eyes. "You need to think about it. I get that."

He makes me a snack plate of apples, cheese, deviled eggs, and pickles. And like everything else, my life changes in an instant. I take a bite of the deviled egg and can't keep it down. I run to the sink and retch. "Were those eggs old?" I ask when I finally catch my breath.

Matt opens the fridge and checks the date. "No, they don't expire for two weeks." He rips off a paper towel, wets it, and wipes my mouth. "I'll start a hot shower for you."

"Okay, but I'm babysitting Witley today, so I don't have much time."

"I'm heading to practice after I get the shower going." He leans down, staying far away from my mouth, and kisses my neck.

Joking, I say, "A real man kisses his girl after she throws up."

"I guess I'm fictional then, because there will be no kissing with throw-up breath."

I chuckle to myself, thinking about how lucky I am to have this man by my side.

When I get to Sutton's, Witley is curled against her chest —tiny and warm, her little fingers twitching and her legs drawn up to her chest while she sleeps. Sutton looks tired but peaceful, a laptop open on the arm of the couch, her world somehow balancing between football operations and motherhood.

"I have food," I announce.

Sutton smiles. "You are officially my favorite person. Texas twinkies?"

I shoot her a look. "Those are for special occasions."

"This is special. Seeing my sister-in-law."

"Next time, I'll order ahead." I take Witley carefully, her weight barely more than a breath in my arms. Holding her feels different now—like my body recognizes something my mind is still trying to catch up to.

"How are you feeling?" Sutton asks gently. "Really."

I hesitate, then shrug. "Some days I feel like I can do this. Some days I wake up terrified."

"That's motherhood," she says softly. "Even after the baby gets here."

I swallow. "I've been reading everything I can, and they make it sound so rigid. I don't remember my mom being scheduled. I made a friend, Clara. She works at the library where I've been researching."

"From what I understand, your mom didn't have the luxury of being strict with routines. With you being so much younger than J.D. and Greyson, she had to take you every-where. She also didn't have every single bit of information at her fingertips. Research first—then decide what works for you. You don't have to do what Birdie or I do. You are the mom of your baby, and what you say goes."

"It's all so much. Vaccinations or not. All or some. All

but spread out. Breastfeed or formula. Don't leave them in a seat once they can sit up for longer than fifteen minutes."

Sutton stops me. "That's where I draw the line. We're mothers, but we are also career women, and if we need thirty minutes to get a presentation done or, in your case, an interview edited, sit them in the damn seat or swing or whatever. You do what feels right for you."

Smiling, I say, "Thank you. I'm so lucky to have you and Birdie." I get choked up looking at Witley and thinking about what happened to my mom during childbirth.

It's as if she knows what I'm thinking, and she rubs my back. "You'll be okay. This baby will be healthy and loved by a big, messy, loving family."

I hold back the tears welling in my eyes and nod.

Sutton quickly changes the subject. "When is your next doctor's visit?"

"Next week."

"Are you going to find out the sex? Oh wait, that's not until twenty weeks, right?"

"Yeah, twenty weeks is what the doctor said. Part of me wants to know everything. Part of me wants one surprise in my life that isn't terrifying."

She laughs quietly. "I completely understand. Either way, you're not doing this alone."

I nod, my throat tight. "Brooks signed the NDA. He gave up his rights."

Sutton's eyes flash with fierce approval. "Good. I'm glad Armadillo Legal could help. That man doesn't deserve access to you or that baby."

I stare down at Witley, at the miracle of her breathing. "Matt asked me to move in with him."

"And?"

"And I'm scared," I whisper. "But I also don't want to be anywhere else."

She reaches over and squeezes my knee. "That's what love feels like when it's real."

By the time I leave, something in me has settled.

> Me: What time will you be home from practice?

> Matt: Seven. Are you making deviled eggs?

> Me: If you're lucky.

At 6:58, I pull into his parking lot, slinging two suitcases from the backseat. I press his number on the pad, and he rings me up.

He opens the door just as one piece of my luggage, the one with the stubborn wheel, gets stuck coming out of the elevator.

"There's more in the car," I say.

He freezes. "Are you—"

"I'm moving in."

He laughs and lifts me right off the ground in those strong, tattooed arms. "You have no idea how happy you're making me right now."

"Oh, I know. Something in your pants is poking me," I cackle as he swings me around.

He presses his groin against me as much as he can. "You want me to poke you?"

"No. Well, maybe."

He puts me down, carrying my luggage inside, and says, "I'll go get the rest. You... make yourself at home."

Home.

"Okay."

When he returns from my car, he looks like a homeless person—my fluffy beanbag on his head, three tote bags thrown over his arms while carrying two baskets of toiletries and pictures.

I pull out my phone and snap a picture before he can protest. "Thank you!" I say, jumping up to peck his lips.

"Is this all?"

"No, we can go get my furniture whenever. I still need to pay my part of the rent until October. That's when our lease is up."

"So are you moving in because you had to move out in six weeks anyway?" His tone hints at disappointment. He sets the baskets down and starts untangling himself from the tote bags.

"No. My boyfriend asked me to move in with him, so I said yes. Sutton said he must love me."

He saunters into my personal space. "I do, but you cannot take over my entire closet," he protests.

"You wear the same Dillos gear almost every day, so I'm sure you have room."

"There's plenty of room. Now let me help get it put away."

I roll my hard-shell suitcase, and Matt brings the rest. We survey the logistics of where things should go. Bathroom stuff in the master. Clothes, half in his closet and half in the guest room. We argue over pillows. Over where my shoes go. Then, we decide to put everything else in his office and spend some time together before I fall asleep. I'm spent from all the travel and the emotion of the day.

The kitchen is open to the living area, so I plop down on

the couch. Matt opens the fridge and pours himself a glass of almond milk. "You drink almond milk?" I ask as he pops popcorn.

"Yeah." When the popcorn's ready, he hands me the glass and says, "Have you tried it?"

"Yeah, and it's not milk."

"Just try it. It goes perfectly with popcorn."

I take a sip, and it's okay, but I don't want to admit it. "It's not good."

"It took me a while to get used to it, but now I love it." He winks at me like he's no longer talking about milk. Matt grabs a bottle of water for me, and we snuggle on the couch, a bowl of popcorn in our laps.

"What do you want to watch?" he asks.

"Preseason football," I say instantly.

He grins. "You're perfect."

After a few bites, we curl into each other, the TV flickering, his arm wrapped around me, my head tucked against his shoulder. For the first time in a long time, the future doesn't feel like someone's waiting to take everything from me. It feels like something we're building.

Together.

THIRTY-THREE
MATT

Game days aren't supposed to start with dialysis.

At least we're playing at home today, which means I don't have to pretend to feel great on a plane ride. But here I am, stepping into the Armadillos' facility, still feeling the faint buzz in my veins while the stadium hums awake around me, die-hard fans filing in three hours early. Sutton set up a meet-and-greet for season ticket holders.

The locker room smells like sweat, tape, and anticipation. Whistles echo. Rookies stretch. Veterans move with the easy confidence of men who know where they belong.

Greyson drops into the chair beside me. "You alive?"

"Barely," I say. "But I think that's just game-day nerves." I don't say how exhausted I feel.

J.D. flops down on my other side. "So how many hours of sleep are you getting now that you live with a pregnant woman?"

I snort. "Define sleep."

"That bad already?" J.D. asks.

"She woke me up at three a.m. because she dreamed she

ate all the deviled eggs and felt guilty about it," I deadpan. "Then she actually needed more."

Greyson laughs. "That tracks."

J.D. adds, "Birdie reorganized our entire kitchen at two in the morning when she was pregnant. Said she shouldn't eat cookies, so she woke me up and made me put them in the highest cabinet. Then the next day I catch her on a ladder trying to get them down and she's really pregnant. We argued about her falling. Trust me. You can't win an argument against a pregnant wife... or girlfriend." It sounds weird coming out of his mouth.

"Wait till the baby needs formula and a clean diaper," Greyson mutters. "You better jump right up."

J.D. agrees as he takes off his Armadillo hat and runs his hand through his hair, shaking his head. "Did you ever think game-day conversations would turn into comparing pregnancy stories?"

I glance between them. "It wasn't too long ago that none of us wanted to be here." I look between them. J.D. was pushed into taking the head coaching role, Greyson got traded, and I needed a coaching job in Austin to be close to my doctor.

Greyson says, "Tragic."

J.D. grins. "It's weird how one day changes the trajectory of your life. I was in Denver, playing for the Vegas Dice, and went out with G and the Denver crew. That's the night I met Birdie, and now we have a family."

"Is she here today?"

"No, she's doing two concerts this weekend. Granny went with her to take care of Henley. She'll be back tomorrow night, so it's only one night without them." J.D. seems conflicted.

Greyson's smile fades just a touch as he looks at me. "Hey." He hesitates, then claps a hand on my shoulder. "Thanks for making our sister happy."

I blink, caught off guard.

"We've never seen her like this," J.D. adds quietly. "Not really."

Greyson nods. "She pretended to be happy with Brooks. We all smiled. Played the part. But it wasn't real. There was no chemistry between them."

"And he disrespected her. We should've kicked his ass a long time ago," J.D. mutters.

Greyson smirks. "I still might."

I swallow around the sudden tightness in my throat. "She deserves better."

"She does," Greyson says. "And for the record... we're glad it's you."

They have no idea how much their support means to me. How disappointing them was the last thing I wanted to do, but as it turns out, they just want their sister to be loved the way she deserves.

Out on the field, quarterback warmups begin, and suddenly it's all motion, muscle, and focus. Whistles cut through the air. Cleats pound the turf. The Armadillo offense looks sharp—hungry.

I step out onto the sideline, headset in place, my heart pounding with something that feels dangerously close to hope.

Then I look up into the stands.

Noelle is in the front row, wearing my Austin Armadillos hat, the one with just the mascot. She's in love with that little guy. It makes me wonder if we're having a boy or girl.

We? Not her?

Our eyes meet. She smiles—soft, proud, just for me—and something in my chest tightens, not with pain, but with something brighter.

For a moment, everything else disappears.

No dialysis.

No fear.

Not the ticking clock in my head.

Just her.

And for the first time in a long time, standing on the sideline of a game I love with the woman I love in the stands, I realize I need to fight harder and don't want to die. I want to be here long term for this spunky, gorgeous, loving woman and her baby.

Maybe true love will overcome, like in fairy tales.

Greyson shows up with a toolbox and the kind of energy that says he's here to fix things.

And he is, but he's also here to check on me. He's the kind of brother a girl is happy to have. Matt has that kind of relationship with his sister, Shelley. I wish she lived here. We've done video calls with her and she seems fun. She's younger than Matt but works a corporate job and says she'll give it all up when the baby comes so she can babysit.

"Where's the crib?" he asks, already scanning the half-assembled chaos that has become Matt's house. Our house. I don't think I'm the one nesting; Matt is. He wants everything put together and organized now.

"In the nursery," Matt says, coming out of the hall with a piece of wood under his arm. "The instructions are lying."

Greyson snorts. "They always do."

I hover in the doorway, watching them work—two men who look like they've known each other their whole lives, like brothers, trading barbs and bolts with the easy rhythm of people who speak the same language.

"Hey," Greyson says suddenly, not looking up. "You remember that third-and-eight play you ran with Logan Warren when you were with the Louisville Heavyweights?"

Matt's hands pause for just a beat.

"The... uh," he starts, his brow furrowing. "We ran an... inside slant?"

Greyson lifts his head slowly. "No. The one in the championship game. You designed it. It was a wheel route. I thought we should put it in for the first game of the season."

Matt laughs it off. "Must've blocked it out. That was a blur."

Greyson doesn't laugh.

A few minutes later, he wanders over to me on the excuse of grabbing a drink.

"Is his memory off?" he asks quietly while retrieving water from the fridge.

My stomach tightens.

"I don't know," I say, but the lie tastes thin.

Greyson studies me. "Because it's not like him to forget something that important. They won the fucking championship on that play."

Worry lines stretch across Greyson's forehead, and I know he wouldn't pull me aside unless he was scared too. He says, "Let's go back, but sis, you need to find out what's really going on."

I look back at Matt. At the way his shoulders slump between movements. At how his skin looks almost gray, even under the warm light.

Severe fatigue.

Loss of appetite.

Brain fog.

Itching.

The words line up in my mind like a verdict. All the things I've noticed but thought he would tell me if something was wrong. I know I need to confront him. He won't let me have a baby on my own, and I'm not about to let him shoulder his illness on his own either.

When the crib is finally finished, Greyson packs up, pretending nothing is wrong. The moment the door closes, the air shifts. "Love ya," he says and kisses me. "See ya at the stadium tomorrow."

"Sure thing. Thanks for your help. The baby has a place to sleep now."

I add, trying to keep it light, "And a place for clothes. Birdie and Sutton have already been buying unisex outfits."

"How much longer until you find out the sex?" Greyson asks.

"Soon. Two weeks."

Sutton calls Greyson, so he waves goodbye, and Matt and I both take a deep breath.

"The furniture looks amazing. You're going to be a great father," I say, wrapping my arms around his waist.

"Hope so."

"Matt," I say, taking a deep breath. "Are you okay?"

"I'm fine."

"What did they say at dialysis today?" I ask.

"I told you. They're sending the labs to Dr. Knupp."

His words cut through me, razor-sharp, and something inside me snaps. The room feels too bright. Too quiet. My skin prickles like I've just walked into cold water. I don't know exactly what I'm afraid of yet—but I know it's coming.

"Call him," I say.

Matt looks at me, startled. "Noelle—"

"Call. Him. Now."

"It's after hours."

"You moved here for Dr. Knupp. Call him. If he thinks it's important enough, he'll answer."

My voice shakes, and I hate that it does. My heart is pounding so hard it's stealing the air from my lungs. Every instinct I have is screaming that something is wrong—so wrong that pretending everything is fine feels like lying to myself.

I think about the way he's been sleeping through alarms. About how he barely eats, always saying he ate at the stadium. About the blank look on his face when Greyson mentioned that play.

Please don't let me be right.

Please don't let me be right.

"Call him," I whisper again, softer now, almost pleading. "I need to hear it from someone who isn't you."

He hesitates, pain flashing in his eyes—not fear, but the kind of resignation that terrifies me most. Then he pulls out his phone and walks into the nursery, as if he doesn't want me to hear what's coming.

And somehow, that hurts even more.

Almost half an hour later, he grabs my hands and delivers the news.

Greyson leans against the doorframe of my office, arms crossed, his eyes sharp in that way that means he's trying to be casual and failing.

"Dad called," he says. "He's having a family dinner tonight."

I don't look up from the film I'm rewinding. "Pass."

"He says since we've got a Saturday game and then a Thursday game next week, he won't see anyone for a while," Greyson adds. "Wants to catch up. See Noelle. Henley. Witley." He sighs into a laugh. "You know how he is. Big softie when it comes to the girls."

"Sorry, designing plays to make you look good on the field," I say. "Your dad's a coach, so he'll understand why I'm not there." Can't he see I'm in no mood or condition to be around his family? Being judged about how sick I am. That I'm worthless to Noelle. I know they probably don't feel that way, but it's how I feel.

Greyson smirks. "I doubt Noelle will allow that."

I glance up. "Allow?"

"Well," he says, shrugging, "I'm pretty sure she's persuasive. I mean…she did something to make you fall in love."

I don't answer that. She did. She cried on my shoulder, kissed me with those tender lips, made me laugh when there hasn't been much to laugh about, and then we shared a hotel room and she asked me to teach her. But what I realize now is that she was teaching me. How to heal a woman from the scars left by a prick of a man. How loving a woman healed me.

Two hours later, we're standing in her dad's kitchen, the house loud with familiar chaos. Henley is sitting up, playing with Mr. O'Ryan and a dancing cactus. Witley sleeps in Paulina's arms. Noelle looks beautiful and anxious, all at once. Her dad pats her back as they talk.

Greyson takes Witley from Paulina and holds her as everyone fills up their plates. Their family reminds me of my own, except larger. Tonight's potluck has all the family favorites—squash casserole, barbecue brisket, mac and cheese, roasted parmesan Brussels sprouts, and five desserts. The O'Ryans love sweets. Until my twenties, I did too, but it was more important for me to be in top condition to play football and stay alive. Okay, that's a little dramatic, but I didn't want to pass out on the field from my sugar going too high or too low.

Everyone takes their seat at the long wooden table with plates piled high. Noelle glances at my plate, shaking her head, and I realize it's half of what everyone else has. Mr. O'Ryan asks about each baby and if they've done anything new for the week.

Sutton says, "Witley is learning to soothe herself. Last night she slept for five hours straight before she needed to eat again."

"When she starts sleeping through the night, it's going to change your life," Birdie says, patting her hand against her chest. "I mean it. Henley is teething, so if she's chewing on your hand, beware—those gums can clamp down hard."

Noelle's fidgeting, and I hope nothing is wrong with the baby. Before I can whisper in her ear, Parker says, "Guess who I have class with?"

Our mouths are all full, so there's a lot of grunting. Finally, Witt asks, "Who?"

"Annika, the waitress from the pizza place. She sits in the front row like we're in high school."

"Maybe she wants to learn and not be distracted by a bunch of asshole football players," Noelle responds.

Well, that startles everyone, including me. Does she still have feelings for Brooks? Her dad surveys the table, and Parker says, "This girl hates everyone."

"She probably hates the way you all act like you're God's gift," Noelle snips and sighs.

Something feels off. Noelle is off. She and Parker are tight. Parker is the gentle one, but he is a little cockier now that he's a college wide receiver for Texas.

Then she drops her fork and presses her hands against the table, bracing herself for what's to come, I guess. It's how she steadies herself. But this time she shouts, "I need you all to get tested."

Tested for what?

"For Matt," she continues. "He needs a kidney."

The room goes still.

It's like the air gets sucked out of the house. I feel it in my chest first—the pressure, the panic, the betrayal. The fear in her family's eyes and in my best friend's.

"What are you doing?" I demand, turning toward her.

We discussed in private what Dr. Knupp said. I've only told her and my sister. This is my news, and I get to decide when to share it.

Her eyes are filled with tears. "I just asked—"

I DON'T LET her finish, storming out the front door, the night air slamming into me like a wall.

Footsteps follow.

"Matt—wait." It's J.D., not Greyson.

"I'm sorry," he says quietly. "I don't know what you're going through, and having it on your mind daily has to be rough, but Noelle just wants you to be healthy."

I rake a hand through my hair. "I'm not taking anything from any of you."

"Why?"

"Because that's not how this works," I snap. "I won't owe my life to your family."

He studies me, his eyes soft. "You're living with our sister. I thought you loved her. If you love her, you'll let each one of us decide to get tested."

"I knew I shouldn't have fallen in love. I should be worrying about her, not myself. I tried. God knows I didn't want to see the distrust in your or Greyson's eyes, but the pull was too strong."

"Just as Greyson and I had to learn to live without our mom who had raised us for sixteen and eighteen years, Noelle will learn how to live with you if that time comes. Dad didn't have the luxury of helping Mom. It was too fast. But Noelle has the inclination to fix things, and you must let her try." J.D. slaps my back, not like at a ball game after a win, but like a brother.

It almost breaks me. I push my hand through my hair, thinking about how to handle this, and I decide to just be honest and open. When I walk back in, they're eating so they don't have to talk. Usually, it's people shouting over each other with lots of laughter, clinking utensils, and second helpings. I did this. I made the O'Ryan family quiet for once.

Grabbing Noelle's hand, I say, "Thank you for caring enough to ask your family, because I know they mean the absolute world to you, and for you to ask them was hard, but I'm not taking any of your kidneys." I let out a shaky breath. "End of discussion, okay?"

No one argues. No one smiles.

The house feels too small now, heavy with things no one knows how to say. Paulina breaks the silence, asking, "Is your baby the size of a tennis ball yet?"

"Usually, the doctors go by fruit," Sutton says with a gentle laugh.

Noelle says, "An avocado, so yeah, about the size of a tennis ball." She scoots her chair back, scraping against the floor. "I'm not feeling well. Matt, can we go home?"

"Sure."

Her family stands to say goodbye, but she waves them off. Greyson shoots a dagger at me for upsetting his sister, a look that says *make it right*.

Later, Noelle and I stand in my living room, the tension stretched tight between us.

"You don't get to decide this alone," she says, tears in her eyes.

"AND YOU DON'T GET to volunteer organs from your

family body," I fire back. "Have you thought about the situation that puts them in? Having to say no?"

"I was asking people that love you to get tested so that the person I love will be around to see this baby born." Her voice catches between words. "And have a life with me."

I reach out for her, and she flinches.

"Maybe I'm not what you need." Every fiber of my being believes this. "You're young and pregnant. You don't need the stress."

If loving her means watching her grieve me while I'm still breathing... I don't know if I'm strong enough to survive it.

"Stress! It's not fucking stress. It's love."

I push my finger into his chest, and he grabs my wrist, holding me in place. Every breath is weighted as our eyes collide. Suddenly, he rips his shirt over his head and puts my hand over his inked heart. "Don't you understand how much I love you? That's why I don't want to be a burden. I should be protecting you," he says, his voice raw and rough.

My thoughts are tornadic. One, I need to be physical with him, intimate with him. Two, I need to make him understand that trying to find a kidney for him isn't a burden. He would go to the ends of the earth to find one for me, so why can't he accept help?

First things first. I make record time getting his clothes off and fall to my knees, sucking him into my mouth. He groans with pleasure, like he needs to prove that he's still a man. Because, God, he is. His body is perfection, and his shaft is hard and thick yet softer than a rose petal. I swirl my tongue over the tip and can feel his blood pumping.

He rattles off my name, stretching it out at times. "Yeah,

Butterfly. So good." I lick and suck and do all the things he taught me until I feel his cock jerk in my mouth. He pistons his hips and pumps into me, filling me. His body releases all the pent-up tension from his muscles and, hopefully, his mind.

I stand up, fully clothed, and he's butt-naked. We usually start the other way around. "Thank you for letting me love you," I say with a smile as I pull off my shirt.

"I don't think you're giving me a choice." Matt wears a sly smirk, his lids still lazy from his orgasm.

"No, I'm not."

My gaze drops to the rubber band barely keeping my jeans closed. I'm in that awkward in-between phase—too big for my old clothes, not quite ready for maternity wear. I slide them down, and I'm left in a tiny thong and a bra that can't keep up with my growing chest.

"Butterfly, your body gets more beautiful each day." His tongue swipes over his plump bottom lip. His eyes darken as he spins me around, caressing my ass. "Goddamn. You should be pregnant all the time. Fucking perfection."

"You got a breeding kink, Coach."

"You want a coach?" he says.

I glance over my shoulder, flinging my hair, relentlessly teasing him. "Can you still coach? Is there anything more for me to learn?"

"Oh, there's more." He sucks on my neck, then strides into the kitchen and back in record time, holding a bottle of olive oil and a bag of salt flakes. He takes my bra off and commands, "Lay down on the rug."

I do.

His body is heavy on mine, but he lifts his lower abs so as not to pressure my belly. I keep telling him it's fine until my belly grows, but he's always thinking of me. Even with our fight, his thoughts were of me.

"What's the olive oil for?" I ask.

He doesn't answer, continuing to trail wet kisses along my neck and boobs. They're so needy, practically screaming for him to bite them. As if he knows what's running through my mind, he says, "Tell me what you want, Butterfly."

"Bite them. I want pressure."

I feel his lips smile on my skin, and he takes my nipple into his mouth, nibbling, grazing, and then biting. I scream. He stops. "I'm drawing up a new play. What should I call it?"

He pours olive oil on my chest and then sprinkles salt on my boobs like he's seasoning his dinner. His head dips, licking the salt off my drawn-up nipples. The slide of his tongue. The sound of his swallow. Perfect. Erotic.

After he's spread the oil between us, he commands, "Show me how wet you are."

My fingers roam to my center, moving up and down. Slow, then fast.

"How does touching yourself make you feel?" he asks as he drives his fingers inside me.

The air in my lungs feels heavy. There's not enough of it. "I... I... feel like a beautiful butterfly."

"You are a beautiful butterfly. Knees parted on the floor. The flush on your face. Sweat dotting your body like spots on a butterfly's wings. Finally, you see it."

My center throbs with need as he teases me, keeping me on the edge. "I want more," I cry out.

"More fingers?"

"I want you inside me. I want you to be relentless." I can't believe the words slip from my mouth. Who am I? I'm carrying a baby, but these hormones are out of control, and I can't stop a runaway train. Better to give in to my feelings.

Matt spreads my legs and bites my bundle of nerves. It's electric and painful yet pleasurable.

But it's still not enough. "More."

He crawls back up my body, kissing me roughly, and growls, "Get on all fours."

"What are you going to do to me?" I lift onto my elbows.

"Ruin you for any other man." He kisses me hard and rough. Urgent and ravenous.

"You already have."

My body goes into orgasm mode immediately. It's a mix of his raw, penetrating words, his body, and the anticipation. I roll over. "I don't want to ruin the rug with this oil."

"Fuck the rug. I'll buy ten more if I can be inside you every night like this."

Suddenly, I feel more oil on my back as he smooths it on my ass cheeks, slides his finger through my folds, then slaps my ass—not hard, but still, I want it harder. "More."

"More is different than harder. Which or both?"

Breathless, I say, "Both."

Who am I with this man?

A woman finding herself. That's who I am.

He gives a firm, heavier slap to my skin and then rubs the oil in. I'm dripping wet, and I want him to see just how much he turns me on, so I arch my back with my butt in the air, taunting him. I want it all.

"Fuck." He devours me from behind, and it feels amazing. My body is shaking, and I can't take much more. "This might hurt, but once we get the angle right, you're going to want it this way every time."

I can't breathe. I'm caught between pain and euphoric

bliss as he pushes in at a snail's pace. The whole time, he caresses my butt and lower back with one hand and holds my hip with the other. He's not all the way in because our skin isn't touching. It feels like a two-by-four between my legs. So why does it feel so good?

Because Matt Stricker is the love of my life. Pain or pleasure. Happy or sad. We belong together.

Matt sinks deeper inside me. His passionate urging rattles me to the bone. I want more, but I feel like I'm popping stitches where I don't have any.

"You fucking feel amazing. Relax. Spread your wings." He wraps my hair around his fist, tugging my head back as he is fully seated inside me. He feels larger than he's ever been. The width is almost too much as he plunges into me. I'm filled with his body and his love.

My lips quiver and my legs quake as he fucks me into oblivion and then tops it off by pressing his finger against my *do not touch hole.*

Not inside. Just pressure.

How can this feel so intimate when I can't even see his face? Then I learn what happens when you block both release points—an eruption. White-hot awareness shatters through me. My vision explodes into a galaxy of shooting stars, bright colors, and then peace. My body slacks a little, but he's not finished.

Matt puts his strong forearm underneath my gently formed belly, holding my ass and belly up, stretching out over my back and making long, lustful strokes. Loving me with purpose.

I don't know if it's my sweaty hair sticking to my face or Matt's body sliding on mine, but it's all-consuming. He makes sure I have another orgasm, and how could I not when he whispers how much he loves me, my body, and our baby while making me feel like the only woman alive?

"Yes, yes. Please. I never want this to end."

His body goes rigid, but he keeps pumping his cock, his fingers attentive to my swollen clit, trying to make it last. Then he pulls out, an erotic growl coming from his mouth, spurting his *happy juice* all over my back, mixing with the oil.

Matt covers my body with his while keeping my belly slightly off the floor, his chest on my shoulder blades. With his mouth on my shoulder, he mumbles, almost inaudibly, "Me either."

THIRTY-SEVEN
MATT

She's warm against me, all soft curves and quiet breathing, her hair fanned across my arm like she belongs there.

Because she does.

I lie still, afraid to move, afraid to break whatever spell has settled over us in the dark hush of morning. My hand rests on her back, just above the gentle swell that wasn't there before. Every time I let myself think about that—about the life growing inside her—something tightens in my chest in a way that hurts and heals at the same time.

I want this.

I want her.

I want the baby.

I want the messy, ordinary future I never thought I was allowed to imagine.

For a moment, darkness and doubt creep in. How can I have this? Or better yet, how long can I have this? I'll take whatever Noelle will give me, but I'm a selfish man. I decide. If I feel decent, I'll be here. I can take the pain.

My body aches, the familiar deep soreness humming

beneath my skin, but today is a day off from dialysis. A small mercy. I don't have to be at the stadium until noon—just a meeting, then practice. The world is giving me a few stolen hours of pretending everything is normal.

Or too much time to think.

Her alarm goes off, soft but insistent. She groans and burrows closer to me, nestling in until she finds a perfect spot. She's so damn cute and sexy at the same time.

"Do you feel better after last night?" she asks sleepily.

I smile despite myself. "I feel... a lot of things." I gently shift her so I can see her, my eyes tracing the curve of her hip, the faint shadows on her skin. My stomach twists when I spot the bruises.

"I'm sorry," I murmur. "I don't know what came over me. I didn't mean to hurt you."

She turns toward me, her gaze steady and warm. "It was the perfect kind of hurt," she says, still sleepy. "The kind that says you need me as much as I need you. We're going to get through this."

The certainty in her voice steals my breath. The look in her eyes steals my heart once more. She's so positive and upbeat even when she shouldn't be.

"We will," I say, confirming her hopes. "But there's something I need to ask you."

Her eyes flicker with curiosity. "What?"

My hands travel a thousand miles up and down her arm before I ask, "Do you want me to be this baby's father?"

The room goes so quiet I can hear my own heartbeat, and I don't know whether she heard me. But then I guess the shock wears off, and Noelle looks at me like I just gave her something precious instead of terrifying.

"Yes. I thought that was understood. You asked me to get

Brooks to sign away his rights, and then you asked me to move in."

My mouth curves into a smile. "I have one piece of advice for you, Butterfly. Dudes need exact information. Don't ever assume we know what's in your head... we think with the wrong one all too often."

She inches closer on the tangled sheets. "I want you to be the baby's father legally. Is that clear enough? I don't want you being able to walk out without a second thought. My baby deserves a fa... father," she chokes, her emotions swelling in her. "You don't have to marry me, but we have to have paperwork to protect *our* baby."

Something inside me breaks open.

We lie there for a long moment, just looking at each other, the future hovering between us like something fragile, yet bright and loving.

"Our baby. No more saying 'Noelle's baby.' Clear?"

This time it's me biting back a rush of tears. I never thought I would have a child once diabetes took hold. Over and over, I told myself I was fine being a bachelor until Noelle kissed me. Those little feelings I had for her before were brief since she was totally off-limits.

"I'm out of town the rest of the week," she says softly. "They're sending me to Oklahoma City to cover their game."

"Scout them for us," I tease. "Let me know all their weaknesses."

She snorts. "I can't. That's against the rules. I'll report on injuries, expectations... and maybe locker room gossip."

I grin. "I'm kidding. I've already dissected every angle of their game. We play them next Thursday."

"Of course you have," she laughs. "You're basically an O'Ryan."

"No, you're basically a Stricker."

We fall back asleep and end up having to race her to the airport to catch her flight. I kiss her goodbye longer than necessary, memorizing the feel of her in my arms. Then I head to the stadium.

What I think will be a meeting with J.D. turns out to be Sutton, Greyson, and J.D. waiting for me in the conference room.

"We owe you an apology," Sutton says. "We're not getting tested. We might need to be here for our kids one day. Or each other. But Dad wants to."

My chest tightens. "I'm still not taking one of your kidneys."

Greyson exhales. "We knew you would say that, but—"

"You all lost your mother in a hospital," I say quietly. "I won't let Noelle lose her father the same way. Not when Witt is just starting to come out of his shell. You all need your dad."

Noelle's words echo in my head—how Witt is finally peeking back into the world.

J.D. nods slowly. "We'll talk about it after practice."

When they leave, I sit alone for a moment, feeling something I haven't felt in a long time.

Hope.

Maybe all I needed was to make love to the woman I love. And have her want me to be her baby's father.

And she did.

THIRTY-EIGHT
NOELLE

Today is the day.

By the time we sit in the exam room for my twenty-week appointment, I already feel like we've crossed into a new season of our lives.

Matt is different lately. Not cured. Not magically healed. Just lighter and living in the moment. He jokes with the nurse, holds my hand without the scowl. He still has dialysis three times a week. His creatinine and potassium levels are stubborn, refusing to fall in line no matter how clean they scrub his blood. But he's stopped acting like every conversation is a countdown.

And that's a win. A huge win.

Our doctor moves efficiently, her voice calm and reassuring as she explains what she's seeing on the screen. I watch Matt's face more than the monitor. The way his eyes track every movement. The way his thumb rubs slow circles over my knuckles like he's grounding himself.

I officially added Matt as the father on the paperwork, so this is now our baby, and he's prouder and more invested than he is when the Armadillos win and their "Broken Play" works even when the opposing teams know it's in their bag of tricks.

These ultrasounds are amazing—3D and color. The doctor follows our baby from all directions and presses until she gets the shot she needs.

She looks at it from different directions and says, "Are you sure you want to know?"

Matt squeezes my hand and peers into my eyes. We nod. "Yes."

Here comes the moment I've been waiting for.

"It's a boy," she says.

Something inside me bursts open. I let out a breath I didn't know I was holding.

Matt exhales a sound that's half laugh, half disbelief. His eyes shine as he stares at the screen like he's memorizing every little curve of our baby boy's body.

"A boy," he repeats softly.

I squeeze his hand, overwhelmed by how right it feels.

Afterward, we go straight to a baby décor store because apparently that's what you do when the universe hands you confirmation that joy still exists. We wander aisles filled with tiny clothes, cribs, and impossibly small socks. Matt picks up a ridiculous football-themed onesie and holds it up.

"I can't wait to tell your brothers," he says, grinning. "Finally, a baby boy in the family."

I laugh, shaking my head. "They're going to hate you."

"They already do," he says cheerfully.

On the drive home, we talk about Oklahoma City—the Armadillos absolutely dismantling them on the field. A bloodbath.

"I hope the network doesn't think I did anything wrong," I admit. "I mean, I reported fairly."

"We beat them last year too," Matt says. "Twice. It's not a scandal. It's a pattern."

That steadiness again. The man who sees the big picture even when his body is fighting him.

"How is J.D. with you taking off half days three times a week?" I ask. "It's been over three months now."

He shrugs. "Winning is everything to J.D. As long as we're winning and I'm doing my job—which I am—he's fine."

Then he smirks. "It helps that I'm his sister's... baby daddy."

I make a face. "No. Just no."

He laughs. "Baby daddy."

"Stop. It sounds like all you are is a sperm donor and we're not actually together." Part of me wishes that I didn't know that Brooks is the biological father. Matt didn't donate the sperm, but he is this baby's father.

"Baby daddy."

"Matthew Allen Stricker."

He goes quiet.

The car fills with something heavier, softer. I don't know what tomorrow holds. I don't know when the call will come or if it will come soon. I don't know how long dialysis will work or what the future will demand of us.

What I do know is that we're not waiting for life to happen to us. We're living it.

"Butterfly," he says finally. "I'd marry you tomorrow. No questions asked. But I'll answer the one that matters and say I do."

"Ready when you are," I tease.

The tires on the car squeal as he does a U-turn. "To the courthouse we go." His smile is wider than a football field.

Is he taking me to the courthouse? I panic. "No, I need a dress at the very least. And there's a very good chance that my family would kill you if we got married without them."

"I know, babe. I'm taking you for deviled eggs."

"Ew, no," I gag. Even the thought sours my stomach.

"Just kidding. We're going through the drive-thru for ice cream before you and I go to work. Your special airs tonight, right?"

My hands fly to my chest. "I forgot in all the excitement."

"Will it feel weird to watch yourself for an entire hour?" he asks, briefly taking his eyes off the road to study me.

The interview is on Oklahoma City's offensive lineman. His family was in a car wreck, his brother was paralyzed, and Amari Brown came out of it without a scratch. There was no alcohol involved, no one to blame. Amari dedicates every game to his brother, who used to play right beside him all through high school. His brother skidded through an intersection on a rainy night, hydroplaning into a light post.

"A little. I hope I portrayed what I felt for him. I teared up three times in the interview. But what made me pitch this story to management was the way he smiles. The way Amari and his brother stay upbeat, positive. Amari says he's blessed that he has the money to buy the things his brother needs. Well, you watch it tonight and see how they play video games together and how they've built a business that his brother runs."

He smiles and says, "I wouldn't miss watching my baby mama." He cracks himself up, and I shake my head.

THIRTY-NINE
MATT

The phone rings at 4:02 a.m.

No one calls at four in the morning unless it matters. Unless it's *the* call—the one you've been waiting for while praying it's not the call telling you you're no longer a candidate for a transplant. That's happened plenty of times to my friends at dialysis. For a split second, fear spikes sharp and hot in my chest.

What if something goes wrong?

What if I don't wake up from surgery?

I shake the negative thoughts loose before they can take hold.

"Hello," I say.

"We have a kidney," the voice says calmly. "You need to be here within the hour. Tenth-floor check-in."

I can't believe my ears. "You have..."

"Yes, sir. Today's the day."

Thoughts swim through my head. My first transplant was from a living donor. A friend of my sister's. A woman who gave me an extra decade of life. Unfortunately, five years ago, the kidney started failing. The failure was attributed to the BK virus.

I roll the name around in my head like it might make more sense if I say it enough times. Something most people get as kids, something that goes quiet and behaves as long as your body knows how to fight back. It just sits there—harmless, dormant—inside healthy kidneys, waiting. But I take immunosuppressants for life, so my body won't reject the foreign kidney.

One thing I'm grateful for is that I have chronic kidney failure, the agonizingly slow kind. But at least it gave me time to meet the woman who has changed my life. My Butterfly.

Everything accelerates. Noelle is already sitting up, eyes wide, hair a mess, joy and terror colliding across her face. "Is it—?"

"Yes," I say, already swinging my legs over the side of the bed. "It's time."

The next ten minutes are chaotic. Drawers open and slam. Zippers scream. Shoes get kicked under the bed. I shove things into a bag without knowing what I'm packing—shirts, socks, chargers, probably something useless like a playbook.

"Greyson will pick up anything you forget," Noelle says, breathless, tugging on a hoodie. "Let's go. Let's go."

I catch her wrists, grounding us both. "Hey. Breathe. We've got this."

She laughs, tears shining. "I know. I'm just happy. So freaking happy."

"Me too." I wrap my arms around her, knowing this is our last squeeze for a long time. I'll have another incision, and I wonder if it will be in the same scar tissue or a brand new one. "Are you ready? If you or the baby needs anything, please take care of yourself first. Promise me?"

She promises, but I can't say I believe her. I call my sister as we pull onto the road and put her on speaker.

She answers groggily, a kid crying faintly in the background. "Matt?"

"I'm getting a new kidney today."

"What?" She's fully awake now. I can see her expression in my mind. Eyes wide open, mouth hanging. "Where are you? Give me the address—I'm on my way."

"No," I say quickly. "Stay. Noelle will keep you updated. It'll take all day to get here."

"No," she insists. "I'm coming."

Noelle cuts in without missing a beat. "Get to the private airport. Greyson will take care of it. J.D. will pick you up."

I open my mouth to argue. To shut it down. To protect everyone from this moment getting too big.

Then I stop.

I need to give Noelle this win. She needs to feel like she's in control, even though nothing about my surgery is in her control.

I lean back in my seat, staring at the road as memory floods in—my sister and me, years apart in age but somehow always orbiting the same world. Poker nights at the kitchen table, playing with nickels because quarters felt like real money. Her trash talk, just as brutal as mine. She loved sports as much as I did—knew stats, called plays, refused to be sidelined just because she was younger. She played football and baseball with all of us guys in the neighborhood.

She was stubborn. Loyal. Always showed up.

If something happened to me... I want her here. I want Noelle to have her. It hits me that Noelle is similar to my sister. Grew up a tomboy in a family of boys. Loves to feel pretty in dresses and skirts. Insanely honest and vulnerable.

The hospital is quiet in that eerie pre-dawn way—polished floors reflecting fluorescent lights, voices hushed like the building itself is holding its breath. They lead me into a room with pale walls and a single window just beginning to glow gray.

Noelle stands beside the bed, wearing a knit dress that hugs her baby bump, her hair in a messy nest on top of her head, her sneakers hastily tied. She looks radiant. Terrified. Alive. We wait. Several nurses come in to take my vitals or insert my ports for the IV bags.

My surgeon enters the room an hour or two later and explains what I mostly already know, since I've been through it before. But I let him go through his spiel, knowing Noelle needs information, direct from the doc.

We have a few minutes just us after the doc goes to scrub in and make sure his team is assembled in the operating room, and I can't stop talking, filling the space like noise might keep fear from sneaking in. Happiness pours from my tone. I have a chance, a good chance at being a husband and father. Of a life still driven by medication and doctor's appointments but not one where that is the focus. The focus will be my family.

The nurse comes in smiling, puts in a port, starts an IV, and gives me some medication. Noelle puts notes in her phone so she can tell everyone who is already gathering in the waiting room.

"Can you give us a minute?"

She smiles softly. "Of course." Noelle squeezes my hand when the nurse steps out.

I lift her dress and lean forward, pressing my lips to her

rounded belly. "Hey, buddy," I whisper. "Daddy's having surgery today. The doctors are top-notch, which is the reason I moved here and met your mom. I don't want you to worry about me. Be good for your mom. I love you, buddy."

She laughs quietly, tears slipping free. "He heard you. He kicked."

"Of course, he did," I say, resting my forehead there longer than necessary. Memorizing this. Just in case.

The transport nurse comes to wheel me out. I crack a joke about hospital gowns being the least sexy thing on the planet. The nurses laugh. Someone tells me to think happy thoughts.

As the sedation creeps in, the world softens—lights stretching, sounds echoing, reality blurring into something dreamlike. Somewhere between consciousness and sleep, I hold onto one truth.

I'm not doing this just to live.

I'm doing it for Noelle.

For the baby waiting to meet me.

And when I wake up, I plan to fight like hell to keep the life we've started building.

FORTY

NOELLE

The waiting room is too bright.

Not the warm kind of bright—clinical and unforgiving, like the lights are designed to give you a headache. And I have one. The chairs are arranged in neat rows that no one actually uses properly. Everyone hovers instead, pacing or perching on the edges, afraid that sitting down means settling into the waiting.

I clutch the water that I haven't touched and stare at the clock on the wall.

Matt went back twenty minutes ago.

The surgeon told us the transplant could take anywhere from four to six hours. That once they connect the kidney, they'll know quickly whether it's working—but that doesn't mean they'll be done. There are steps. Monitoring. Waiting. Always waiting.

Everyone is here except Paulina and J.D. She's at the tennis academy with her best friend today, and for once I'm grateful. She's too young for this kind of fear. Too young to sit in a room and wonder whether someone she loves will come back out alive. J.D. is picking up Matt's sister.

We are that kind of family. One that drops everything when needed, and today is one of those days. The quiet celebration with a side dish of fear of the unknown.

Dad sits stiff-backed in a chair, hands folded like he's bracing for bad news. Parker and Witt stand near the windows, talking quietly about nothing and everything. I've noticed they talk more since Parker said he wanted a relationship like Greyson's and J.D.'s. It's a start that both deserve.

Greyson paces, unable to stay still for more than thirty seconds at a time. Sutton rocks Witley gently in her carrier, murmuring to her like babies can absorb reassurance by osmosis.

When J.D. arrives with Matt's sister, I run to her. I don't even really know her. She's breathless from travel and adrenaline; I don't even say her name.

We just collapse into each other.

She sobs into my shoulder like she's been holding it together for years. Like she's finally letting go. I cling to her, our grief and hope tangling together until neither of us knows whose tears are whose.

"He taught me how to throw a spiral," she says through tears. "I was ten. He refused to let me quit until I got it right."

I smile weakly. "He's stubborn like that."

She laughs softly. "My feet are always cold, and we would sit at the kitchen table for dinner, and I would slide my toes under his thigh. At first he would jump, making some comment that he thinks I might be dead. My feet are like ice. I don't know if you know, but we're both sci-fi lovers. After school and practices, we would lie on the floor on our stomachs watching television together."

Piquing Witt's interest, he says, "Matt? Sci-fi?"

She grins. "He's always loved television shows, but sci-fi and of course MTV were the staples during the week at our house, leaving the weekends for live sports. And Saved by the Bell. I almost forgot that one. You must be Witt. He said you were the youngest sibling."

Witt's eyebrows raise. I think he's surprised that Matt would mention him.

Pointing to my belly, I say, "He still loves TV. We've been watching true crime lately, because we've had a lot of other things going on."

After introductions, Birdie clears her throat gently. "Okay," she says. "While we're all here losing our minds... let's talk about the baby shower."

The shift is subtle but intentional. A lifeline.

"Where do you want to have it?" she asks. "Your place? A venue?"

"And who are we inviting?" Sutton adds. "Because this family alone is a crowd."

"What about a theme?" Birdie presses. "Classic? Sports? Something neutral?"

I blink at them, startled—and then grateful. Matt's sister chimes in, "Matt had a best friend growing up who was a girl, Steph. She's already been blowing up my phone wanting details of the transplant. I know she would love to come celebrate the baby, and don't forget about Mom."

"I would never leave either of you out. We're practically family." Mrs. Stricker is coming to stay with us during Matt's recovery. She'll be here tomorrow. "Oh, and I'd like to invite my friend, Clara; she's been checking out baby books and bringing them over. And my producer and cameraman. That's it."

The women lean in, voices overlapping as they debate colors, decorations, and whether a football theme is too on-the-nose. Dad and the boys huddle a few feet away, talking quietly, their low voices a constant murmur of support.

I glance back at the clock.

Time hasn't moved nearly enough.

But for the first time since the doors closed behind Matt, I feel something steady settle into my chest.

We are not alone.

And when he comes back to us—because he will—I want him to know that his life is already surrounded by love, laughter, and plans for the future.

I press a hand to my belly and whisper silently, *Your daddy is coming back.*

Hours pass, gallons of coffee consumed. We've all taken turns grabbing lunch or a snack. There's no need for everyone to be here, but I'm glad they are.

Finally, the surgeon appears in his blue scrubs and takes off his paper hat, holding it in his hands. "Noelle," he calls out, and I stand up.

"Is he okay?"

"The surgery was flawless," he says confidently. Matt would like his cockiness. I know my family does. They want to be around people that are sure of themselves. "He'll be under sedation for another couple of hours so we can monitor him, and if anything changes, we can go back in without starting all over."

"What are the chances of something going wrong?" I hear the crack in my voice and try to stuff it down. He'll be fine.

"It just takes a while to see if his body is accepting the kidney. It's early. Don't worry. So far, it's been perfect."

Emotion overwhelms me, and I dive straight into his stomach, hugging him. "Thank you."

Tears fall. Right now, we can breathe.

Finally, the operating nurse comes out and says, "Noelle, you can see him now. He's very groggy, but he said your name, so I'll give you fifteen minutes. Then someone else can go in for a few minutes. I'm sorry everyone can't go in. His immune system will be really compromised for a while."

I can tell that Greyson really wants to go in, so I say, "You should go. I think his sister should be the one."

He shakes his head in agreement. "I'll get Witley and Sutton home. Tell him we were here, and if either of you needs us, call. Promise?"

"How about I tell him you love him?" I laugh as a happy tear slips down my cheek.

As I walk down the hallway, nurses and technicians are everywhere. What a difference from five in the morning until three in the afternoon. The nurse says, "He's in here. Here's a mask. Sanitize your hands. Fifteen minutes. I'll be back."

I take a deep breath and peek my head inside. Matt is lying flat on his back, eyes closed, and his head is raised just a smidge. As I get closer, he moves his head toward me like he hears something but isn't fully aware yet. I survey the room and him. Every monitor beeping, tracking. A pillow placed under his knees. And the gown he's wearing is different from the one he went into surgery with—it's blue with little ditties on it instead of the gray one he had on earlier. It makes me wonder why they changed him. Blood?

Pushing the thought from my head, I sit in the teal-green faux-leather chair with wooden arms. I caress his hand until his eyes flutter open. The smallest grin appears. "Hey."

"Hey. Don't talk. Just rest."

"I..."

"Shh... let me talk. The doctor said it went swimmingly. He was cocky."

Matt murmurs, "I... like... that."

"I knew you would. That's why you picked him, right?" His head moves minutely up and down.

"Greyson and his family just left, and he wanted me to tell you he loves you." Matt grins again.

"In fact, everyone was here. Even Witt. Parker said something about getting a tutor who he hates. The girls want to plan a baby shower. And your sister told me that you always kept her feet warm and that you're a secret nerd who loves sci-fi." Another grin.

Is he still drugged? No comebacks?

"Are you in pain?"

"Not yet. Are you okay?"

"I'm fine. You just had a transplant. Don't worry about me."

"Worrying about you is my job. A job I want. I applied for it, remember?" he asks, his voice weak and frail.

"When you became my coach?"

"Yeah, and then I fell in love with a girl who sits on the counter and swings her feet, who loves milkshakes and deviled eggs." He laughs and yelps in pain.

"No joking right now. I'm not sure how many stitches you have, but for now, you just lie there."

"I love you, Butterfly."

"I love you, Coach." I lean down and kiss his forehead through the paper mask. "Your sister is champing at the bit to see you, so I'm going to let her come in before the nurse kicks me out."

The couch creaks when I shift, and for a second, I'm back there again—flat on my back, the bed tipped just enough to keep me still, pillows wedged under my knees like they were afraid I'd break myself if I moved wrong. I remember the way the incision pulled every time I breathed too deep, the weight of my own body feeling foreign, fragile, like I was being held together by instructions and IV lines. Five days in that room. Nurses in and out, numbers on screens, someone always reminding me not to twist, not to sit up too fast, not to rush what couldn't be rushed.

I'm home, cleared from the hospital but not free. No lifting. No driving. Pills lined up like soldiers, alarms telling me when my body needs help staying alive. Recovery isn't dramatic—it's slow and quiet and measured in small wins.

Standing without bracing my hand against the counter.

Falling asleep without feeling like I'm guarding something fragile inside me.

The kidney is working. I'm healing. But everything still feels careful, like one wrong move could send me right back to that bed, staring at the ceiling, learning how to trust my body again.

A month after surgery, I walk a mile every morning.

Not fast. Not like I used to. Just steady laps around the park's walking trail while the sun is just coming up, when there are fewer people around. I have to be careful, and so does everyone around me. The doctor said walking is encouraged, if I listen to my body. I've become very good at listening. This time, I'm older and listening.

I can shower on my own now. That felt like a victory I didn't know I'd crave so badly until I had it back. No baths yet. No soaking. Just warm water and careful movements, one hand braced against the wall while I wash around the incision instead of over it.

Independence comes back in pieces.

I still can't lift more than ten pounds.

Which means I can't help Noelle the way I want to.

She's getting bigger every week, the curve of her belly unmistakable now. Watching her struggle to bend over while I stand uselessly beside her might be the hardest part of recovery. My body is healing, but protecting the people I love is an instinct, and sometimes I do normal things that set me back.

My mom's in her late fifties and can bend over much easier than Noelle or me. She's been staying with us since the surgery, moving through the house like she's always belonged here. Cooking. Folding laundry. Sitting with Noelle, getting to know the woman I love when I need to rest as they video-call with Shelley. Mom doesn't hover—she never has—but she watches me with a quiet awareness that reminds me she's been here before. Hospitals. Waiting rooms. Fear dressed up as patience.

"She's glowing," Mom says one afternoon, nodding toward Noelle as she shuffles past with a basket of laundry.

Noelle scoffs. "That's sweat."

Mom stops and smiles. "No matter. You're still glowing."

"She's in love with you, you know," I say as I saunter toward her, wanting so much to show her how much I love her but knowing I can't. It doesn't stop her from flashing me her boobs. Talk about incentive to recover quickly. Her ta-tas are the best medicine.

"Not as much as you love these." Smirking, she dares me to touch her while my mom is in the other room. I waste no time, squeezing her mango-sized boobs. I kiss the space above her chest. "I can't wait to be inside you again. Mom is going out to dinner tonight. Evidently, she met a friend at the café down the street, so we can have some alone time."

"A guy? Did she meet a guy or a girl?"

"She put on makeup and jewelry, so I think it's a man."

"Could be a woman. But probably a man. I'm so excited. She shouldn't have to go through life alone. She's too fun. Like the mother I didn't have."

Gingerly, I tuck her under my arm. "She's happy to play any role you want her to."

She presses to her toes and places a sweet, slow peck on my lips.

Each day I'm getting better but also bored. Noelle works and travels. Greyson gives me the idea to run Zoom calls with the quarterbacks, receivers, and tight ends. We review film of their footwork, timing. Greyson stops by daily, either before practice or after, bringing updates and pretending he's not checking my color, my energy, the steadiness of my hands.

Life is moving forward.

"So, I think I'll be ready to go back to the facility in a few weeks," I say, testing her reaction.

Fear sits like a veil over her face. "It's too soon. Too many people," she says, putting her hands on her hips like it's settled. "You're not risking it yet."

"Not on the field or the sideline. Meetings first, in person. I'm not risking anything," I argue. "I'm easing back in."

Noelle hates that plan.

She gives me *that look.* "We were given a second chance. You almost died."

"I didn't."

"You were *close enough.*"

I shut up after that. It's a month away, so we can decide then. No sense in arguing over something so far down the road.

Her baby shower is next Monday. Mom leaves afterward —she insists she doesn't want to overstay her welcome. And Noelle and I need time alone. We're both desperate for some intimacy, even if it's just kissing. I don't want her thinking she's no longer desired because she's pregnant. In fact, it's the opposite. If I wasn't recuperating, she would be begging me to leave her alone.

I'm mid-Zoom call when Noelle appears in the doorway, arms crossed.

"Are you working again?"

"I'm coaching."

"You're tired."

I am.

The kind of tired that settles deep in the bones. The kind that doesn't show up until you stop moving. I close my laptop. "Okay."

She softens instantly, crossing the room and pressing a kiss to my temple. "Rest."

I lean back, watching her waddle toward me, my hand instinctively finding her belly. "Okay." I need to be what she needs right now. A month ago, I wasn't entirely sure I would survive a second transplant. Now I'm planning a future.

When she leaves for work, I lie down and email the jeweler I have designing an engagement ring. I can't help but smile. It's perfect, like my girl.

I click the remote from the couch and catch Noelle on the broadcast of our game against the New Orleans Blacksmiths. J.D. and Greyson assured me they would watch out for Noelle. You never know what Brooks will do or say. I just hope the NDA he signed means something and he won't let anything slip.

The analysts throw it to Noelle at halftime as she asks J.D., "How are you containing the New Orleans offense?"

"We're taking the long ball away from them. And our G is performing out of this world."

"Coach, I know who G is, but the audience may not."

He chuckles. "Sorry, Greyson."

The third quarter starts, and the New Orleans quarterback throws it to Brooks. He jumps to catch the ball and is hit from both sides by the Armadillo defense. He lies on the ground. Not moving.

I wait in front of the television for Noelle. What's her reaction? Will she run to his sideline? She's carrying his baby. Fuck. Finally, they help him off the field and take him into the injury tent. The game continues, and the Blacksmiths punt to us. We take over the ball on the forty-two-yard line.

"Cinderella 42 Black," I shout at the screen. "Call it. Call it, J.D.!"

Great minds think alike because Greyson throws a low stinger to the running back—which is why it's called **Cinderella**, because it's at the receiver's shoes; **42** is for four yards downfield; and **Black** means we're making money on this play. The defense is pulled to the left while the running back is going right. He gains ten more yards after the catch for a first down. Greyson drives the field in eight plays for another touchdown.

When New Orleans's offense takes the field, there's no Brooks. At the next television timeout, two faces fill the screen: Noelle and Brooks.

"I wanted to give you an update on the injury from Brooks Pendleton from the man himself. What happened out there?" She maintains a steady voice, but I heard the hitch when she used the word *man*.

His eyes are trained on her baby bump. All I can think is for him to hold up his end of the NDA.

"A dirty play by the Armadillos, that's what happened."

"No doubt the secondary hit you hard, but that's their job," Noelle says matter-of-factly. "Are you in concussion protocol?"

His eyes narrow. "No. Broken ribs."

"How long will you be out?"

"I'm going back in on the next series," he claims. There's no way they'll put him back in when they're down by twenty-one points nearing the fourth quarter.

Brooks takes a few steps backward. Noelle lifts her shoulders and lets them fall as she says, "That doesn't seem smart. That's all from the New Orleans sideline. Armadillos

35, Blacksmiths 14. We'll have to wait and see if Pendleton gets back into the game."

Noelle O'Ryan is one hell of a reporter. Knowing Brook's baby grows inside her, she's a complete professional. There wasn't a hint of a flirtatious smile or one that showed she regrets any of the choices she made.

I text her.

Me: That must have been hard to stand beside him, pregnant.

Noelle: He's a mentally stunted jackass.

Me: He's regretting not treating you like the woman you are.

Noelle: Honestly, I don't care. I hope he finds someone to change his ways.

Me: You're way more forgiving than I am.

Noelle: He doesn't have someone that loves him like I do.

Me: True. No one could love you more than me.

Noelle: It's time you show me how much ;)

Me: Thought you would never ask.

Noelle: I'm not asking. I'm demanding. I need to feel your touch.

Me: My hands are ready to meet your demands.

Steph arrives.

She's Matt's childhood best friend and I have to admit, jealousy clogs my throat. "I brought the chips," she cackles as she flashes a contagious smile. "It's a perfect time to play. Who's in?"

Matt says, "After the shower, we'll play for quarters."

"Come on, Matt. We're adults. Let's up the ante."

"I don't think I should let you take my wife's money the first time you meet her."

They tell a million stories from middle school and high school and how she would wreck every hookup he had. I like this woman. Shelley and his mom explain to me when they can't because they're laughing nonstop.

I never had a friend like that. I was always friends with guys, but I never had one special best friend. I hope my son is like Matt.

The baby shower feels like a celebration and a victory lap rolled into one.

Everyone wears a mask, except for me. My doctor

doesn't want me to wear one. I love her because she's sensible. But Matt's eyes are bright, his posture stronger than it's been in weeks.

He stands off to the side with Greyson, J.D., and Parker, all of them balancing plates piled high with brunch food like it's a competitive sport, lowering their masks when they shovel food into their mouths.

"Winning streak," Greyson says, shaking his head. "Maybe we should keep you virtual."

Matt chuckles. "Don't get used to it."

J.D. grins. "I don't know. The team's doing great. You sure you want to mess with the chemistry?"

"Stop needling my boyfriend." I nudge Greyson's arm.

Greyson laughs. "Hear that? Boyfriend."

I roll my eyes. Surely they're used to our status by now. I know they are, but my brothers love to tease. The smiles between them. I'm not sure if I should be happy or fearful.

I feel a prank coming.

Once Clara shows up and I make introductions, everyone piles their plates high—Texas Twinkies, grilled chicken dippers, zucchini fries, fruit, and way too many desserts. The room hums with excitement and anticipation of the baby to come.

Matt clears his throat. The conversation fades.

He reaches for my hand and draws me beside him. My heart starts racing.

"I'm not great at speeches," he says, his voice steady but soft. "But I'm great at knowing when something matters."

He turns to me. "Noelle, you came into my life when I wasn't looking for anything. You made me laugh. You challenged me. You taught me how to love when I didn't think I was allowed to anymore."

A tear slips free before I can stop it.

"You gave me a family," he continues. "You gave me a future. And you're giving me the greatest gift of my life."

He drops to one knee.

The room gasps as he opens the box. Inside is a ring—an oval center stone, flanked by diamonds shaped like butterfly wings.

"Butterfly," he says softly. "Will you marry me?"

I can't breathe. I can't think. I can only nod and whisper, "Yes." I break into tears. So happy. So fulfilled. I'm in disbelief that he managed to pull this off while recovering from a transplant.

"How?"

"I'm capable of online shopping and emailing the jeweler to give you a ring as unique as you. Your brother picked it up for me."

We kiss like no one is in the room, and when we part, the room erupts—cheers, tears, applause. He slides the ring onto my finger, stands, and kisses me like this moment is etched into his bones.

When the congratulatory hugs are finished, I open gifts. A hand-knit blanket from Birdie. A framed family tree print from Sutton. Tiny boots from Paulina with a note that says *for my first little buddy boy.*

My producers and colleagues sent a huge chenille basket full of clothes, baby toiletries, toys, and teethers with a gift card.

Matt bends to grab the next bag and begins to sway.

"Matt?"

He crumples in slow motion.

The room explodes into chaos. Someone calls 911. Greyson drops to his knees beside him. I'm frozen, my heart pounding so loud I can't hear myself scream his name.

The paramedics move fast. Blood pressure cuff. IV. Calm voices over panic.

"His blood pressure is dangerously low," one of them says. "We're stabilizing him now."

Matt's eyes flutter open. He looks at me, pain and sorrow flooding his gaze.

"I can't do this to you," he whispers. "To you and the baby. It's too much."

And then they wheel him away.

And everything I thought we had secured slips through my fingers.

FORTY-THREE
MATT

By day three, I don't recognize myself.

The numbers on the monitor refuse to cooperate—blood pressure still too low, alarms chirping like they're mocking us. The doctors have tried medication after medication, adjusting doses until my body feels like a chemistry experiment gone wrong. My veins burn, my head swims, and they've switched IV bags more times than I can count, since I'm asleep more than I'm awake.

No, that's not right.

It feels like I'm suspended between consciousness and sleep, never fully in either one. And I'm afraid if I let my mind relax and stop fighting to stay present—I won't be strong enough to come back.

The doctors speak in careful voices just outside the curtain, as if whispering will keep the truth from being true. They have no idea how to help me. They're out of meds to try. Doc has called in the top cardiologist in Texas, and still, I'm dying.

I feel it in my bones.

The weakness.

The fading.

Noelle sits beside me, her body curled into the hospital chair that isn't made for a pregnant woman. She's afraid to leave even for a second. Her hair is pulled back, with dark circles under her eyes, one hand always on my arm, my chest—anywhere she can remind herself I'm still warm.

Alive.

I hate that I'm doing this to her.

"Butterfly?" When I speak, my voice sounds smaller than I expect, like it's already leaving me. She turns, only half awake herself. Her lids open sluggishly, searching for my face. "You need to listen to me," I say.

Her head snaps up, suddenly fully present. "Don't."

"I mean it," I push, even though it takes more effort than it should. "You don't get to pretend this isn't happening."

Her eyes are veiled with tears, defiant and broken all at once. "I'm not pretending. You'll be okay."

I shake my head slowly. "That's the problem. You're not allowing yourself to see what is happening. I'm... dying."

She stands so fast the chair scrapes loudly. "You are not. Do not say that."

I look at her—really look. The woman carrying my child. The woman I love more than my own heartbeat. The woman who deserves mornings and decades and a man who can stand beside her without monitors and nurses and fear.

I lie quietly as my own tears roll down my nose and over my lips. "Noelle, loving you was a forbidden play I wasn't supposed to make," I say quietly. "But I'd call that play again. Every time. But I won't let it cost you your life, waiting for me to die, or cause stress on our baby."

She shakes her head, tears spilling. "Stop talking like this." Her words are broken and weak.

"I love you," I say. "God, Noelle, I love you. But you don't deserve a dying man. You deserve someone who can lift you when you're tired. Someone who can chase our son through the yard. Who won't make you count pills or watch numbers on a screen."

Her hand presses over her mouth, a sob breaking free, an ugly cry that shows her soul.

Her love.

Her beauty.

"I wanted forever," I admit. "I wanted to be your husband. I wanted to be in the delivery room when our son was born. I wanted to throw touchdowns with him and have birthday parties for him. Drench you in whipped cream and... but wanting doesn't change biology. Or fate. Or the fact that my body keeps failing me."

She leans over me, forehead pressed to mine, tears falling onto my skin. "You're not allowed to leave," she whispers. "You promised."

I close my eyes because if I don't, I won't be strong enough to finish this.

"I'm not leaving you because I don't love you," I say. "I'm leaving because I do."

And when she finally breaks—when the sound she makes rips through me deeper than any pain—I know I've shattered both our hearts.

But loving her was never a mistake.

FORTY-FOUR
NOELLE

I'm not leaving him or this hospital.

No matter what he says. No matter how tired he looks. No matter how gently—or not so gently—he tries to push me away.

When Matt finally dozes off, his breathing uneven but steady, I slip out into the waiting room. My legs feel hollow, like if I stop moving, they'll fold beneath me.

His mom looks up immediately. So does my dad.

I don't bother sitting.

"Why is he doing this?" My voice breaks on the last word. "Why is he pushing me away like he's already gone?"

Mrs. Stricker's face softens in that way only mothers can manage—like she's carried this fear longer than anyone. "Because he's scared," she says quietly. "He doesn't want to see the finality in your eyes if this doesn't go his way."

I swallow hard. My future hangs in my throat.

"He's tired," she continues. "Exhausted from years of managing this. But I promise you something—" She meets my gaze. "I have never seen my son happier. Not when he won the state championship in high school. Not when he dated other women. Not when he won the Super Bowl with the Heavyweights."

My chest tightens painfully.

"Why are you giving up?" I whisper before I can stop myself. "My mom wouldn't have—"

I freeze. "Oh God. I'm sorry. I shouldn't have said that."

My dad steps forward, steady and calm. "Your mom would tell you the same thing Mrs. Stricker just did," he says gently. "Give him room. He only wants your happiness."

I shake my head fiercely. "I'm not letting him die. Not like this. Who can we call? Can he get another kidney? Can one of you—" My voice rises, desperate now. "Matt doesn't get to die on me."

I glance down at my ring. At my belly.

"Not when we have so many milestones left."

We stand in silence, and my dad holds me, rubs my back, strokes my hair, and assures me that Matt loves me. I don't know how much time has passed when the doctor approaches.

"Noelle, we're not sure how long this will hold," he says carefully. "And we're still fine-tuning the medication. But his blood pressure is rising into normal ranges. We're not quite there yet... but there's reason to be hopeful."

Hope.

The word nearly buckles my knees.

I hug my dad hard. "Call Greyson and J.D."

Parker appears then, backpack slung over one shoulder, eyes wide. "Can I see him?"

"Wash up," the nurse says. "Mask up. I'll sneak you in," she adds. "If it's all right with Noelle."

When we reach Matt's room, Parker drops his bag with a soft thud. I hold up a finger. To be quiet.

"Do you mind if I talk to him alone... if he wakes up?"

I nod. "Of course."

Matt stirs, and when he opens his eyes, I hover just outside the open door, listening.

"You better not be missing school because of me," Matt murmurs. "I'm not that important."

"Oh, you're important," Parker says without hesitation. "I can't imagine my sister if you die."

The word lands like a punch.

Die.

Parker said it out loud. Maybe I'm the only one still pretending it's impossible.

"I'm fighting," Matt says quietly. "I just don't know if it's enough. Talk to me about school. I'm sick of talking about me."

Parker sighs. "Well, I'm failing physiology. The athletic department assigned me a tutor. They want to make sure I can play in the championship game."

"Okay?" Matt asks.

"The waitress from the pizza parlor. She's in two of my classes and she sits in the front row. Passes me like she doesn't remember me. Smartass. Kind of bland. Nothing special."

Bland? Nothing special?

Is that really my sweet brother talking like that?

Matt huffs softly. "Sounds a little harsh."

"She thinks I'm a dumb jock."

"Honestly," Matt says, "you sound like one right now. Want my advice?"

"That's why I'm here talking to a half-dead man so he can't tell my secrets."

"Your dad doesn't know you're failing one of four classes?" Matt's voice sounds like he's finding his footing. Not quite as strained as four hours ago.

Parker mumbles, "No, and I don't want him to find out."

"Then suck it up. Do the work. Graduate. Not everyone makes it to the NFL—the average career is two years. Did you know that? Put in the effort with your pizza parlor tutor."

I step back into the room, unable to stop smiling. "You haven't talked that much since you told me you were dying," I tease softly. "Which I didn't listen to, so it doesn't count."

Matt reaches for my hand. "Come here. I feel better. For some reason."

"Divine intervention," I say, squeezing his fingers. "The doctors say your blood pressure's improving. They might've found the right cocktail."

I turn to Parker. "And you—check your attitude. Don't be a Brooks. Be Parker. You've got so much love to give."

He nods quickly. "I'll call everyone."

After he leaves, Matt runs his hand over my belly. "We're getting so close to meeting our son."

"He's been tossing and turning. He may be a platform diver."

"He's telling you to go home and get some rest. Little buddy is smart."

The doctor steps in again.

"Did you tell him the good news?"

"I did, but I'm sure he wants to hear it from you."

"If your numbers stay up for two days," the doctor says gently, "we'll let you go home."

Home.

The word barely registers at first. I look at Matt then—really look at him—and for the first time in days, he doesn't feel like he's slipping through my fingers. The gray tint that haunted his skin has softened, warmth slowly returning to his cheeks. His eyes lift to mine, tired but unmistakably present, holding me like he's anchoring himself here. His breathing evens out, his shoulders sinking into the pillows instead of fighting them, and something tight and crushing in my chest finally loosens.

"Home?" Matt asks, with a lift in his voice.

"Yes," the doctor confirms. "Your blood pressure is the only concern now. Every other marker looks excellent."

Matt's fingers curl weakly around mine. "You hear that, Butterfly?" he murmurs. "I'm still stubborn enough to stick around."

I press my forehead to his, swallowing past the lump in my throat. It's not a miracle. It's not the end of the fight. But it's hope.

It's a start.

And for the first time since the ambulance doors closed, Matt is letting himself believe we get the future we've been dreaming of.

The field feels different under my feet.

Not unfamiliar—never that—but sharper somehow. Like I'm more aware of every step, every breath, every inch of space between me and the players I'm coaching. I keep my distance, careful, deliberate, except for the quarterbacks. Greyson. The backups. And J.D., who hovers close enough to check my face every few minutes like he's waiting for me to vanish again.

I hold the tablet up, drawing lines with my finger. "They're going to blitz. Over and over. They think they can rattle you early. You see this?" I tap the screen. "That linebacker cheats left every time."

Greyson nods. "So, we burn them?"

"We punish them," I say. "Quick release. Trust the read."

The public address announcer cuts in. "Fans, please direct your attention to the video board as we celebrate one of our own—"

I keep talking. "If they bring pressure on third—"

"Matt," Greyson says.

"Are you listening?" I snap, eyes still on the tablet.

He jerks his chin upward. "Are *you*? We're supposed to be looking at the Jumbotron."

I look up.

And the world tilts.

My face fills the screen—older, thinner than I remember, but unmistakably me. Then Noelle's voice carries through the stadium, calm and strong and steady in that way she gets when she's telling a story that matters.

"Matt is probably going to be upset about this," she says, smiling softly at the camera. "But my career is about finding stories. Reporting on stories."

My chest tightens.

"This one will be airing in its entirety on the Sports Network this Tuesday at nine p.m. But since my brother coaches this team, my sister-in-law is the general manager, my brother is the quarterback, and my fiancé is the quarterbacks coach... I thought it was important that you see first what Coach Matt Stricker has gone through—and survived."

Images flash.

Me on dialysis.

Me hunched over a tablet, working when I shouldn't have been.

Zoom calls from my living room. Hospital rooms. IV lines.

"This game gave him something when his body was failing him," Noelle continues. "A distraction. A purpose. Something to hold onto during weeks in the hospital and months of recovery."

Noelle's cheeks have rounded now that she's in the third

trimester, her hair is thicker, and she really is glowing. She's been my rock. Never giving up on me. Never.

The screen shifts.

The proposal.

The embrace.

Her face when I collapsed.

The terror in her eyes—I have to look away for a second.

Then surgery. Recovery. Pictures with the O'Ryan clan. My sister. My mom. Noelle laughing again.

"All of you," she says, her voice breaking just slightly, "your messages, your letters, your support—it gave me the strength to help him fight. And I hope seeing his story reminds you that whatever you're facing... you can make it. You can beat it." She chokes up.

Silence crashes over the stadium.

Then the chant starts.

"MATT! MATT! MATT!"

Then a live feed flashes to Noelle in her seat with her hands tenting her nose. I can't imagine how hard this was for her to put together. And the emotions she's had to relive. She continues to amaze me. Not that long ago, she was a scared, beaten-down young woman in need of comfort and a kiss. Who knew that would turn into fake dating and then to where we are now.

Engaged.

In love.

A baby on the way.

And the strongest woman I've ever known. A woman I know is strong enough to weather any storm that comes our way.

I stand there, stunned, lost in thought, as the camera zooms in on me and captures the tears I didn't even realize were there. Greyson grips my shoulder. J.D. clears his throat and pretends he's fine.

The announcer comes on again. "Thank you for sharing your journey, Coach Stricker. Now it's Dilllllooooo time."

Greyson runs out on the field with the other captains for the coin flip. We win the toss and elect to receive the ball. The roar of the crowd races through my veins. I laugh to myself.

Life is good.

Late in the fourth quarter, we're down by four. I lean in, heart pounding, and call the play I drew up months ago—back when I wasn't sure I'd ever stand on this field again.

Greyson and LaRue execute it perfectly. Touchdown.

We win. The crowd jumps and dances, and the guys hoist me on their shoulders when it should be Greyson or LaRue. And the fans refuse to leave, chanting my name. A name they may not have known before my kidney failed and failed again. I stand in the back of the locker room—I really shouldn't even be in a confined area with all the sweat and germs—but I want to see the celebration in the guys' eyes. This is why I love football.

Later, Noelle and I celebrate somewhere quiet, away from cameras and noise. She's glowing, hand on her belly, her eyes bright. We drove out to Andy's Deli. It's far away from the city lights and people.

"I want pickles dipped in a chocolate shake," she announces.

I grimace. "That's disgusting."

She arches her brow. "You made me drink almond milk for weeks."

"That was for the baby."

"This is for the baby," she says sweetly, sliding the glass toward me.

Although I'm very strict about what I eat, I'll do anything for this woman, and this proves it. I take the pickle spear from my plate and dunk it into the thick chocolate. I was right. Disgusting. The two should never be eaten together.

She laughs like she's won something important.

But I'm the winner of this game. I scored her.

FORTY-SIX
NOELLE - SIX MONTHS LATER

Two things become apparent.

One—our son has lungs like a stadium full of fans on third down.

Two—Matt Stricker is *never* right when he questions me. Even when he absolutely thinks he is.

"See?" I say smugly, shifting our sleeping newborn in my arms. "I told you he'd like the noise."

Rocking the bassinet with his foot, Matt whispers, "He staged a protest for nearly an hour." He shakes his head, smiling down at our baby. "O'Ryan drama genes."

I grin as we sneak out of the nursery. "We are not dramatic."

"Your family—*our* family—is the very definition of dramatic. A picture of the O'Ryan clan is next to the word in the dictionary. J.D. proposes on a concert stage. Dramatic. Greyson runs off the field like a knight in shining armor to save his boss. Dramatic. You make a video about me and share it with the world. Dramatic."

"Well, Parker and Witt aren't."

He lets out a hushed scoff. "Maybe Witt isn't. We'll see, but do you remember that Parker quit the UMich hockey team because his girlfriend cheated, and how he hates his tutor and is always talking about it? Dramatic."

"But you love us," I smirk.

"I do, and I wouldn't have it any other way." He leans over and gives me an open-lipped kiss, slightly damp with a little bit of tongue, and I moan into his mouth.

It's been a while since we've had sex. Months, in fact. His recovery. My delivery was harder than expected, and pure exhaustion has won this game.

Our living room looks like a baby store exploded—tiny jerseys, burp cloths, and diapers tucked into every possible drawer. The Armadillos logo is everywhere because apparently, my family believes football loyalty should begin at birth.

The baby monitor crackles. Our son sighs in his sleep. My heart melts instantly. "Look at him. He's perfect."

He really is.

Dark hair. Long fingers. A grip that already feels like he could throw a spiral fifty yards. When Matt holds him, I see it—the quiet awe, the gratitude, the way he looks at our baby like this moment is stitched into his soul.

"You okay?" I ask softly.

He nods. "Yeah. Just thinking about how I almost missed this."

I press a kiss to his jaw. "But you didn't."

We didn't rush anything—not the wedding, not the season, not the healing. Life slowed us down whether we wanted it to or not. And somehow, that made everything sweeter.

Matt's back at the stadium full-time now. Stronger.

Healthier. Slightly more annoying, according to Greyson. The doctors call it a miracle.

I call it stubbornness, love, and a hell of a support system.

I stretch beside him, yawning. "When he wakes up again, you're on diaper duty."

"I changed the last one," he says.

I lift a brow. "When you married me, I had 'do everything I say' added to the marriage license."

He laughs and pulls me close. "We'll see about that."

We can't take our eyes off the monitor. Our son stirs, fists waving, already demanding attention like he owns the place.

"Thank you for letting me be his father."

I don't have time to respond before Matt kisses me, and my heart feels so full it almost hurts. Our need is hot and desperate. And even if our bodies aren't ready, we're ready to risk it.

Some plays are risky.

Some break every rule.

But the forbidden plays?

They're the ones that change your life.

EPILOGUE

PARKER – THREE YEARS LATER

The ball hits my hands—and drops.

Not a bad throw. Not wind. Not sweat.

Just me, a professional wide receiver not being able to catch a damn football.

I stare down at the grass like it personally betrayed me, my chest tight in a way that has nothing to do with conditioning and everything to do with fear. The kind that doesn't hit all at once but creeps in, quiet and relentless.

Not the awkward kind. The heavier kind.

Matt doesn't react. He never does when it matters. Just bends, picks up the ball, and hands it back to his kid. "Again."

My jaw tightens.

He rears back and throws it to me.

Same thing. My timing's off. My hands don't trust what my eyes already know. Something I never had to think about before.

I step back, drag my hands down my face. I mutter, "Need water."

Matt studies me like he's watching film. Doesn't push. He never does. Always positive and calm, but I can see the worry lines stretching across his forehead.

"Again, Daddy!" my nephew shouts.

Matt grins. "All right, all right. Last one. Then it's bath time."

I walk to the patio, running my hands through my hair. My body feels fine. Strong. Fast. Healthy. I've passed every physical, every drill, every metric the Austin Armadillos care about.

But lately, when it matters most, when instinct should take over—I hesitate.

That half-second is everything in this league.

Noelle appears beside me, carrying a tray of lemonade like this is just another late summer evening and not the slow unraveling of my career. She searches my face the way she always does, like she's reading a story no one else notices.

"You want to talk?" she asks gently.

I exhale. "I've talked to everyone. Dad, J.D., Greyson. Matt. Even Witt." My family hasn't been able to help.

"And?"

"Everyone keeps asking if I'm overthinking." I swallow. "I don't think I am. I think something's wrong."

She doesn't dismiss my opinion. That's her gift.

Before she can say anything, my phone buzzes in my pocket.

Sutton: Call me.

Sutton's the general manager of the team and my sister-in-law, so I step away and call. "What's up?"

"We made you an appointment," Sutton says, brisk but kind. "Sports psychologist. Tomorrow at ten."

My stomach drops. "I didn't—"

"You didn't ask," she finishes. "But you didn't have to. This isn't punishment. It's support."

I glance back at the yard. Matt has his arm around my nephew, his other hand steadying his kid's tiny throw. Just like Dad did with me.

"Okay," I say finally.

"Good. You'll get a text."

The call ends. A second later, my phone buzzes again.

ANNA MORROW, PSYD — APPOINTMENT CONFIRMED

Tomorrow | 10:00 AM

I walk back toward Noelle, already annoyed at myself for the tension climbing my spine. For somehow getting into this situation where I need help.

"Who was it?" she asks.

"Sutton set up an appointment with a... sports psychologist."

Noelle tilts her head. "Who?"

"Anna Morrow."

Her brows lift slightly. "Oh."

"'Oh' what?" I ask, hiding my fear in a glass of lemonade.

"I know her," Noelle says. "From work. A lot of guys swear by her. Say she helped them through career-ending stuff."

Great. She helps desperate players.

I barely sleep through the night. Nervous about my career. Afraid of being mocked. More afraid of a doctor digging around in my head. An O'Ryan should be able to fix it themselves. I mean it's fucking football—my family's legacy.

The next morning, I sit in my truck outside her office, gripping the steering wheel like it might keep me from bolting.

This is stupid.

I don't need this.

Still, I go in.

The waiting room is quiet. Too clean. Too calm.

"Parker O'Ryan?"

I look up. The doctor's gaze locks on mine.

Recognition hits.

Annika stands in the doorway with a tablet tucked to her chest, hair pulled back, posture controlled. Same warm eyes. Same closed-off calm that always felt like a challenge.

My college tutor.

Who hates me with a passion.

"You've got to be kidding me," I mumble under my breath.

Her lips press together. "I could say the same." Then she locks back into professional mode. "Come on back."

I follow her down the hall into an office that looks intentionally neutral—no sports posters, no motivational crap. Just space. Silence.

I stay standing.

She notices. "Have a seat."

"I'm good."

Her eyebrow arches. "You're here because you're not."

She settles across from me with a tablet balanced on her knee. "Before we start—this is confidential."

I'm sitting across from Annika once again. She never

bought my bullshit in college, and although I passed the class, she didn't make it easy on me.

"I'm not here to relive senior year tutoring," I say.

Her jaw tightens. "You always reduce things when you're uncomfortable."

"And you always psychoanalyze when someone disagrees with you."

Her eyes flash. "I was right about you back then."

"And you were annoying," I shoot back. "Always acting like you had me figured out." My eyes daring her to kick me out.

She exhales slowly. "You didn't make it difficult."

I scoff. "I showed up."

"Late."

"I passed."

"Barely."

"I went pro." I twist my lips while strumming my fingers on my knee.

"And yet," she says evenly, "you're sitting in my office."

Silence slams between us.

She studies me, then asks calmly, "Why are you here, Parker? The Armadillos made the appointment and wanted me to go in blind without any preconceived notions of what you need."

Something snaps.

I stand so fast the chair scrapes loudly across the floor.

"Forget it," I growl. "This was a mistake." I head for the door, anger burning hot in my chest—not at her, not really, but at the fact that she sees me too clearly.

I yank the door open.

"Parker."

I don't stop.

The door slams behind me, echoing down the hall. "Run if you want," she calls after me, her voice sharp and steady. "But you'll be back."

I pause, fist clenched at my side.

"You can't stand not knowing why you're stuck," she continues. "And you hate even more that it might mean you're not automatically better than your brothers."

Well, there goes her professionalism.

Her accusation hits hard. My feet stutter as I walk out, letting the truth follow me all the way back to my SUV.

She's right.

I'll be back.

THANK you for reading Forbidden Play, a love story very dear to me. Read the dedication if you want to know where the inspiration and raw emotions came from.

Next up is:

Head Play, Parker and Annika's enemies-to-lovers showdown. Claim your copy now.

Need more of Matt and Noelle? I've got you covered. It's ten years down the road, and Matt still knows how to make her feel special. Click here for the **Forbidden Play Bonus Scene.**

<u>All Your Fault (Hagan/Adalee)</u>

<u>On My Knees (Logan & Harper)</u>

<u>On Icy Ground (Reed & Brooke)</u>

<u>Out of Bounds (Dane/Lettie)</u>

SARASOTA SHARKS SERIES

<u>Stealing a Second Chance (Wils/Kenni)</u>

<u>Sliding Headfirst (Patrick/Avery)</u>

<u>Scoring the Boss (Archer/Megan)</u>

<u>Swinging for Love (Tackett/Talynn)</u>

SOUTHERN SOULMATES IN KISSING SPRINGS

<u>Secret Santa</u> (Axel/Alice)

<u>Sunshine & Saddles</u> (Maverick/Jessica)

<u>Bourbon & Brawn</u> (Beau/Vanessa)

<u>Ride with Beckett</u> (Beckett/Tessa) — Yes, this is Beau's twin brother.

<u>Midnight and Mine</u> (Scott/Wynter)

RACING HEARTS SERIES

<u>Always With Me (Brandon/Gracie)</u>

<u>Let Me Love You (Ben/Mia)</u>

<u>Come On Baby (Nic/Kaylee)</u>

Standalone:

<u>The Billionaire Proposal</u> (Winslow/Cameron)

ABOUT THE AUTHOR

Kristin Lee is a USA Today Bestselling Author and writes heart shattering, heart melting romances with a shot of humor and a twist of suspense.

Her books feature Forbidden, Second Chance, Friends to Lovers, Enemies to Lovers, Age Gap, Brother's Best Friend and Forced Proximity.

If she isn't writing or reading, you'll find her streaming her favorite shows, or attending sporting events. Did I mention she loves having a Bourbon cocktail while at the horse races?

If you haven't found your match, don't worry, you will. But for now, take a romantic journey in one of her romance novels, where you are sure to meet a swoon worthy book boyfriend.

ACKNOWLEDGMENTS

Believe me when I say, I could not do this without the support of my husband and family. From writing in the car line to posting on social media while waiting to check out in the grocery store to hooking my hotspot up to do admin research or my newsletter on the way to my son's games.

Being an author is all consuming, and my family takes tin stride so that I can be PRESENT during games, dinners and other events. So from my whole heart, I thank my family for giving me endless ideas and encouragement.

To my beta readers, Alyssa, Mindy and Thorunn, thank you for making my love stories stronger, deeper and more enjoyable.

And to my ARC team of loyal readers, I stand and applaud you. You also strengthen my stories and the end product that's released to the world. You message me, and email me to offer an idea. You help name my characters and locations. You support me on social media. And I feel your love. Thank you for everything you do for me and this book community.

Wishing you all the love and romance you can handle!

Kristin Lee